BODYCHECK

Steven Owad

Steve Owad

RENDEZVOUS
PRESS

Text © 2005 by Steven Owad

Cover art: Trudy Agyeman

LE CONSEIL DES ARTS
DU CANADA
DEPUIS 1957

THE CANADA COUNCIL
FOR THE ARTS
SINCE 1957

We acknowledge the support of the Canada Council for the Arts
for our publishing program.

Napoleon Publishing/RendezVous Press
Toronto, Ontario, Canada

Printed in Canada

09 08 07 06 05   5 4 3 2 1

Library and Archives Canada Cataloguing in Publication

Owad, Steven, 1967-
        Bodycheck / Steven Owad.

ISBN 1-894917-22-7

        I. Title.

PS8629.W33B63 2005   C813'.6   C2005-903469-6

This story would not have become a book if not for Sylvia McConnell and Allister Thompson. What for them is all in a day's work is for me a very big deal.

Thanks also to the world's best editor, Knox Burger, whose willingness to guide a neophyte will always be the highlight of my writing life.

Most of all, thanks to my beautiful wife Aleksandra. Books are great, but the love and support of an exceptional woman are even better.

One

Behn McAvoy drew the fishing rod over his head and launched the treble-hooked lure into the foamy water at the lip of the weir. Reeling in, he glimpsed the iridescent flash of a rainbow trout swirling for the lure. The fish flopped once behind the bait and fled, leaving the metal to shimmy in alone. Behn leaned the rod against the safety rail, lit a cigarette and peered out at the tumbling water.

The fish were rising today, but they weren't feeding, not with ice coalescing into glassy crystals in the current. The poor angling prospects felt fitting. The seasons set the conditions. The seasons gave you rare days like this, with a scrubbed-grey sky and a high-altitude bite that felt more alive than any tropical seaside. Behn turned his glance to the open prairie, a quick scan for signs of life. There were no birds, no rabbits or coyotes snuffling the frozen alkali slough that stretched southward to the hills. The movement he did glimpse felt wrong the moment he caught it. The distant figure of a man, the first person out here since the weather had turned. He was maybe a half mile off and heading this way, taking cautious, city-dweller steps along the river's rocky embankment. Beige overcoat, shoes covered by what looked like rubbers. Wherever he'd come from, he'd made a good part of the journey by foot; there was no car at the outcropping of trees that lined the path back to Highway 22x.

A reporter, maybe. Tracked Behn down for an impromptu interview. The reporters had been popping up lately, gophers attracted by the morning sun. The *Hockey News* had run a "where are they now" bit on Behn Thomas McAvoy in its last October issue, describing the "hockey dinosaur" as the Boston Bruins' "worst ever first-overall draft choice." Also calling him a "grizzled warhorse and infamous recluse of the Central Hockey League"—as if avoiding the spotlight made one a recluse.

The story had piqued a local cosmetics company's interest. A call had been made to the Agrodome, where the Renfrew Cowboys played their home games, and Behn was offered a TV commercial for Nothing But Natural Hair Colouring for Men. Which Behn respectfully declined. It would be woefully depressing, hawking junk on TV. Channel surfing, he'd once caught Dick Butkus selling barbecues on a Channel 54 infomercial. The image had stuck with him for a long time afterwards. A man on the back arc of life. A disposable hero drawing on the last vestige of a tenuous fame.

The stranger finally closed in, stopping at the safety railing to the right of Behn. "Cold out here," he said, breath misting the air. "November and already a deep-freeze."

Now a flash of jumbled memories. *Here* had been *hee-a.* Boston accent, long-ago cadence. *November* had been *Novembuh.* Behn studied the man. Age: forty, forty-five. Face: ruddy leather, rugged angles. Boston. The man leaned against the railing and struck a pose of contrived leisure.

"Maybe you can help me out," he said. "I'm looking for someone. Fellow who lives in the woods close to here. Name of Behn McAvoy."

Behn took a pull from his cigarette. No reporter.

"They say there's this path to his house, but hell if I can find it..."

The path was in full view. Behn plucked more names and faces from his memory. "Behn McAvoy the hockey player?"

"That's right."

"Right wing for the Cowboys?"

The man chuckled. "You catch on."

"Why don't you just phone him?"

"Not listed." A yawn, then a flashy grin. Boston knew who he was talking to. And he knew that Behn knew it—he had to. "So you're saying you don't know the path?"

Boston rubbed his hands and straightened his collar against the wind. Then he leaned forward and cast an intimate glance. "You know, I got a picture of him. So maybe you could recognize him. I mean, if he turned up right now and asked for a quarter or something." He undid an overcoat button and reached into a pants pocket. "I got this O-pee-chee hockey card."

He glanced at the card, which he had pulled from the wallet, then looked back at Behn, eyes scrunched. He made a show of checking the photo a second time. "Uncanny," he said. "Striking."

"What do you want?" Behn said.

Boston flipped the card over and read the back. "Behn McAvoy, Bemidji, Minnesota. Sure is a long way from Minny-sota to the Renfrew Cowboys, wouldn't you say?"

Behn crushed out his cigarette, then waited out another of Boston's I'm-in-control pauses.

"Actually, it's not a question of want," Boston said, "more like need. I have a mortgage back home, can't keep up with it."

"A mortgage?" Behn said.

"And you're going to help me pay it."

Boston shrugged, the statement being a natural product of a logical development. Then the hand that had extracted the wallet reached into the coat and jerked out a pistol.

Sensation fled. No more icy breeze mingling with cigarette smoke in Behn's lungs. No tactile contact of feet touching ground. The only thought that flared was how fast everything could change. In a heartbeat.

Behn raised his hands and stepped back. Boston inched forward, brushing the butt of the fishing rod with his foot. He held the gun just out of reach.

"You know, I went to a game once, I think in your second year with the Bruins. Man, did you stink. Bumbling around like a retarded monkey. You looked drunk or something."

I was drunk, that was the problem.

Behn's gaze darted along the horizon. No one there, no options presenting themselves. There was the stranger and the water, neither less deadly than the other. Every year the weir killed a guy or two. There was always some thrill-seeking dimwit tying to shoot the rapids in a canoe, or a boozed-up fisherman wading in to rescue a snagged Panther Martin or Buzzbomb, $3.99 at the local Mohawk.

Behn swallowed sandpaper and took another step back. Boston again loped forward to close the space. Careful. Watchful. The foot that had brushed the rod now slapped it forward and the pole tipped over, the eyes skipping on the railing as it fell. Boston snapped his head to the jangling, and Behn reacted without thinking, leaping at the brief chance to close the distance.

The gunshot at his ear sounded oddly distant. He clamped his hands around Boston's wrists, then slid his left hand upward toward the gun. Driving his knee into a soft, ample stomach, he heard the gun clatter to the concrete. One hand slipped free, and Boston threw an ill-aimed roundhouse right, fell off-balance against the railing and shot the free hand into a coat pocket for another gun or a knife or some other weapon. Still without thinking, still without feeling, Behn reached down behind Boston's knees and pulled the would-be killer up and over the railing.

The stranger didn't surface from the churning foam for a full ten seconds. When he did come up, it was feet first, held quick to the froth like one of the soft-buffed logs bobbing near the wall. His body submerged twice, briefly, then was sucked back for another prolonged washing.

Behn's heart pounded. The clarity of fast action was gone, coherent thoughts were impossible. This couldn't have happened. Not *this*. He picked up the gun like a robot and peered down the barrel. The cold silver felt heavier than it looked. He pocketed the piece, then picked up the wallet, which was lying half-open on the pavement, a few American twenties sticking out.

There was also that hockey card, a rookie card of Behn McAvoy, right wing for the Boston Bruins back in eighty-eight. The young Behn McAvoy was in mid-stride, taking a pass outside the Washington Capitals' blue line, a lion of a defenseman named Rod Langway bearing down on him.

He went through the wallet with trembling hands. Massachusetts driver's license for one Randolph Skalky. AT&T calling card with the same name. A few other cards, including a receipt from the Horseshoe Casino downtown. Behn knew the place. He pocketed the wallet, leaned against the railing and tried to catch his breath. Something wet dripped down his neck, bringing him back from a fumy distance. He peered down at the water again. Randolph Skalky was either still tumbling in the countercurrent or had started to drift downriver. A fish jumped near where his body had last surfaced, and Behn found himself thinking that it was a good one—meaty girth, a potent leaper. Then he linked thought to bodily action. He picked up his gear and headed for his house in the woods.

Two

Twigs of green ash and Russian poplar crunched underfoot. He heard noises behind him—or thought he heard them. Adrenaline fired off jumbled thoughts: *You killed a man, you ended a man's life, this cannot have happened.* He kept his head on a swivel, searched the area for more Randolph Skalkys. He fought to slow his mind and his feet, told himself to calm down, go call the cops.

But it had happened so fast. He had to replay it, rethink it, convince himself it wasn't a hallucination. How could this thing be what it was? These things did not happen to people.

Nearing his house, he spied a line of smoke winding upward from the chimney. It was more of a cabin than a house, built as a retirement retreat for an Edmonton lawyer who'd died of prostate cancer a month before he could move in. Behn had come across the listing in the *Renfrew Herald* by happenstance, while leafing through the Sunday edition in a quest for the Music section. After glancing at a black-and-white snapshot of the one-bedroom bungalow with a sprawling deck and no other houses to spoil the neighbourhood, he dialled the number in the caption. A few details later, he told the lady at the agency that he wanted the place. That simple. The lack of phone lines and roads in the vicinity as well as the brick fireplace and the gas-powered Black and Decker generator in the shed made the purchase more attractive. It took less than a week to have the paperwork done and to move from his eighth-floor apartment in downtown Renfrew, where he'd been living for seven years. The cabin sat on Blackfoot land, so he found himself with the last ninety-eight years of a ninety-nine-year usufruct, which seemed like more than enough time. There were no kids, no wife, no worries about the future.

Rico—bought to guard the place—lay in front of the woodpile, his tail tip flopping like a fish on land. A pair of squirrels scurried past the German Shepherd in a break for a distant tree, inspiring a pricking up of ears. Behn dropped his rod and tackle box by the door and stepped inside to an aroma of eggs and bacon.

A bearded man with patches of grey hair over his ears stood at the gas stove watching over a skillet. The man looked anaemic, forty going on seventy, in baggy khaki sweatpants and a black, hand-woven shirt he'd received from a Maos hilltribesman in Laos.

"Great white hunter catch breakfast?" he said. "Great white hunter get some moose meat to add to the pot?"

Behn's voice came from far away. "Jimmy, I just killed a man."

"Yeah? That some kind of idiom for getting skunked? Pull up a chair. Can't start your day without some nice saturated fats." Then: "Neck's bleeding, by the way."

Behn reached up and felt a gummy trickle of half-dried blood. The neck was numb, along with the rest of him. Jimmy dipped a fork into the pan, speared eight strips of bacon and set them on a plate.

"What'd you do, hook yourself with a lure?"

"Jimmy, he pulled a gun on me." Behn pulled off his boots and sat down. Mechanically, he took out Randolph Skalky's wallet and flopped it onto the table. "I was standing there having a smoke, nothing biting. He shows up and asks me where Behn McAvoy's place is. But he has this look on his face, like he already knows it's me he's talking to. He pulls a gun, he says..." The words sounded irrelevant. "I killed him."

Jimmy was now searching the wallet with his hands but not his eyes, which remained locked on Behn. When he finally spoke, his first question was oddly practical.

"Did you call the cops?"

"Battery's dead on the cell."

"So charge it."

"Charger's broken."

"Since when?"

"Last week."

"Jesus, Behn..."

"I'll drive into town after breakfast."

"After?"

Behn let the question hang. Stupefaction looked wrong on Jimmy. The man was unflappable to a fault. He'd passed fifty without trading off the speed at which he'd always lived his breakneck life. Still smoked copious amounts of dope, still believed in thumbing his nose at all authority real and imagined. Those gaudy shirts and khaki trousers—clothes a backpacking teenager would wear in the tropics. Some folks saw him as pathetic, but Behn suspected the impact was calculated. People underestimated Jimmy, and Jimmy liked it that way. He liked the role of the outsider.

But now he was in blunder mode. His current sum of wisdom: "I cannot believe this."

"He's from Boston," Behn said.

"What?"

"He said someone was paying him to kill me. Or implied it."

"Jesus, Behn, do you realize you're sitting here wolfing down breakfast?"

Behn looked down at the bacon on his fork. He stopped

in mid-chew. *So this is what it's like to be in shock.* He pushed the plate away and crossed the floor to the window. The woods outside were calm, frost and snow pellets clinging to the moss and crabgrass. There were no footprints apart from his own. Rico lay at his post in front of the woodpile, oblivious.

Jimmy said, "I'll ride into town with you."

"No, that's okay." Behn donned his jean jacket and stepped toward the door before pausing in mid-step. "Strange."

"What?"

"I killed a man. I ended the life of a human being."

Jimmy sucked in his breath. "If you're feeling guilty, now's not the time to—"

"No, not guilty. More like..." The right word took some finding. Reactions were still settling, sediment in a current. "More like angry."

The feeling had crept up on him. How could he be steamed at a man he'd just killed? Opening the door, Behn looked left and right outside. With everything calm, he jogged to his Cherokee, searched his pockets twice for his keys and started the engine.

*　　*　　*

Larry Coyne did not just sit down on coach Ken Duguay's living-room sofa. In kicking his feet onto the coffee table and stretching his arms, he appropriated half of the room.

Ken Duguay entered from the den and glared at his top-scoring centreman. It was a clear rule, a rule of military gravity: players were not to bother him at home. They were to catch him at his office at the Agrodome, where he spent twelve hours a day anyway.

"What," he asked Coyne, "is so important that it couldn't wait until practice?"

The player lounged, looking right at home. "I want more ice time. I'm averaging fourteen minutes a game. That's grinder time."

"You can gripe about ice at practice," Duguay said. "You didn't have to defile my personal space."

"Don't change the subject, coach. Vancouver won't call me up unless I score more. How do I score more unless I play more? You know how it works. My agent says—"

"Your agent?" Duguay said. "Christ, kid, show some savvy. Save the agent for contract time."

Duguay had trouble locking eyes with him. The twenty-year-old forward from Piapot, Saskatchewan, was not conversing here, not in the conventional sense. He was eyeing a reflection of himself in the china cabinet—and was impressed with what he saw. Duguay remembered how Red Kelly, an old coach with the Toronto Maple Leafs, had categorized hockey players. Kelly's belief was that every team had its carriers of water and its choppers of wood. Coyne carried water. He scored enough goals to demand more money and more ice, but he shrunk from the game's physical side, leaving teammates to chop the wood. The little runt had plenty of habits to learn—and maybe he would learn them if he worked hard enough—but like too many Canadian kids in the game today, he chose to whine instead. Fall back on his rights. *Call the agent.* Guys like this wondered loudly and incessantly why they were still in the minors when the answer was right before their eyes. They turned the normal coach and GM's fear of getting axed into a never-ending ordeal of Chinese water torture.

"Last I heard," Duguay said, "the coach decides who plays

and when. You don't like it, you can pack up and go play in England. I hear they started a league over there."

"Let me make it simple, coach. Play me or trade me. Tell Vancouver that's my line."

"Trade you for what? A skate sharpener?"

"I'm serious."

"You're a crybaby is what you are. Your linemates never gripe about ice time."

"They play the power play and kill penalties."

"Would McAvoy bitch? He'd work harder."

"That's another thing," Coyne said, "I want that asshole off my line."

"Oh?"

"The bastard's always at me. He doesn't respect me."

Ken Duguay took a deep breath. "Larry, he plays hard. He feeds you most of your goals and keeps you from getting thumped. You need a big guy on your line. You should be goddamn appreciative."

"He calls me 'Beaker'."

"He...what the hell does that mean?"

"Beaker. Says I'm always 'beaking off' about something."

Duguay buried his head in his hands. "For God's sake, Coyne, you *are* a beaker. Now stop looking at yourself in the glass. It's embarrassing."

The player turned his eyes to his coach, but only for a moment. The lure of his reflection was too much. He knotted his jaw and swept his hair back with his hand. "You're great for a guy's ego, coach. Dale Carnegie of the Central League."

The phone rang. To coach Ken Duguay's ears the ringing was salvation, the bells of heaven carrying him away from a purgatory peopled by numbnuts like Larry Coyne. Reaching for the receiver, he said, "Now would be a good time for you to leave."

Coyne didn't stir—wouldn't stir. Instead, he tried a new china-cabinet profile: stern eyes, trouble a'brewin' beneath the surface.

On the line was Patrick Bouchard, a journeyman left-winger from Trois-Rivières, Quebec: "Look at de TV, Channel five."

"What for?"

"Just look at it. McAvoy he kill a man. A man come to visit him, and Behn use him for fish bait over dere at de weir."

Mary, mother of... Duguay snapped up the remote. What the hell kind of thing was that? Killed a guy?

"What is it?" Coyne asked as the coach's ancient Hitachi buzzed through its warm-up.

Finally the box beamed an image of Behn being led into the Buffalo District Police Station by a pair of cops. TV and print reporters were being held at bay by other officers. The reporter was saying:

"...at seven o'clock this morning at the Carseland weir. The victim is one Randolph Skalky, an aluminium-siding salesman from Boston. Police are not commenting on the incident except to say that the hockey player is being detained. McAvoy, a first-round draft choice of the Boston Bruins in 1985, is best known for his battle with alcoholism, which forced him to retire briefly in 1988. A minor-leaguer ever since, he has made only sporadic appearances in the NHL with the Vancouver Canucks, the Cowboys' parent team."

Larry Coyne was no longer giving himself the eye. Transfixed on the screen, he crowed, "My God, he actually killed a guy! Murder!"

What a ghoul.

Anchorwoman Marilyn Biddle was now enunciating through surgically enhanced pearly whites: "...and no comments on what relationship McAvoy had with Skalky. Detective Edward Woo of the Renfrew Police Department would only say that an investigation is underway and that further information will be made public shortly. Now we return to our regularly scheduled—"

Duguay clicked the "off" button and sank into his seat. When the day turned bad, it turned bad. This was an almost mystical kind of bad. Wherever Larry Coyne slithered, slug trails of misfortune followed.

Coyne's eyes were silver dollars. "That's gonna screw up his book deal!" He thrust out a middle finger. The guy was actually flipping off the TV set. *The Behn McAvoy Story,* hah! Booze and rebirth, hah! It's being ghosted by a burnt-out freaking academic!"

"Academic?" Duguay said. "What do you care?"

"I don't. But I guess he won't be writing any life story if he's making license plates up at Drumheller, eh?" He paused and thought up something that made him smile—cheesily. "And I guess he won't be my winger, either."

Duguay hadn't looked at him for a while. He was afraid he'd strangle him if he did. "Get out of my house, Coyne, I have some calls to make."

"I bet that's an understatement. Damage control. Forget that sitting-out threat, eh? Maybe think of Halkidis, put him on my line instead of Mac. Keep me from getting, quote unquote, thumped."

He left with a gaudy spring in his step. He could always turn it off at that moment just before you throttled him.

Ken Duguay poured himself an orange juice and half-hoped the folds of his sofa would swallow him up. In sixteen years as a pro coach in Canada and the States, the worst crime he'd known players to commit, apart from the usual booze-related infractions, was assault. The worst incident under his own stewardship occurred just two weeks after he was named general manager of the Carolina Longshoremen of the Eastern League. A pair of defensemen had pummelled a bouncer in a Baltimore bar after a stripper complained they were shooting wadded paper at her through the straws from their margaritas. And now his hardest-working player, a man with sixteen years of pro experience and a touchingly foolhardy desire to make it back to the big league, was courting a murder rap.

Ken Duguay wished he'd followed Daddy's advice and got an education. He'd been fired from seven teams in three different minor leagues. The Renfrew Cowboys would one day become team number eight—such was the business— but he was tiring of the revolving-door career. He liked it in the city on the banks of the Clear River. In the last year or so he'd harboured the foolish coach's dream of not getting gonged again. He wanted to settle here, take advantage of the small-town temperament and simpler living. The thinly spread population of 900,000 seemed about right. Paul Anka had once told a talk-show host that Canada's gentler pace lent perspective. Duguay, an American, believed that. Renfrew was big enough to have once had an NHL team, the Stormriders, but not big enough to have kept it. The Stormriders had moved to Houston in '98 and become the Meteors, and Renfrew was still intensely sore about it. The cry around town was that they didn't know the first damn thing about hockey in Texas. There were bigger markets and lower taxes in the States, but those baseball freaks and gridiron-crazy Jethros wouldn't know a two-line pass if it hopped up and bit 'em in the ass.

Which was another thing Duguay liked about Canada. Maybe anti-American sentiment was fermenting over the loss of the national sport, and maybe Ken Duguay was from Binghamton, New York, but the Canadian bitterness over losing pro hockey to U.S. money was a sign of stubborn pride. Renfrew was not a complacent city, never would be. Like a sharp goalie behind a crumbling defence, it would always be poised, always looking out for the Yanks, or the Japs, or whoever the hell else, because the foreigners were always on the power play, the bastards, and they always had the puck.

Thoughts of duty shook Duguay from his reverie. Tonight's game with the Tacoma Titans was scheduled for seven thirty but had been pushed ahead to five o'clock. (The Harlem Globetrotters were in town the following morning, and the Agrodome maintenance staff had been decimated by a flu epidemic caused by a sharp upswing in the temperature last week. They needed extra hours to put in the floorboards.)

Which meant Ken Duguay had to get himself over to the rink. Rousing himself from the chair, he decided that what he'd seen on TV had to have been some sort of mistake. Mac killing a guy? There was an explanation—somewhere. He stepped into his boots, pulled on a coat, and walked out of the house half-wondering if he would draw fire from unseen enemies squatting in the bushes. It was still only eight-thirty in the morning.

Three

Behn knew what they were doing. The cops at the Renfrew Buffalo District Police Station were taking their time with him, giving him ample chance to hang himself with his words. The cop in charge was a detective named Eddie Woo, a plump, moonfaced man of maybe fifty. Running down fleet-footed felons would not be Woo's forte, but he exuded a silent authority that had the two other cops in the interview room standing at deferential attention. Woo listened to Behn's story about the encounter with Randolph Skalky, jotted down bits of his statement, then told the hockey player that this fabulous tale of a strange would-be murderer-turned-victim sounded like a crock. From where did Behn really know Skalky?

"I don't know him."

"So basically," Woo said, "he showed up, said you're a lousy player, took a shot at you, and you put him in the river. Then went home for viddles."

Behn nodded.

"And you have no idea who in Boston might dislike you enough to send a man like that."

"If I had an idea, would the story sound so absurd?"

Woo chuckled. "You were in rapturous love with everyone in Beantown? Not a single enemy?"

Behn chose not to answer sarcastic questions.

"You've so far waived your right to have counsel present. May I ask why?"

"Because I don't need someone to help me lie."

"You can do it fine by yourself?"

"I'm not lying," Behn said.

Woo leaned forward. "Turn your head to the right." He reached across the table and put two fingers to Behn's neck, below the nick from the bullet. "The gun was fired at close range?"

"A couple feet. Arm's length."

"There's some tattooing. Looks like you haven't tried to wash it."

"Tattooing?" Behn said.

"Gunpowder. I'm gonna have the doc look at it."

"It's a scratch. It doesn't need a doctor."

"Not that kind of doctor," Woo said.

He got up and left, followed by the two cops who'd stood at the wall behind him, listening. As the minutes passed, Behn knew someone was watching him through the camera hanging from the ceiling. He imagined pot-bellied homicide vets in an adjoining room. Their lines: "Do you buy any of this?" "This guy's yanking Ed's chain." "Book him."

When the "doc" arrived, he looked like a run-of-the-mill detective, clean cut, badge on his belt. The only difference: prophylactic gloves. Woo stood aside while the doc studied the wound, probed the tattooing with a tiny metal pick, and pronounced that if the gun fired had been the 9 mm Sauer that Behn had turned in, the wound was caused by a blast maybe two feet away. For the wound to have been self-inflicted or otherwise planned, the gun would have to have been held at arm's length. Only a lunatic would attempt such a risky cover wound.

The doc was still talking when the rap sheet on Randolph Skalky came in. Woo read it silently and then, oddly, recited it aloud. Until six weeks ago, Skalky had been incarcerated at the Cedar Junction Prison in Massachusetts. The crime: burglary. There were other crimes dating back twenty-one years. Assault and battery, burglary, assault again, more burglary. A small-time felon. Homicide looked like a big leap.

Where was the utility in this? Reading the rap sheet to the suspect? Behn soon saw why the cop was doing it. He was watching for a reaction.

"When's the last time you were in Boston, Behn?"

"Not for a decade."

"So if I check airline records, I won't find that you went down there?"

"What you'll find is that Skalky came up here. My guess is, very recently."

"Why do you say that?"

"He didn't seem like a guy to fly in early and spend some time taking in the sights."

He told the cop about the receipt from the Horseshoe Casino. Woo thought the tidbit over, then reapplied the suspicion. "I have a hard time buying that you have no enemies in Boston. Everyone has enemies. Spinny here"—one of the cops at the wall— "has a guy he sent up on armed robbery. Guy's making threats from prison. Me, I have an ill-tempered ex who thinks she's getting a raw deal in alimony. What do you have? Former teammate? Aggrieved ex-chippie? Do share."

"Tell us about your wife," one of the other cops said. "Pure bliss?"

"Wife?" Woo asked.

"Mr. McAvoy was married in Boston. As it were."

"As it... Spinny, I hate phrases like that."

Behn said, "We were married for three weeks."

Woo laughed, as did the other cops. "Terms of length, that must be some kind of record."

"You want the short version or the long version?"

"The useful version," Woo said.

So he told them about Maria Blackwell, the caretaker of his frazzled body during a three-week drunken blowout. He'd picked her up in a Worcester pub, a nineteen-year-old kid who was slow and buxom and thrilled about seeing a Bruin in person. She didn't know that this particular Bruin had two days earlier been demoted to the Albany Wallbangers of the Eastern League. She didn't know he was currently AWOL from the organization. After extracting her from the pub, he married her in Atlantic City. Because she was amenable. Because the idea was outrageous. Also because he'd taken thorough leave of all sensible thought and wasn't about to accept a stint in the minor league. He drank, she drove. They hit the casinos and bars, stayed in an expensive Marriott. He lost eleven thousand dollars betting on the Tampa Bay Buccaneers, then ran out of stamina, sobered up and annulled the marriage. It was time to quit hockey and save himself from himself. Time to seek help.

"You guys are the specialists in finding people," he told Woo. "If you're asking me if I know who has it in for me, I've already answered that."

The cops looked like all they needed right now was buttered popcorn.

"You ever fall off the wagon, Behn?"

"Only when I'm out murdering ex-cons from Boston."

Woo glanced at the cop who'd brought up the marriage, then looked back at the suspect. "You have much money?"

"I'm well off."

"So was Gandhi, in his opinion. How well off?"

"Two point eight million. Maybe it's up to three now."

"Well," Woo said, clasping his hands behind his head. "Well, well."

Now it was Behn's turn to laugh. "So this has to do with

money?" It didn't take much to perk them up.

"Where are these humble savings? In a bank? Investments?"

"Some in T-bills, some in mixed-risk trust funds. A little in a Russian oil company."

"Sounds prudent."

"I have a half million sitting in Citibank in Bemidji. Term account."

"You saved all that money from the Boston days?"

"Some I saved. These days I make a hundred sixty a year —if that's important."

Woo's eyebrows jumped. "A hundred and sixty in the minors?"

"The benefits of collective bargaining." Even with the new CBA, there were guys in the league making more than a million. Few non-hockey people knew that.

"Salaries," said the other cop at the wall. "Salaries and strikes and lockouts. That's what did in the Stormriders."

"Detective, is there any chance you'll get to the bottom of this?"

"Choose optimism," Woo said. "Choose to believe we always get our man."

"I thought that was the Mounties."

"Us too. I want you to move into town for a while. Stay somewhere accessible."

The suggestion made sense, but not for the cop's reason. Every sports reporter in town had at one time or another shown up at the cabin for an interview. Today they'd all roll out there, Rommel's boys with flashbulb artillery.

"I'll stay at Jimmy Teal's place," Behn said.

Woo paused over the name, then scanned Behn's statement. "The writer you ate breakfast with? Guy who's helping you write *The Behn McAvoy Story?*"

"That's only a working title," Behn said.

"So how's it work? You talk, he writes it down?"

"More or less," Behn said.

"From the sounds of things, you've got some grist for a good tale. Where would Teal be right now?"

"He would be at class. He teaches English at the university."

Woo scribbled down a few more lines and indicated the cop who had brought up Maria Blackwell. "All right. This is Detective Dante Spinetti. He's going to sit with you while you read over your statement for accuracy and sign it. You want to change anything"—he turned his eyes to his subordinate—"Spinny, any changes, I want you to let me know before you let this guy go."

"You got it."

"Sign this one, too, Behn." Woo slid a slip of paper across the table. Behn turned it around and saw that it was a Consent to Search form. His address was on a line near the top. "I'm going there whether you sign it or not. Please don't make me go rile up a judge for a warrant."

Behn signed the form, and Woo snatched it up and stalked out of the room.

Behn read the statement. Woo had done a fair job of writing facts and omitting tangents. The whole thing ran barely three pages. He signed it and asked if he was free to go.

Spinetti nodded, so he pushed his chair back and sought out the police entrance, which he found at the rear of the building. He peeked outside the door and was pleased to see no reporters milling around. Small comfort. He didn't know what bothered him more: having killed a man, or being suspected of murder.

Four

Robbery-and-homicide detective Edward Woo stepped into the office of Lieutenant Lloyd MacKenzie, the head of Major Crimes. Woo had always seen MacKenzie as more of a paper pusher than a cop. The boss wore flashy suspenders, rarely left the office, and kept his nose snuffed closely up to Chief Sandra Laller's ass. The last time MacKenzie had hit the streets on a case, Eddie Woo was eleven years younger and wearing a blue uniform as a General Patrol officer. At the time, Renfrew was six years away from having the first woman police chief in Canada, and Lloyd MacKenzie was compiling a decidedly average closure rate as a detective in Major Crimes.

He hadn't done much since then to win his detectives' respect.

"Why'd you assign me to this case?" Woo said, sitting across from the boss.

"That was sharp," MacKenzie said, "reading him Skalky's priors like that."

"Lloyd, I'm already working a case."

Three days ago, a homeless woman named Susan Welter had been found in a dumpster behind Albert's News with a broken hyoid bone and steel baling wire around her neck. Seventy hours later, the leads on the murder were nil. Woo still didn't know where Welter had been staying in the days before being garrotted.

"In case you need reminding, Eddie, the good folks in this town don't commit a lot of murder. We need an experienced man on this one. Postpone Welter."

"Lloyd, she's a clear-cut homicide. This Skalky, if McAvoy's on the level, isn't."

MacKenzie flashed a toothy smile. "And you're just the man I want to address that question. None of your esteemed colleagues have your experience."

What was he talking about? Three Major Crimes guys had seniority. They were good men who could handle Skalky just fine—assuming someone here *should* handle him. "It's a case for the Mounties, Lloyd."

"The Mounties haven't expressed an interest."

Now Woo caught on. A Skalky closure would be high-profile, lots of press. A Welter closure would go unremarked. In MacKenzie's books, that was what mattered. But why him, Woo?

"I've called Boston," MacKenzie said. "A detective Samuel Cullen has the case there. You two will share. Here's his number." He slid a slip of paper halfway across the desk, then leaned back and locked his hands behind his head.

Woo said, "You still haven't said why it has to be me."

"Look Eddie, this one came down from the top. Laller wants us to close it. If the RCs get interested, we can't stop them from taking it over. In the meantime, you've got the lead. Period. The department's called a press conference for three o'clock. If you'll allow me, I'd like you there so I can introduce you as one of our brightest, most upwardly mobile detectives."

So that was it. "Lloyd, would I be sitting here right now if I had a European skin tone and blond hair?"

Sometimes the hardest answers were right before your eyes. Chief Sandra Laller had been on an affirmative-action kick ever since arriving in town, and MacKenzie was an embarrassing kiss-up for the crusade. A memo two months ago had instructed all department employees to act conscientiously on requests for cooperation from the Municipal Committee for Cultural Diversification, a body of well-intentioned blockheads who promoted multiculturalism by trumpeting the successes of minorities on the city payroll. The committee ran celebrative PR campaigns and persuaded city offices to hire as many minorities as possible. Important posts had been filled with people who were as unqualified as they were unWASPish.

Woo did crave a promotion, but he wasn't about to cut ahead of men who'd paid their dues. He felt sorry for the minorities who'd been forced up the ladder and were now struggling; it wasn't their fault. He also felt sorry for MacKenzie. If you couldn't judge a guy by his merits, you were a chapter short of a book.

"Postpone Welter," MacKenzie said. "First freed-up detective takes her on. We're finished here, Detective."

He slid the Boston cop's number the rest of the way across the desk. Woo took it up and pushed his chair back. Before reaching the door, he turned to face his boss. "Aren't you worried, Lloyd, that one day they're going to give me your job?"

At his own desk he called Cullen, a thirty-year robbery-and-homicide vet with the Boston PD. Cullen said Records and Information was now putting together a file on Randolph Skalky. He also asked: "How many hours of daylight do you people get up there in Alberta?"

Woo got rid of him. The crime scene unit would soon head out to the Carseland Weir to fish for a body. There was also the one and only suspect's house to search. He pulled on a ski jacket and stepped out to the winter morning.

The temperature was falling fast after a jolt of warm air

from the Rockies yesterday. The Chinook. Every so often it sent Renfrew a spring wind. Minus fifteen one day, plus fifteen the next. Then, when Mother Nature was feeling cruel, back to minus fifteen the day after. This was the day after. Woo stopped off at his one-bedroom apartment in Glenwood Heights and swapped his ski jacket for a down-filled parka. It would be a forty-minute drive down Highway 22x to the weir. And today he'd already wasted a lot of time.

Five

Behn walked toward Jimmy Teal's apartment, which was just a few blocks from the station, on Fifth. Jimmy was still at the university for American Literature 311, teaching tomorrow's local literati that Allen Ginsberg and William Burroughs were gods (while Jack Kerouac, contrary to his reputation, qualified as an apostle, a Wolfe impersonator). Jimmy would enjoy having Behn as a roommate. He'd always told Behn he was doing the ghost of Thoreau proud by living out at the cabin. The thing to do was to shun the crude and unlearned mob, ignore the rabble of the lobotomized mainstream, rise above any society that made sages of omelette-brains like Oprah and Dr. Phil.

Dodging a speeding car on Fourth, Behn felt a slight tug from such reasoning—though last night he'd felt only indifference. Last night—the night before Randolph Skalky showed up and tossed his life into a blender—now felt like forever ago. Lounging at the cabin, Jimmy had told him, "You don't owe them, Behn. You don't owe anyone a single thing."

Behn was tying flies at the kitchen table; Jimmy was rolling a joint.

"Cash it in," Jimmy said. "Retire. Stop striving."

Behn said, "Like you're gonna do, right?"

"Yes, like I'm going to do, just as soon as I'm rich enough."

"The authorities in the Caymans know you're coming yet?"

"Hey, I even looked into citizenship. Why not? I do plan

to devote my every waking hour to the noble and righteous pursuit of being an islander."

"Sounds noble," Behn told him, wrapping the tail of a dobsonfly. "Your students must positively swoon when they hear your plans to just drop out."

"Hey, you don't impose reality upon toddlers. Let 'em find wisdom when they're ready for it." Then: "You, however, are no toddler. It's time you sought some wisdom for yourself. Don't let guilt get in the way of making yourself happy."

Behn looked up from his fly. "Me, Jimmy? What are you talking about?"

"That 'noble' crack proves it. I say something that makes you uncomfortable, so you trot out white liberal angst in the form of sarcasm. It's so very predictable."

"That's what I like about you: your insights."

"There you go again," Jimmy said, "deflecting things. Guilt. You've got it like haemorrhoids—can't sit still. You're still lacing 'em up, still playing the game because you think you owe the world something." Now a pause to light the joint. "Drank it away when you were young, so now you have to atone for it, give something back."

Behn now worried that his plastic insect's midsection looked too hellgrammite-ish. "You want to put that in the book?"

"All I'm saying is, stop carrying loads. Guilt is no good. I say play out the year—"

"Yes, yes, yes," Behn said, "play out the year, then pack it in."

"Spend some of your lucre and get fat and careless. You'd have to be insane not to."

A car horn bleated. Behn realized he'd wandered aimlessly into the street while replaying last night's talk. He also felt less dismissive of Jimmy's cynical wisdom. Jimmy had been axed from three universities for various grades of "misconduct", and as a rule he tended to try to beat you over the melon with his astuteness, but he did have a way of raising issues that might otherwise not get considered.

Behn finally reached the apartment and got the doorman to let him in. First move now: call Tornheim & Ellsworth in New York. Editor Frank Sparrow was a no-nonsense man who saw books as business and wouldn't cross the street for "art". He was expecting the latest chapters of *The Behn McAvoy Story* yesterday.

Sparrow answered the phone sounding hurried. "Obviously," he said after Behn told him about Randolph Skalky, "the book'll now have to start with what happened this morning. Tell Jimmy that. Let the cops do their thing, but keep writing those Renfrew chapters. When the cops find out what's going on, you can go back and revise. We'll use this incident as a...call it a controlling metaphor for your life."

"Thanks a lot."

"Hey, we wanna sell this thing or not? Everything about you is fair game. How's Jimmy?"

"Full of lectures," Behn said, "and hungry as ever to scrape together his nest egg. But he writes it up with real clarity."

"Last two chapters he e-mailed were absolutely pellucid. He gets home from school today, tell him to keep it up. Most colloquial academic I've ever read."

"Okay, Frank."

"What's he doing up there in the sticks, anyway?"

"It's a city of almost a million."

"He should be haunting some grungy coffee shop in San Francisco, writing a history of the Beat Generation."

"He says he's mellowing, 'riding the great Canadian wave of carelessness' while he saves his pennies."

"He smoke dope while you two are working?"

"Would that be a good thing or a bad thing?"

"I don't know," Sparrow said, "maybe a good thing. He's got a real voice on paper. Hell if I'm gonna try to change him this late in the game."

Behn cut the conversation short. He stepped into the kitchen and flipped open cupboards. Canned soups, Aunt Jemima pancake mix, junk food like Snickers chocolate spread and Pop Tarts and Beefaroni. No fruit or veggies, no fresh meat or even canned tuna. Jimmy didn't care what went into his body so long as the body got up in the mornings.

So a trip to Safeway. Behn pulled his coat on again and took the elevator down to an unsettled breeze outside. The sky was a dead kind of grey, looked like a storm coming. He climbed into the Jeep and pulled the door closed. A sharp clink of metal against metal rang out, prompting him to peek out the window and open and close the door two more times to listen for the sound.

It wasn't until he was at the Safeway on 18th Avenue, sauntering toward the strip mall and glancing back, that he saw the hole.

A round dent with a pinprick hole, the mark of a bullet, broke the paint a few inches below the mirror. His feet stopped moving. He surveyed the parked cars and the people around the strip mall. No one was watching him, no one looked dangerous—which made everyone look like killers. He stepped quickly toward the Safeway and bypassed the strip mall's outdoor telephone. The phone was at a brick wall between a convenience store and a drugstore. It looked like a good place at which to get shot.

Six

Alicia Fournier jerked the pillow off her head, blinked open heavy eyes and checked the clock.

Ten past ten. Earliest day this week. She slogged herself to upright status and made the odyssey to the mailbox.

A brittle kind of cold today, maybe go for a run, blow out the cobwebs.

Or maybe not.

The mailbox held an envelope with a cheque and a postcard from Vai, Greece. Palm trees, white roofs, the sapphire hues of the Libyan Sea:

Those chocolate bar commercials on TV? They film them here. It's absolute paradise, hon. I'm putting it in the next novel. Can't you at least answer the phone when I call?
Love,
Walter

She tossed the thing aside and scooped out the cheque. Six thousand two hundred. Conscientious with the alimony. She fluttered the paper onto the coffee table, where it came to rest with the cheques from September and October, which she hadn't gotten around to cashing.

Then she crawled back into bed.

This couldn't go on. How many decent nights' sleep had there been this month? Five? Six? Lately the insomnia had been followed by deep sleeps that came on just before sunrise and lagged into the early afternoon. Last night she'd popped a Seconal, picked up a hardcover copy of *A History of CBC Daytime Television* (a suitably tedious book) and pictured herself snoring within minutes.

But sleep didn't close in until six in the morning, until she'd learned more than she ever wanted to learn about *Coronation Street*—which wasn't even produced by the goddamn CBC!

Jesus. She was twenty-seven, but soon she'd look fifty, easy.

Ghosts. That was the problem. Ghouls haunting her like some psychic illness.

The ghost of ex-human Walter, who'd celebrated publication of his surprise bestseller, *Squeaky Wheel,* by bringing home two hookers and a bottle of Gibson's. The ghost of her brother Normand, dead at thirty-one because of the sport of hockey. Normand deserved better than hockey—which felt as tragic as his suicide itself—which in turn was no less tragic than Walter.

Walter. Wasted time. Insomnia. Ghosts.

So break with it all. Exorcise.

In the spare bedroom, she dug out a shoe box full of wedding photos. Using her wedding gown as a limpid kindling, Alicia fed the photos into the fireplace one by one, first time she'd used the thing this winter. Curious relief, a feeling both welcome and despised, washed over her as the lace and cellulose sent fumes up the chimney. She sat with the flames for a few minutes, then stepped down to the basement, which was still packed with clothes and furniture from Normand's apartment.

It made a damn morbid museum, that mini-apartment in her basement. It had provided just the right setting for impromptu crying jags in the weeks following Normand's funeral.

Well, no more mourning. The Salvation Army would take the clothes, maybe the community association would want the hockey gear. She began sifting through boxes.

The first carton produced snapshots of men getting blotto at a country bar: a teammate's stag, if she surmised correctly. There was a stage and pitchers of beer and men hooting at out-of-frame sights. A life for the lobotomized. Drinking, chasing bimbos, blowing your salary on dumb fun until they sent you back to your farm or small town or whatever else you had before hockey claimed you.

It was a hard thing to think about, given its awful proximity to her life. She swept the photos aside and began bagging up Normand's clothes. She separated the socks from the pants, stuffed them into Glad bags, then dug into the blazers.

Fifty? Hell, she was twenty-seven going on *eighty*. She searched the pockets like Grandma searching for proof of Grandson's misbehaviour.

The first two coats were empty. The third held a velvety jewellery box. She snapped it open and saw a ring, small and lustrous. Also expensive. Wedding or engagement? She rolled it in her hand, felt its weight, peeked under the felt lining. There was a slip of paper with a print-out: *GH243R*.

The blazer's other pocket produced two quarters, a comb and a piece of paper with scribbled handwriting: *Caesars, April 3*.

Vegas?

Okay, so he'd been planning a gambling trip, for gambling was what Normand did best and most prolifically. He'd been addicted for years.

But a ring? Like this? He hadn't had a girlfriend since being dumped by a bulimic model named Randi, who'd lucked into a gig with Sonja Rykiel in Milan. And he certainly would have told her, Alicia, if he was getting heavy with anyone. She'd had her differences with him, but some things in life were certain.

So Normand had been holding the ring for someone, maybe for the groom in those stag photos. But why hadn't that person stepped forward to claim the thing? It looked expensive.

Expensive yet a little tawdry.

But at least it helped peel the exhaustion away. Alicia forgot how tired she was.

Seven

The cops didn't show for twenty minutes. Behn bought a Montreal smoked meat and ate it standing up at the Safeway deli.

"You Behn McAvoy?"

"Yeah."

A guy in dirty jeans and a Mack cap thrust out a pen and a copy of the *Hockey News*, an autograph seeker—thankfully without asking questions about what he'd likely heard on the radio this morning.

Skalky was probably still in the river, and now someone else was out there. What did they have, a team? One assassin stumbles, another grabs the baton? It looked like Mafia, or CIA, or whoever it was that carried out hits these days.

Hits of nonoffending hockey players? Maybe Woo was right: someone was gunning for Behn's money. But how would that someone gain access to it? The money was secure.

An unmarked car pulled up in front of the Safeway. Behn recognized the detective behind the wheel as one of the cops from the interview room. He chomped down the heel of the sandwich, stepped outside and showed the cop the bullet hole in his Jeep. Then he climbed into the Jeep and followed him down to the Buffalo District station.

Inside, the detective—Dante Spinetti—paraded Behn past a line of cops who stopped what they were doing in order to see Behn McAvoy in the flesh.

"The Jeep's gotta stay here for the techs," Spinetti said. "And this Jimmy Teal, his apartment isn't such a good place to stay."

Nice deduction, Einstein. "If Woo's in charge, shouldn't I be speaking with him?"

"He's at the weir with the techs." Spinetti stuffed some papers into a desk drawer. "You guys have a game tonight, right? Who's in town?"

"Tacoma Titans."

"Playing in that game would not be a good idea," Spinetti said. "In fact, it'd be a bad idea."

The idea got stuck in Behn's throat on the way down.

"The Agrodome could be a go-to place for whoever's after you," Spinetti said. "Best if you sit tight while we work this. I'm gonna arrange security, find a place for you to stay."

The cop stood up and ambled down a hallway. Behn drank some of the coffee they'd poured for him. So that was his fate, being holed up while they sought a gunman. Dark hotel rooms, greasy fast food, cops sitting in a car out front chugging coffee.

A bearded hulk near the Complaints desk was pressing a towelful of ice to his forehead. Beside him stood a woman waiting for a constable. She looked familiar. A wife of a teammate, maybe, or a girlfriend. It took a few seconds for the names to come.

Allie. Alice. Alicia.

Alicia Fournier. That was it. He'd met her at Normand's funeral, and once before that, with her husband and Normand at the Tony Roma's down on Harwich. Normand had introduced her, and she was polite but cool. The husband smiled and cracked jokes, sounded vapid. Normand later said she'd drawn snake eyes in the marriage department, working double shifts at a greasy spoon so the bum could sit in the basement and pound out this novel that everyone doubted he'd ever finish.

A cop led the bearded man to a desk, and Alicia stepped forward. Behn skipped over to her.

"Alicia?"

She wasn't cool this time, just surprised to see him. She said the TV this morning had told a very odd story about him.

"Odd is a conservative way of putting it," Behn said, unable not to stare at her. She looked good, one of those rare women who were one hundred per cent there, all the time. She didn't have to do anything to win your attention. Behn said, "Normand used to use your name to threaten the guys during practice."

"He what?" she said.

"Yeah. Bungle the left-wing lock, he'd say Alicia would come to you in your dreams, kill you and toss your carcass onto a pile of all the other hockey players she'd massacred."

She laughed in spite of herself. "He spoke highly of you, too."

"Yeah?"

"He said you were about the only guy who'd keep working his ass off, even though he knew he wasn't going back to the big league."

Behn felt a little smaller. "Normand never did sugarcoat things."

"Yeah," she sighed, "at least there's that."

An awkward moment passed. Behn said, "What brings you down here?"

"I found something strange in Normand's things."

She pulled out the ring. Behn didn't need to look closely to be impressed.

"Normand had this?"

She nodded.

"I didn't know he had a girlfriend."

"He didn't. I think he was holding it for someone. I mean, you guys had this stag, right? It'll belong to one of your teammates. I figured the cops'll call around, get in touch with the players."

"Why not call around yourself," Behn said, "instead of coming down here?"

"No desire to."

"No desire to?"

"'fraid not."

To what? Endure the self-mortifying act of spending face time with a hockey player? It was that painful for her? "You said something about a stag," Behn said. "What did you mean?"

"I meant beer and strippers. Slurring players groping at silicone."

"I meant what did you mean by—"

"I *know* what you meant," she said. "God, there's no fooling with you people, is there? I hate that mindset about hockey players. Coach tells you to run through a wall, you do it."

"You take things literally," Behn said, "when literal things happen to you."

Now she surprised him and gave him a sympathetic look, an understanding look—which was good, because he wasn't sure what he was talking about. He sensed that she wanted to ask him about Randolph Skalky. *Why'd you kill him, Behn? What did that man do to you to deserve it?*

"I never met him before," Behn said.

"Who?"

"The guy I killed. It was self-defence."

She shrugged nonchalantly—*Why would I care, pal?*—but he knew she was glad he'd made the statement. She dug a heap of photos from her purse. "That stag. Normand had these in a shoe box."

Behn riffled through the photos. A country bar. Men half-cocked. One shot showed the victim of honour being smothered in a stripper's bosom. Another showed Normand lapping at the orange body paint on another stripper's hip.

Curious. "Apart from Normand," he told her, "these aren't Renfrew Cowboys."

She gave a double-take. "They have to be. I assumed..."

They did look like hockey players. They were the right age, the right shape and size, and they had quintessential hockey noses. Most of them were wearing baseball caps.

Caps with Boston Bruins emblems.

"What is it?" Alicia said.

Two shots showed a Bruins wall-lamp behind the bar. Another showed Old Milwaukee on tap. "This bar's in the States," Behn said. "Boston." Then: "Certainly no shortage of Boston being mentioned these days. You know when these photos were developed?"

"They were in a plain brown envelope."

"Just keep the ring. Sell it. Buy yourself something nice."

"It's not mine."

"How very Canadian of you."

"How Canadian?" she said.

"Find something that isn't yours, seek the rightful owner. Obey the rules."

Alicia sucked in her teeth. "Sorry to prove myself such a square."

"It wasn't an insult. I just meant that where I come from, possession is ten-tenths of the law, and that's in the so-called law-abiding heartland. No matter how long I live up here, I still can't get used to how decent people—"

Now something was wrong. Something didn't fit, but he couldn't put his finger on it.

"What's wrong?" she said.

He thought about it. "Normand. Something he said to me." He scrutinized the top photograph. Boston, yes, and Normand, troubled little Normand, imbiber of thousands of drinks, committer of suicide at age thirty-one, had told Behn—just a couple days before he died—that he'd never been to Boston.

Alicia said, "What? What is it he said to you?"

"Nothing. Just that... I remember him asking me what is was like to play in the Boston Gardens. He said he'd never made it to the great state of Massachusetts."

"Meaning what?"

Behn shook his head. "Nothing. It's odd, that's all. I'm sure he had his reasons for lying about going there. Good luck finding the ring's owner. If I were a betting man, I'd say the odds of you finding the owner are—" *That was it. Gambling. That was what bothered him.* Normand used to gamble at the Horseshoe, same place Skalky gambled. Odd coincidence number two. At what point did "odd" morph into "noteworthy?"

A constable showed up at the desk and addressed Alicia: "How can I help you, ma'am?"

Spinetti was back at his own desk, drumming the blotter with a pen.

"I'll be back in a minute," Behn told Alicia.

He walked over to Spinetti, and the detective said, "We want you to check into the Rancher's on Broadway. We'll have a car outside to watch you while you're there."

"Why the Rancher's?"

Spinetti scratched his scalp. "Why not the Rancher's? You can stay anywhere we can park a car out front."

"How about if I skip out your back entrance and call you when I get to a place?"

"Wouldn't you rather have us take you there?"

"No, I wouldn't." It would be hard to take, being carted around town by the police. Something about the backseat of a police cruiser would only worsen his suddenly constricting sense of liberty. Sitting back while others looked into the mess that his life had become was not a digestible option.

He stepped back toward Alicia, who was leaning on the counter. He asked her, "What did the cop say?"

"That they have a lost and found."

"Would you mind giving me a lift?"

"A lift?"

"To a hotel." He considered telling her about the second attempted hit this morning, about the bullet hole in his Jeep. "If you like, I can also help you find out who this jewellery belongs to."

Alicia scrunched her nose. "What's so intriguing about my little mystery? Don't you have bigger things on your mind?"

Now he spoke before he could stop himself, his mind's eye seeing Randolph Skalky being spit feet-first out of the water: "Normand going to Boston—why would he lie about that?"

Hand to her chest, eyes shooting fire at him: "My God, did your mother make you wear your helmet off the ice, too? He lied about taking a trip, so by default he had something to do with the man who attacked you?"

"I didn't say that."

"Yes, you did. That's precisely what you said."

"Maybe it's the other way around. Maybe Skalky had something to do with him."

She gaped at him. "There's a thing called plausibility. There's a thing called logic. You can't just decide what people did and didn't do."

"No, I can't. But since I can't for the life of me understand why anyone in Boston would have it in for me, I can't let myself ignore even the far-flung coincidences."

"'Coincidences?' Why are you using the plural?"

"When Skalky came to town, he gambled at Normand's favourite casino."

"Yeah?"

"Yeah."

"That's it?"

"Afraid so. It's nothing, I know. Less than nothing, maybe – me feeling paranoid. The cops are going to laugh when I tell them that, but I've got to tell them anyway. Whether it means anything, whether these pictures mean anything—"

"You want to give them these pictures?"

"Wouldn't you?"

Alicia buried her face in her hands. "Oh, Lord..."

He knew what she was thinking. She'd been planning to hand over the ring, not the photos. She could see some reporter getting his hands on the snapshots. She could see the resulting headlines. *Normand Fournier's Revised Autopsy Report: Death by Debauchery!* In the eyes of the world, Normand would cease to be a tragic suicide victim and become another fatally depraved athlete. A woman-objectifier. A drinker. An *alcoholic.* Another John Kordic or Len Bias. What a fantastic epitaph. What a way to be remembered. Certain newspapers wouldn't let a thing as simple as objectivity stand in the way of a juicy story. They'd crucify him. No, let him rest. Let her rest.

Alicia sighed heavily. "Listen, I can make some phone calls. Maybe my parents know something about a wedding in Boston."

"Okay," Behn said.

"I don't want you telling anyone about these prints." She filed the photos back in her purse and slapped the flap closed. And she glared at him. "Well?"

"I know where we can have that diamond looked at. Can you bring your car around back?"

"Why around back?" Alicia said.

"Someone—I mean, reporters could be following me."

"Don't you have a car of your own?" she said.

No, definitely do not tell her that someone's been shooting at the Jeep. "It's out of commission."

She started to say something, but backed off and recast the statement. "In your last life, I bet you were a Bible salesman."

"A Bible salesman?"

"Bend people to the word of God. Win over the heathens. I'm driving a black Jetta. If I see any reporters out there, you're on your own. Normand will not—I repeat, *not*—be on the evening news."

Sure, Behn thought. The news could be an unpleasant place.

Eight

Alf Lundgren slid his gun and silencer between the mattresses, then flopped onto the bed and told himself two things.

One: good boy, you lifted this pistol.

Two: dipshit, use the thing right or go back to chasing chickens for a living.

What was the guy, thirty, thirty-five yards away? Should have been a kill, not paint work for the Jeep. Now McAvoy knew, or would know once he saw the dent, that someone was after him.

Alf Lundgren yanked a bottle from the bedside table and popped two vitamin E pills—for fertility and the vascular system. He imagined the pills dissolving in his bloodstream, fortifying an already well-steeled body. Then he reached for the phone and told the desk to put a call through for him.

"I screwed it up," he told Ed Newby. "I blasted his damn car." The line buzzed. "I stole this gun, this old Browning down at the gun show. I figured I'd—"

"What the hell are you telling me for?" Newby said.

"What?"

"You want the rest of the money, do the job. Bailing out, giving the money back, if that's what you're thinking, isn't an option."

"I didn't think it was," Alf said.

"You can't come crying to me when things go wrong. I'm not your daddy."

"I'm just giving you an update, Ed. Jesus, I'm on top of it."

"You spend the cash yet?"

"No," Alf said.

"Good boy."

"And it isn't worth anything without the second half," Alf said, "so don't worry, I do plan to collect the rest."

A chuckle from Ed. "Yeah? What's so expensive?"

Alf was happy to share. Plan was to rent a room in a small but not too small town—Cranbook maybe, something fairly ignored—and start a business pitching mail-order sex toys. Pump fifteen grand into billboards and ads in women's mags, set up a bogus bank account and have housewives send him money for dildos and feather dusters that he'd never deliver.

"Alf," Ed Newby said, "you are nuts."

"Sure I am. I read that dildos are the world's top-selling mail-order product. Women are too chicken to buy 'em in stores."

"I stand corrected," Newby told him. "You've really thought this through."

Twerp. See who's laughing when the money gets tripled.

"They'd catch you," Ed said. "Stunts like that, they—"

"Not if I hightail it back east before the heat comes. I mean, look at it. How many women are gonna complain that their rubber willies haven't arrived? They'll be too ashamed."

Now a clucking sound from Ed. "Okay, do whatever you want to do, but do your damn job."

"Count on it," Alf said.

He recradled the phone, feeling optimistic. Then he remembered his failure today.

McAvoy would turn careful, hard to get to. Which meant wise up. Maybe you *tried* to miss him. Maybe you can't follow through on this.

Jesus, what if it turns out that you're actually a chickenshit?

Partly to punish himself and partly to chase the doubts away, Alf pulled the Browning and pistol-whipped his own nose. He did it much harder than he'd wanted to, but he figured he had it coming. Don't let your mind do gymnastics. Don't think too much. Just do. Just act.

He gulped three vitamin P pills. Toughen up the cell walls and capillaries.

He had to get out of bed to get the phone book, but the number to the Renfrew Cowboys' front office was a quick find. He asked the lady who answered the phone when the Cowboys' next game was.

"Tonight, sir. Why didn't you just check the newspaper?"

"Why?" he said. "What makes more sense, picking up the phone or going out, finding a stand and paying fifty cents for something you'll only read one line of?"

No answer. He hammered down the phone. That was precisely the kind of tensed-up broad who bought mail-order dickies. Hopefully, there were plenty more like her.

His nose really throbbed now. He laid down and wheezed in a long, deep breath. He tried to force himself into a nap, a recuperative slumber that would translate, later today, into a calm head, fast reflexes and a clear purpose. Especially a clear purpose. The hockey player wasn't lost yet. He was still around.

And today was game day.

Nine

Behn climbed into the Jetta and told Alicia to cross the
alley and enter the Blackie Tower Parkade. She rolled down
her window and took a ticket from the machine, and he told
her to head for the exit on Whitetail Trail.

"Throw the reporters off," he said.

"You're kidding. Do you actually go around 'throwing the
reporters off?'"

Back out on the street, he looked back for tails every few
seconds. The cars on Whitetail Trail moved at a crawl,
spewing exhaust into the winter air. A billboard showed a
snarling hockey player riding a high-kicking bareback bronc
—helmet, stick, skates and all. Bold script beneath the piece
read: *Ride 'em High, Cowboy! AM 109.* On the flipside: three
gophers wearing hats and scarves, sitting before a warm
fireplace with glasses of beer in their fluffy mittens. *Chase
the Winter Woes. Prairie Dog Ale.*

Not subtle. The Prairie Dog brewery was owned by the
same woman who owned the Vancouver Canucks and the
Renfrew Cowboys. Behn had beaten the bottle in the States
only to earn his paychecks from the biggest-grossing beer
seller in Western Canada.

Heading past a block-long strip mall, he told Alicia the
noteworthy thing that he'd been holding back: someone had
shot his Jeep this morning, which meant someone was still
after him. Hearing him say this, she nearly rammed the car
into a furniture truck.

She said, "I guess the rules of decency don't apply."

"How's that?"

"No point being straight with me back at the station. I mean, you're looking into my brother's filthy past and all..." For the moment, she left it at that. Then, "You and Normand, were you good friends?"

"From a distance, if that makes sense."

"He was your linemate. I thought maybe—"

"He was my roommate on the road for a few weeks," Behn said. "Then we decided to switch with a couple other guys."

"Why?" she said.

"Because he liked staying out late, I didn't. He drank, I used to. Gambling ditto. There were temptations. I don't do well around temptations."

Alicia just kept driving as if he'd commented on the weather.

"Sorry I wasn't straight with you," Behn said. "I knew that if I told you someone was following me, you'd take off."

"Behn, I'd have left you standing there staring into your melting ice cream. In fact, why don't I stop the car right now?" She did just that, parked at the curb and drummed the steering wheel with her fingers. Her gaze told him it was time to get out and hail a cab.

"No one knows I'm with you," Behn said. "Not even the cops know. No one's going to find me."

Other cars groaned past. "Yes. That makes me feel all fuzzy inside."

Behn reached for the door handle, but then found himself pulling up.

"I lied to you about Normand," he said.

"You lied to me?"

"Normand and I were never roommates. Truth is, I never liked him."

"Tell it to your bartender," Alicia said, putting the car in "drive" but keeping her foot on the brake.

"Because it's hard to watch a guy self-destruct, especially when you've done plenty of self-destructing of your own. Normand's drinking and gambling, it was like watching a train wreck in slow motion. Like being forced to watch your own ruin in replay."

"Mr. Behn McAvoy, I really do not care what you think about Normand or me or anyone else."

"And it was bad for the team, too. That's more to the point. A hockey player gets shipped to the minors, the last thing he needs is a teammate who doesn't care about his career. The young guys in the minors, they're delicate. They're busy figuring out where they went wrong. So yeah, I didn't like Normand, didn't like what he did to guys who were very breakable. The whole time I knew Normand, I hoped he would be cut or traded." Behn watched her shift in her seat. Now she was avoiding his gaze. Now she flicked on the defrost.

"But you know what," he continued, "even while I hated him, I felt sorry for him. He was a guy who couldn't handle his own problems, a guy who, for whatever reason, couldn't look in the mirror. And all I could do was look at him from a distance and wait for the inevitable to happen." He fell silent. *If she says anything, cut her off. Tell her to stop behaving childishly.* But she didn't say anything. So: "What do you do for a living, Alicia?"

"I cash alimony cheques. None of your business."

"You waited tables when you first came here, didn't you? Normand mentioned that." No answer. "And your family's from Quebec City, right?"

"Shawinigan. We—" Her mouth stayed open. She seemed to know what he was driving at.

"I know why Normand came to live out west," Behn said. "He came because the Canucks sent him here. But why did *you* come here? Renfrew isn't exactly a haven for Quebecois."

"Why would you care about that?"

"I'm getting the sense that you came here more or less at the same time he did."

He watched her check the side and rear-view mirrors as if something interesting was out there. She was bad at faking preoccupation, inexperienced at it.

Behn said, "You followed him out here, didn't you? You came here to take care of him."

She laughed—too strongly. "Don't be absurd."

"A guy with an addiction," Behn said, "has no idea what kind of signals he's giving off. When I was drinking, I got maudlin at the drop of a hat. It was easier to handle life by dealing out sloppy hugs and soliciting affection than by earning approval honestly. Normand, when he was gambling, he went the other way, turned sullen, didn't talk much to the guys. And the more he tuned out, I'm sure the more he needed approval from...somewhere."

Alicia's eyes narrowed, as if Behn had morphed into something surprising.

"This doesn't make me a philosopher," he said. "It makes me a drunk. After a while you begin to spot the ways in which a drunk keeps it together. I always wondered where Normand had his refuge. Now I know."

Alicia said, "I fed his dog when he was away on road trips. This does not make me his keeper."

But she peered down at the floor mat, and Behn knew what she was thinking. Bad memories were bubbling up. Memories of hockey players and perhaps of the reason that she had begun to hate them. Not because of anything they had done to her, but because of what they had done to Normand. Or what she told herself they did to him. Behn watched her chew her lip, watched her wrestle a demon. He let a long silence pass before saying, "Sorry for lying to you," and opening the door.

He had one leg on the pavement before he heard her say, "Wait a minute."

"Yeah?"

"You really think Normand might have known Randolph Skalky?"

"I doubt it," Behn said. "It's like I said, it's the only thing I have right now."

She nodded forlornly, then lowered her forehead to the steering wheel, rested it there, sighed heavily. "His crying bouts were a sight to behold, you know that?"

Behn stayed silent.

"He worried that if he breathed a word about how—well, about how he felt his life was getting away from him—the guys on the team would have laughed him out of town."

"A lot of the guys knew how he was feeling," Behn said. "Some things you can't hide."

She shifted her head, and the car horn bleated, snapping her upright in her seat. Her eyes had watered up, and when she blinked, a tear trickled down her cheek. She made no move to wipe it away. Behn liked that.

"Okay," she said.

"Okay?"

"Let's find out why he had this ring."

He closed the door, directed her left, then right, then left again and into the parking lot of Kruk's Jewellers.

"Why here?" she said. "You know these people?"

"No," Behn said, "but I don't know much about diamonds either."

The air inside the overlit shop smelled like money. An overdressed man stood with his hands folded atop the counter. His smile looked plastered on.

"May I help you, sir?"

"We'd like you to appraise a diamond."

"I'm afraid we don't do appraisals."

"We don't need official," Behn said. "A ballpark figure will do."

The smile faded.

"Say fifty dollars?" Behn said.

Instant smile retrieval. Alicia slid the stone onto the glass countertop, and the clerk pulled out a magnification loupe.

"If I could take the stone out of the setting," he said, "I'd know better what you have."

Alicia shook her head. "The stone has to stay where it is."

He hunched over and squinted. He took his time, more time than seemed necessary. Behn glanced around the shop, then noticed that Alicia was watching him. He let her do that, study him without being caught doing it. He pretended to care about a watch display.

The jeweller finally spoke up: "You see these symmetrical cuts? All the light comes out the tip. There's not one blemish on this thing. I haven't seen one this nice in a while."

"Can you put a price on it?"

"It's the setting, the setting's a problem. I'd have to weigh it."

"It's missing its owner," Alicia said. "I don't want you to mess with it."

"Missing it's owner?"

"Yes."

"How unfortunate."

"A ballpark figure?" Behn said.

"Six or seven. Minimum. Maybe up to ten, depending on the carat."

"Thousand?"

"There's not a single inclusion," the jeweller said. "Someone put some real care into it."

"Could you buy a ring like this anywhere?" Alicia said.

"Anyplace they care about quality."

Alicia snapped the felt lining from the box. "There's this number. What is it, a serial number?"

"That's a certification. GIA."

"Huh?"

"Gemological Institute of America. Every stone over half a carat, they give it a grading report. Clarity, carat, colour. All our stones go through the GIA. Sir, have we met before? Something tells me I've—"

"So I could call them," Alicia said, "and find out which jeweller sold it?"

The clerk rebedded the ring in its felt cushion ever so gently. "I'm afraid not. They deal mainly with wholesalers. The wholesalers bring in their stones. Basically, they're buying a guarantee of quality from an independent source."

Alicia snapped the box closed. "You've seen him on TV," she said. "He plays for the Cowboys. Want an autograph?"

The jeweller shook his head. Behn approved of the candour.

"Thanks for your help," Behn told him.

He skimmed a fifty onto the counter, but the clerk was too dignified to pick it up until they left.

Back in the car, Alicia pulled a fifty from her purse and tossed it onto Behn's lap while she watched the road.

"I pay my own way."

"So if we ever go on a date, I can choose something twice as expensive."

"What now?" she said.

"You know the Horseshoe Casino?"

Her eyes shot suspicion at him. "Normand's favourite place."

"His favourite place," Behn said. "Like I said, it's probably nothing."

*   *   *

The Horseshoe hadn't changed much since Behn was a Bruin in town to play the Stormriders. Road trips back then weren't for playing hockey, but for finding new and better ways of spending money and murdering brain cells. When the Bruins had a layover in Renfrew, blackjack at the Horseshoe was a must. It wasn't a splashy place. It had more video poker than slot machines, the drinks were expensive, and you'd never see many extravagant spenders.

But the owner, a guy named Tony Tran, kept a room off to the side where high-rollers could get together and bet whatever amount they wanted. The house brought the parties together and supervised. Each player paid the house a four-hundred-dollar fee. Everything was off the books.

Alicia waited in the car while Behn asked a security guard for the head man. Tran wasn't in. Instead, the guard took him to the manager's office, right next to the unmarked door to the same room where Behn had lost some of his Bruins salary. The nameplate read "Marshall Toby, Executive Manager."

As Behn walked in, a dumpy, balding man in grey pinstripes looked up from his paperwork. He looked like something straight out of *The Sting*.

"Behn McAvoy. Well. What brings the Renfrew Cowboys down here?"

Either he hadn't been watching the news or he was being

tactful about Skalky. Behn shook his hand. "I used to get in on your poker games."

"My poker games?"

"Next door, the unlicensed stuff. Maybe that was before your time."

Toby laughed and shook a naughty finger. "Now, even if we did run something like that, you wouldn't expect me to come right out and admit it, would you?" He leaned back in his chair. Confident. "We run a clean business here."

"Of course you do." Clean. Tony Tran was into dope trafficking and cigarette smuggling, as mobby as a guy could get in a smallish city like Renfrew.

"You gonna light many lamps this year?" Toby asked. "My brother has you in his pool."

"I'll try."

"Gonna make the playoffs?"

"You can bet on it."

Another laugh. "I'd make a killing if I did. The board outside has you as twelve-to-one underdogs. Drink?" He motioned to a walnut liquor cabinet against the wall.

"Actually, Mr. Toby, I have someone waiting outside for me. I was hoping you could answer a few quick questions about a friend of mine."

"Oh?"

"Normand Fournier."

Now a twitch at the guy's lips. "The hockey player? A tragedy, that. A real sad story..."

"He used to gamble here," Behn said, "religiously. You being up on the Cowboys, you'd know that. You'd also know if he ever showed up with a guy named Randolph Skalky."

Toby thought about it. "I don't know what you're driving at, but—"

"I don't have time for foot-dragging, Toby. Be straight, or I'll turn what I've found so far over to the cops."

Toby gawked at him. Toby didn't look used to pressure. Toby looked like he'd lived a lucky life, not much stress. His copious fat was worn proudly.

"Cops?"

"Skalky's dead," Behn said. "The cops'll be by to ask you some have-you-seen-this-man questions. Tell me what I want to know, and I'll keep mum about the back-room stuff.

Toby's cheeks flushed like bloated crabs. "But what exactly do you want me to tell you?"

"What I just said, that you recall seeing Normand and Skalky here."

"But I've never heard of this Skalky."

"Normand would have been one of your best customers. He have any powerful friends? Or enemies?"

Toby shook his head.

"Toby, it was a long time ago, but I remember sitting down with a certain alderman. And a certain high-ranking cop whose job was to ensure that all proceeds from gambling went to government and to charity. But that's no problem for you. That's water off your back."

Behn headed for the door.

"Look," Toby said, "I won't confirm that Normand or anyone here ever gambled illegally, okay?"

"That's not what I'm after."

"But what if I pass on a rumour? It's a rumour you could have heard from anyone. Understand?"

"Sure," Behn said.

"Normand was in debt. A lot of people were unhappy with him."

"Including Tony Tran?" Behn said.

Toby shook his head.

"Including Randolph Skalky?"

"I already told you, I don't know any Skalky."

Then what good was this? Behn moved to leave, but Toby blocked him again.

"Look," the fat man said, "names of players are supposed to be confidential."

"I'll keep them confidential."

"Tony wouldn't like you messing around with his customers. He's likely to give you some trouble."

"Worse than the trouble I'm already in?"

That stumped him, but he soldiered on. "Okay. You need someone who knows more about Normand than I do, try Jack Brigham."

"Who's that?" Behn said.

"He used to be a partner at Pullman and Shantz. Lawyer. Normand and Brigham always seemed to be in on the same games. Rumour had it Normand was so overextended that Brigham was funding him. Big-time."

"Another rumour, huh?"

"You're looking for dirt on Normand, that's all I can give you. I swear, there's been no Skalky at any of the games. Tony doesn't let just anyone play. He's afraid of—"

"Of guys like me," Behn said. "Guys who'll squeal to the cops. Only I'm not actually going to squeal. Where can I reach Brigham?"

Toby looked away. "I'm not sure you can. He went bust last year. Quit the law firm and ran away."

"Toby, why do I get the feeling that the good Mr. Brigham doesn't exist?"

"Really, he hopped into his Caddy and poof, good bet he left town. He had it bad, gambling. He owed more money than he could ever repay." Toby finally looked Behn in the eyes. "And yes, he owed Tony, too, if that matters."

It didn't. None of this tied Skalky to Normand. Toby stood anxious and oval-eyed, dreading everything that could or might be done to him. He clutched the door handle, holding Behn prisoner.

"Okay, Toby, I'm sorry for coming on so strong."

"And the cops?" Toby said.

Woo and Spinetti would have their own way of looking into Skalky's presence at the Horseshoe. Behn said, "There's nothing for me to tell them."

"Fine," Toby said, scraping up some poise. "It's all such unpleasant business. An innocent game of cards, and the potential for embarrassment is so great that—"

"Toby?"

"What."

"You can take your hand off the door so I can leave."

Toby stepped aside. On his way out, Behn heard him say something about not letting Tony Tran know they'd had this talk.

Tran would go ballistic.

*   *   *

Alicia's house wasn't large or splashy. There were three bedrooms, a modest living room and a kitchen with a half-eaten bagel crumbing the counter. She led Behn down to the unfinished basement and started in on Normand's belongings. Between sipping coffee and digging into a stack of *Sports Illustrated*s, Behn figured, briefly, that a drink would go down nicely right about now. The notion fired recollections of the rehab days in New York. Drying out, he'd met plenty of celebrities. Actors and singers, mainly, with a few writers and well-known ballplayers for variety's sake. It was the same story with each of them—big paychecks, bigger egos, zero willingness to look inward for the source of their troubles. Being with them was therapeutic, because to be with them was to look in the mirror. Nancy Reagan was right: just say no. Simple didn't always mean easy.

On her third box, Alicia unearthed more photos. She sat next to Behn, and they riffled through them together. Most were old family snapshots. A few were of Randi, the model who'd given Europe a crack. Nothing had anything to do with Boston.

"That's all," she said. "All the other boxes have kitchen stuff and furniture."

"You're sure?"

"I went through them this morning." She wiped her forehead. "This feels wrong anyway. Seeing if he chummed around with murderers."

Behn scanned the incredible mess around them. She had Normand's whole life down here. "Why do you keep all this stuff?"

She shrugged. "Why does anyone keep anything? What's a collection? What's an heirloom?"

"It happened almost a year ago, Alicia."

"I know." Fatigue crawled into her features. "A year or a century?"

He gave her some time to get over a private thought.

"You're not like the rest of them, Behn McAvoy."

"Thank you. I think."

"You haven't told me how great you are, and you haven't made a pass at me. Usually by this time I'd know your stats, your salary and just how much of a bitch your ex-wife is."

"The ex-wife's a saint," Behn said, "and I assure you the stats are exceptional."

"Of course."

"And I give my salary to lepers."

"I wouldn't doubt it."

"In Mongolia. Fly to Beijing, hike the rest of the way."

She laughed, then remembered why they were here. She tossed the photos aside and expended great effort in gaining her feet. "So what do we do now? Call Skalky's family, see if they had Normand over for dinner and plotting?"

The furnace behind her kicked in, sending a tinny rumble up through the ducts. "You're tired," Behn told her.

"I'm tired?"

"It's the impression I get. You're tired of Normand."

She was also very hard not to stare at. Which was a complicating thought. He pulled the original snapshot of Normand from his pocket and said, "Let's keep things simple. Let's find out where this bar is."

Ten

The Renfrew Cowboys' first game without Behn McAvoy was a case of men playing against boys. The Tacoma Titans scored on a lame-duck wrist shot forty-nine seconds in. Number nine earned a game misconduct for pounding on number seven, who had pounded on number four. Number three was concussed when he tripped on a teammate's stick blade. Number sixteen scored the Cowboys' goal, but did so blindly, deflecting a slapshot while trying to duck it. The Cowboys lost seven to one, and owner Pamela Wells, who had flown in from Vancouver to buy out Behn McAvoy's contract, felt that the score was flattering.

This despite the fact that Pamela Wells paid little attention to hockey games per se. She considered hockey a pointless spectacle of vanishing Canadian machismo. Slashing. Charging. *Fighting.* Fighting on skates. Pulling the jersey over your opponent's head and pummelling the blind bugger senseless—to the uproarious approbation of six thousand beer-guzzling, blood-sniffing subhumans. No, hockey wasn't sport, it was the modern version of gladiator school.

But it was also wonderful business. And it just so happened that the business was at a point in its development where it could bring her an obscene and beautiful profit. The Canucks had come cheaply back in eighty-nine, only twenty-one million U.S., including the minor-league affiliate, then in Medicine Hat. Pamela Wells made the purchase knowing full well that the organization, properly managed, could go in only one direction. An American city where they'd like their own team—a Cleveland or a Portland—would one day pay a bundle for a club.

Because in recent years there'd been a market shift. Second-tier Canadian towns like Quebec and Winnipeg and Renfrew had lost their teams to U.S. cities. The league's appeal down south was dubious, but, thanks to a new, owner-friendly collective bargaining agreement, the business was still a cash cow. The NHL had expanded into Florida, of all places, and though it wasn't profiting there, there were plenty of overzealous American zillionaires clamouring to throw funny money at underperforming Russian superstars and Canadian prima donnas who could count only as high as the number of teeth still left in their mouths. If the sport— the *business*—could attract such interest in the sunbelt, then the time to sell was approaching. Only a week before hearing that Behn McAvoy had killed a man, Pamela Wells had decided she would soon put the Vancouver Canucks up for sale. Throw in the Renfrew Cowboys, too, assuming anyone would want them.

But now, having on the payroll an ex-drunk who might be a murderer wouldn't do much for her portfolio in the eyes of potential buyers. Especially when that man was now writing a biography about drinking and debauchery in pro hockey. Everyone would want to read his story. Aspersions would be cast. So move the story out of the organization. Be cold but careful. Run your hockey teams the same way you run your brewery. Get McAvoy gone.

Pamela Wells stayed in her SkySuite for a full hour after the game. While the players showered and dressed and told the reporters their clichés, she went over McAvoy's contract to inspect the termination clause.

All the zeros in his salary leapt off the page. A hundred

and sixty thousand a year? In U.S. dollars? And a no-trade contract with almost two full years left on the current deal? Who had negotiated this thing, the team mascot? The deal was structured so that she wouldn't save a dime on a buyout. The word "loss" came to mind in writ-large letters.

The stands were empty when she stormed down to the concourse to find coach Ken Duguay. A big man stopped her outside a canteen. He was pale, with thinning blond hair and pink rabbit eyes that seemed to move in all directions at once. His nose was swollen.

"How's a guy get a autograph?" Alf Lundgren asked nasally, thrusting out a pen and paper. "I come lookeeg for players, but I guess they go out some differett exit."

Wells said, "Have you seen a doctor about that?"

"Never mide the node," he told her.

Creepy. "The Agrodome is closed after games," she told him. "I hope you enjoyed the game."

Trailer trash. Minor-league hockey. She slipped past him and found Ken Duguay in his office jotting something on a portable chalkboard for tomorrow's practice. When Duguay told her he didn't know where McAvoy was, and that a detective Woo would make sure Behn called in tomorrow, she told him to have Behn phone her, ASAP.

"Why?" Duguay asked, moving his chalkboard defenseman from the blue line to the enemy crease.

"Because I asked you to."

When she left the office, the blond man was gone, but now one of the players was waiting. Larry Groin, or Coyne, something like that. He'd been the miraculous architect of the Cowboys' lone goal this evening. He thrust out his handshaking hand and stated his name. A cloud of cologne clogged the air.

"What can I do for you?" Wells said.

"Well, Miss Wells, you might have noticed that the Cowboys are, how shall I say, really shitty?"

She didn't answer.

"Well, it's because of the atmosphere in the dressing room. I mean, you wouldn't know this, not being in Renfrew on a daily basis, but hockey players need some...encouragement sometimes? We're as emotional as the next guy."

"And the point is?" she said.

"I'm saying we have no morale."

"No?"

"No. Because the coach is brutal. And that's something you maybe oughta think about addressing."

She couldn't believe it. Was a player standing here grinning and telling her to fire the coach? A basic instinct kicked in. "What's your salary, Coyne?"

"You pay me. Don't you know?"

"How much?" she said.

"Fifty-one thousand plus incentives. Canucks call me up, it goes up to six-hundred. But I'll never make the Canucks, not under this coach."

"Aha," she said, "so you're the one with the problem, not Ken."

Coyne's hands swatted away bees. "No no no, you got me all wrong. I just mention it as a—"

"Young man, if there's one thing I can't forgive, it's backstabbing."

She started past him, but he stepped around her and blocked her way. The gall. He looked a little like the actor Christian Slater. Compact body, big mouth.

"It's like with this McAvoy fiasco," he said. "Fans like him because he played for the Bruins, got lots of press. But let's face it, the guy'll be thirty-six next year. Only place he's going is retirement. Yet Duguay's giving him twenty-six minutes a game. Twenty-six. Guys' asses are bonded to the bench. I thought the farm team was supposed to develop young talent for the parent team."

"It is." She wouldn't begrudge him his rare moments of insight.

"So yeah, get rid of Mac, too. Who's to stop you?"

"You're a funny little man, Coyne."

"Yeah?" he said. "You might think you're stuck with him —he's got that no-trade clause and all—but you're not."

"Oh?"

"Uh uh. Maybe... I mean, maybe I got an idea."

"An idea," she said.

"Yeah."

Clearly, the idea was still coming to him. She checked his ears for smoke.

He said, "How about you let me buy you dinner or something?"

"Not if you were the last person on—"

"Let's not shit each other, Miss Wells, you'd like to get rid of Behn, wouldn't you? Because that's what you do, you think about money, which he costs you a lot of. No shame in thinking that way as long as you admit it."

Candour was an odd trait for a backstabber. Three-hundred and twenty thousand dollars for Behn McAvoy over the next two years. Three twenty, non-disposable.

"And hell, it's not like I'm the only guy on the team who wants him gone. Just yesterday Arch threatened to murder the bastard."

"Arch?" Wells said.

"Halkidis. Archie. Archie's going nowhere fast, thanks to

Mac stealing his ice time. Arch does everything—hits, fights, plays it tough—but he can't get anything going with the coach."

"At least he doesn't complain to the owner."

"Just give me a ride home, Miss Wells, that's all I ask. I don't even have my car here. It's on the fritz."

She wondered. The buyout—McAvoy's contract—would look irresponsible to prospective buyers. Maybe if she gave Coyne a ride home, she could keep the tinted windows on the limo rolled up?

"If I give you a lift," she said, "will you promise to never bother me again?"

"Fabulous," he told her.

She regretted the move. There was more to Larry Groin—Coyne—than she wanted to experience. Fighting his cologne fumes, she walked with him to the exit. The white-haired man with the swollen nose was there, still loitering. His hands were jammed into his pant pockets. He gave off a long sideways glance but didn't say anything. He was trying to listen in on their talk.

She also noticed that he didn't bother asking Larry Coyne for his John Hancock. Odd for a guy who was seeking autographs. Something about him told her to give him a wide berth.

Leaving the building, she gave herself over to a shiver of fear.

*   *   *

The obvious truth was this: she hated Mac, and she wasn't about to say why. With the limo rolling between the perimeter of Chinatown and the downtown Sheraton, Larry Coyne let Pamela Wells blow smoke. She said she had the team's best interests in mind, she only wanted to win, to make the playoffs. She didn't know why she was willing to listen to him, Larry Coyne, right now. My, how she was full of it.

There had been no Pamela Wellses back in Piapot, but if there was one thing the prairie hamlet gave Larry Coyne growing up, it was the time and the space to learn how to judge things objectively. There wasn't a lot to do in town. There was the Royal Bank, the Co-op, Harry's Bar. There was a Chinese restaurant that served congealed MSG, a wheat elevator where the old boys hung out and smoked and talked about how the goddamned Liberals were screwing Saskatchewan sideways with their goddamned Wheat Board. People trusted you. You didn't lock doors. You spent more time on the farms than in town, even if, like Coyne, you were one of the seventy-six who lived in town. The nearest hockey rink was in Tompkins, twelve miles away, and Coyne had no childhood horror stories about having to trudge through three feet of snow, thirty below, to get to practice at six o'clock on Sunday morning. If his dad couldn't drive him, a neighbour could. Everyone was dying to make a star of the kid who showed such promise on the ice. They were all so damn hopeful for you, so accommodating and starry-eyed about the NHL and absurd contracts and appearances on *Hockey Night in Canada*. Coyne figured they didn't know their asses from their elbows.

Even his parents—or his old man, to be precise. Jake Coyne had been a laconic man who ran the local gas station and spoke in aphorisms. He worked hard and played by the rules, and what did he get for it? Achingly slow business, robberies every two years, abominable provincial taxes that helped drive him damn near insane before a stroke put him out of his misery eighteen months ago. All of the old man's farmer ethics, his proudly hayseed view of the world ("Our town is so small that we gotta step outside of it to change our minds!")—it was a loser fib he'd sold himself to keep the truth at bay.

Jake Coyne had been two hundred thousand dollars in debt when he died, and as a point of honour, son Larry knew he had to pay the money back. The loan had been his, Larry's, idea; he'd advertised it around town as such. It had gone toward jazzing up the gas station with smart pumps that accepted credit cards, and toward installing a snappy neon sign out front, U Save Gas, and a deep fryer, oven and walk-in cooler in the back, the main implements for a gas-station restaurant at which hardly anyone ever ate. Larry had thought the renovations would attract more business off the Trans Canada, and he'd been dead wrong. It had been a dumb idea, seriously dumb. It—he—had basically killed his old man.

Wells was telling him something.

"Huh?"

"I said, would you like some brandy?"

"I prefer beer," Coyne said. "Your beer, in fact." He launched into her company's most famous jingle: "I really go-pher Prairie Dog." He watched as she poured herself a drink in a hoity-toity glass as the limo rolled. "What do you have against McAvoy, Miss Wells?"

"Nothing, I—"

"The second I mention he's a problem, you can't get nice to me fast enough. I thought you were gonna give me a big wet one."

The car stopped at a red light outside an Arby's, and Larry Coyne figured she looked a little afraid of him, like he was unbalanced or something.

"Here's what I'm thinking," he said. "I'm thinking I can get Mac to waive that no-trade clause."

"I think I should let you out right here," she said.

"You hear what I said? I can help you save a lot of money. I can help you unload him without paying a dime."

"What makes you so sure I would want to do that?"

"The fact that I know what he makes. And because I've been hearing rumblings. Rumour has it you're looking to sell the Canucks."

"Do you always listen to rumours?"

"And if you're looking to sell, you wouldn't want his embarrassing stories about booze and blackjack hitting the headlines—at least, not while he's in one of your uniforms. I mean, no one would've cared about his book before, but now that he's messed up in this Randolph Skalky thing, he'll be a media pet."

She sighed heavily, but she didn't protest. She was just now understanding that he was not a moron. He was used to being underestimated.

"So," he said brightly, "what I can do for you, I can make Behn amenable to a trade."

"Oh yes?" she said.

"Yes. And all I ask for in return is a shot with the Canucks. Say, ten games."

She laughed uneasily. "This is crazy."

"Sure. Life's crazy."

But not that crazy. Either she agreed or she didn't. If she did, a couple of months from now he'd have the Royal Bank paid off and a big-league career kick-started in the bargain. He was already thinking up ways of ruining Mac's love affair with Renfrew. Plant kiddie porn in his duffel bag. Pay some ultra-skanky hooker to take him to a hotel. Tell her to leave the door open, tell the press photographers where to find them going flub-flub. All it took was imagination.

"I can make it in the NHL, Miss Wells. All I need's a chance."

She still looked as though he were Medusa and she'd been caught gaping. This woman wasn't in the habit of letting others set the conditions. She was the type who always had to be in control. He pulled a cigar from his blazer pocket. She took control of her tongue long enough to tell him not to light it, so he took great pleasure in lighting it anyway, cracking the window as a compromise.

She said, "You misunderstand me. I would never, ever, sanction any such plan that even remotely resembled—"

"Tut tut," he said, holding up a stop-sign hand. "I'm talking win-win here. I deliver for you, you deliver for me, we're both happy. I don't deliver, no one has to know we had this talk. You'd have no trouble getting the Canucks to call me up. Simple phone call. Now tell your driver to slow down."

"You're not listening to me. You—"

"Driver, stop this tub right now." *Now get out before she makes the wrong decision.*

The driver pulled up near a group of kids playing roller hockey in an icy 7-Eleven parking lot. Coyne tapped his cigar in an ashtray. "Nice talking to you, Miss Wells."

She just sat there shaking her head, flabbergasted. He stepped out of the car and looked back in. "I'll be in touch then. You still have that big mansion here in town?" If memory served, she'd moved out to the coast after buying the Canucks. Her house in Renfrew was a local landmark, having been lived-in by the town's first mayor. Now her daughter lived there.

She nodded.

"Then I'll be calling you."

She shook her head as if to say "Please don't," but he slammed the door and the car rolled away, and he *knew* she was looking back at him through the window. Since she didn't have to do or risk anything until he, Larry Coyne, had fulfilled his end of the bargain, the idea of the deal would grow on her. It would have to. He would make it grow on her.

He straightened his collar against the cold. The hockey-playing kids were veering around the parking-lot ice, fighting for balance, missing the orange ball. They needed ice skates, not in-line skates. A boy of twelve or thirteen recognized him. The kid hacked out a few strides to reach him. Panting, the kid asked for an autograph. He was bow-legged, wobbly on the spot, snot running from nose to mouth.

Biting down on the cigar, Larry Coyne asked the kid if his parents knew their kid was out here acting like an idiot.

Eleven

Eddie Woo picked over Behn McAvoy's statement—someone potshotting his Jeep outside James Teal's place—only to be interrupted by the phone. He knew who was calling.

"We missed you at the press conference," the caller said.

Harlan Pertemby, chairman of the Committee for Cultural Diversification. The cops called him Snarlin' Harlan for his tenacity in promoting the "Canadian mosaic".

"Harlan, I've been too busy playing cop to lend my racial profile to a press conference."

"I'm sorry to hear such sarcasm from you, Eddie. Your work to promote multiculturalism in the past was vitally—"

"The key words there," Woo said, "are 'the past'."

Once in the past, actually, and it wasn't multiculturalism that had floated his boat anyway. A rookie constable, who through no fault of his own was Chinese, had shot a man in the heart during a domestic violence call. An ex-felon fresh out of Bowden had been hammering on his wife, and when the cops arrived, he threatened everyone present with a paring knife. In the process, he hurled at Constable James Chan as many racial epithets as his tiny mind could produce. Chan instructed him twice to put down the knife, and when the man refused, he plugged him. The cop argued later that there had been sufficient danger to warrant the shot, but a paramedic who'd witnessed the incident told the papers Chan had blown the guy away because scum was scum, and he didn't like being called a hopsing. In the aftermath, Woo vouched for Chan. He'd believed the constable's story. Ever since then, Snarlin' Harlan had hounded him.

"Eddie, I know that Lieutenant MacKenzie likes his people to be team players. If you're not willing to go out into the community from time to time, then I have to tell you, it doesn't reflect well upon you."

"I think the boss is in his office," Woo said. "If you call him up, you can tell him how disappointed you are."

He slammed down the phone, then asked himself why he let a nut like Snarlin' Harlan bother him. He sat back in his chair, peeled some plastic wrap from a ham sandwich, and finished McAvoy's statement. A second gunman shooting McAvoy's Jeep. This was going to take a while. He slid Stevie Ray Vaughan into his Walkman. After a fast-gulped dinner and two tracks from *Texas Flood*, he pulled off the head phones, picked up the phone and punched in Detective Dante Spinetti's extension number.

"Spinetti."

"ME's report come in yet?"

Spinetti said not yet.

"Then let me know when it does."

"You got it."

He hung up. Randolph Skalky's body had drifted two kilometres downstream before washing up. There had been no visible head injury, no gunshot wound, no sign of incapacitation before the man was sent swimming. Looked like death by drowning, but the medical examiner was the only one who could say so with a degree of confidence. The autopsy was expected by seven thirty, meaning twenty minutes ago.

Woo slipped open his notebook and went over his field notes. The search of Behn McAvoy's cabin had turned up nothing beyond the facts that the suspect listened to country music, read voraciously and didn't have a television. And the scene at the weir had yielded nothing to contradict McAvoy's story about his encounter with Randolph Skalky. There was one set of footprints—Skalky's—in the frost leading to the weir's gravel and concrete. Skalky's car, found parked on the shoulder back at the highway, was a rental from Tilden. Nothing pointed to more than two people being out there, and there was one 9 mm cartridge lying where the weir's retaining wall met the concrete ground.

The phone rang.

"Woo."

"Report just came in." Dante Spinetti.

"And?"

"Cause of death: cerebral anoxia. Weeds and gravel in the lungs. Which can't get there unless he breathed them in himself. Also minor ATP depletion because of the icy water. No chlorine in the lungs. The man died of drowning. In that river."

"Time of death?"

"You'd have to guess. Water was so cold, rigor hadn't set in."

Swell. Even the stiff served up no clues. "Spinny, I want you to call the National Crime Information Centre."

"The FBI, Eddie?"

"They keep a database on stolen weapons in the States. See if they can trace our Sauer."

"Maybe it wasn't stolen."

"Which would make it easier to trace. And check the airlines, see when Skalky came up here, and if he rented that car from Tilden himself. When that's done, find out if he had any money in the bank or if he was in debt."

"Cullen's men'll take care of that," Spinetti said.

"Then you know who to direct your questions to, don't

you? And find out where McAvoy's ex-wife is."

"Okay."

Woo cut the connection and put a call through to Boston. Lieutenant Cullen came on the line sounding downright frisky.

"Hey, Wong, talk about timing. Read in the paper this morning, the U.N. did this rating of the world's countries. You know what, you guys came in first. Third year in a row."

"So our government likes to remind us. How'd you guys do?"

"Third, behind Norway. Apparently balmy weather isn't one of their yardsticks."

"I forgot Boston was in the tropics," Woo said. "You have anything new for me on Skalky?"

"Uh-uh, still tracking down friends and relatives. It seems Skalky doesn't have many buddies outside of Cedar Junction. His wife, she's crazy with shock right now. They've got her sedated, so we'll have to wait awhile before we get anything sensible out of her. How about you? Any leads on whoever blasted your hockey player's Jeep? Sounds like you got an action-rich environment."

War lingo. An ex-soldier. "Action yes, rich no. Talk to you later, Cullen."

Hanging up, Woo sifted through the pile on his desk for Randolph Skalky's mug shot. Time to flash the dead man's face around the Horseshoe Casino.

* * *

"Do you have a computer?" Alicia said.

"There's no phone line or cable at the cabin," Behn said. "But when I get to the motel, I'll hire a P.I. firm in Boston.

74

You can scan the photos and send them to him."

"You think they'll really track down this bar?" Alicia said.

"I don't know."

He wasn't optimistic. He asked Alicia to call him a cab.

"You're a cab," she said, and from her expression he saw that the lameness in the joke was intended. She wanted something sour in the air, something to keep her from feeling comfortable with all of this.

The last few minutes in her living room were awkward, the kind where you can hear clocks ticking. The setting, her own home, weighed her down. Thoughts of things unpleasant. Memories. For a moment Behn wanted to take her in his arms. He wanted to be dashing, her saviour, "swaive and de-boner." He probably would have made a move if he hadn't been sure that she would've welcomed it by kneeing him in the groin.

When the cab arrived, they both jumped to their feet.

In the car, the feeling that he was being followed grew slowly. The car turned a corner, a black Taurus turned with it. The taxi changed lanes, the Taurus stayed two cars behind. Being shot at twice in one day didn't help Behn's analytical skills at such moments. Every car on the road was a threat. He had the taxi drop him off at the Sears building downtown. The Taurus pulled up to a loading zone half a block back and killed its lights.

The Sears revolving-door entrance was crowded with shoppers. Behn watched the car from amid the throng. A dark windshield concealed the driver. A moment later, the headlights flashed on and the Taurus made a U-turn and disappeared.

He found a pay phone and called Alicia, told her they'd been followed from the police station.

"Thanks a lot," she said, and he heard the line go dead.

He fished out another thirty-five cents and called Jay Ireland, a reporter on the Renfrew Cowboys beat at the *Sun*. Ireland was that rare thing for a sports reporter, a man of integrity. He had contacts at the phone company who could check for listed or unlisted phone numbers for Jack Brigham, Normand's putative gambling partner, nationwide. Ireland would keep the favour off the record, but the check would take a day or so.

Then Behn called Scotia Bank and asked for Mariola Lacroix, the wife of teammate Benoit Lacroix. She would run a credit check on Jack Brigham in exchange for Chinese and a movie, just her and Benoit—Behn would get the kids for the night.

"Deal," Behn said. Then he used the last of his change to call the Buffalo District Police Station. Woo and Spinetti were out of the office, so Behn said to tell them he'd be staying at the Western Holiday down on Eleventh Avenue Southeast, a few minutes west of the Agrodome.

He cut through downtown and kept his head up for the Taurus. He almost wished the car would return. The Western Holiday was going to be a prison. He'd never sat back before, never removed himself from the game like they were asking him to do now. What kind of person twiddled his thumbs while someone else cleaned up his problems? Worrying would become an unwelcome pastime.

The suspense, quite literally, could kill him.

Twelve

Jerry, this scruffy rink rat, kept staring at Alf Lundgren's nose, which was ironic given the juicy bomb of a wart on Jerry's own nose. At first Jerry wouldn't talk, but a little persistence had made him nervous and agreeable. Some of the Cowboys liked to unwind at the King Eddie, a strip joint down on Eleventh.

Alf found an exit and decided to cover the eight blocks to the bar by foot. But first give the players some time to get lubricated, some time to slow the reflexes. He stepped into the first fast-food joint along the way: MJ Submarine. The teenager behind the counter had a name tag that read "Bill". Alf told Bill he wanted a club sub, extra bacon. Then he sat down in a booth and waited.

A dumpy old guy in a turban pushed a mop around the floor. He moved in slow motion, his back to Alf. He couldn't care less whether his mop picked anything up.

"You look like you got the low-downs," Alf said across the floor.

The man turned and leaned on his mop. "Huh?"

"I said you look depressed. And watching you be depressed makes me depressed."

The guy shrugged.

"What's your name?"

"Kamil."

"Well, come over here, Kamil."

Alf held up his right hand, his fingers spread out as a display. Kamil squinted, not understanding. Rolling the mop and bucket closer, Kamil finally made out the display: the hand had no fingernails. Kamil's nose crinkled.

"Stinson's poultry," Alf said. "It's from the bacteria in chicken carcasses."

Kamil didn't reply.

"You got yourself a cruddy job, guy, but mine was worse. So buck up."

"Gross." It was Bill, looking up from the sandwich in progress.

Alf explained that he'd worked as a catcher at the poultry plant, which was out in Brooks. Spent nine hours a day picking birds from the floor of 40-degree Celsius holding pens. "I'd stuff the little fuckers in these containers, then they'd go on to the hangers."

"The hangers?" Kamil was now interested. Bill was back on the sandwich.

"They're the guys who string the birds up so this razor wire can slice their heads off. Day I started there, two other catchers were off sick with salmonella. An hour into the job, I'd been pecked at and pissed on by so many birds, I didn't know up from down."

Kamil commiserated. "A man's got to work."

"Don't I know it," Alf said, "don't I know it." They shared a moment of mum solidarity. "They spread this ammonia around. It got so I couldn't tell the smell of chicken shit from a cheeseburger in the cafeteria."

"Awful," Kamil agreed.

Alf leaned forward. "Would you believe I picked up four thousand birds a day?"

"You did?"

"It was supposed to be eight, but the foreman didn't care. Hell, I had the job no one else wanted. Hey, Bill."

Bill looked up.

"A coffee and club for Kamil here. Let's give him a break, okay?"

Bill said hell if he cared, and Kamil wiped his hands on his apron and slid in across from Alf.

"Luckily," Alf told his new pal, "I got rescued from all that."

"Rescued?"

"Yeah. Better job offer."

"Where?" Kamil clearly hoped there was another opening.

"Can't tell you."

Won't tell you. Rescued by Ed Newby, friend and old cellmate from the Bowden Penitentiary. Alf still felt intensely lucky about the whole thing. Newby had heard from Gary Grant, who Alf had done some hitchhiking with, that Alf had fallen on hard times. He said he had some contacts in Peru. Guys brought merchandise up through Brownsville and Laredo, Newby distributed it. Instant profit margin. You wanna kill a guy, Alf?

"All done," Bill said from across the counter. "You want that heated?"

"Nah." Alf got up and retrieved his meal while Bill got to work on Kamil's sub.

"Excuse me," Alf told Kamil, "I'm starving."

He chomped off a good quarter of the sub and did some crocodile swallowing. The guy to be killed was a hockey player for the Renfrew Cowboys. Lived in a cabin out in the woods—no address for it, but there was an address for this apartment he hung out at in downtown Renfrew; chummed around with this writer. So you, Alf, do the job, don't ask who's footing the bill, never visit me in person. Those were the only ground rules. Follow them and the second ten grand would find you at the Regent Hotel.

Fine. Alf figured he could kill a guy.

He hoped.

Kamil watched Alf eat for a while—gaped at him with lost-puppy eyes. "I could use a better job."

"Sure you could." Alf sniffled and coughed over his sandwich. It was a light cough, but a cough nonetheless. He dug into his coat pocket and popped two vitamin C pills.

"I have four children," Kamil said. "My wife, she doesn't speak English so well. She can't find a job."

"That's too bad, but I can't get you a job."

"The government used to help us, but now I work two jobs, and the bills just always get bigger."

You bought a guy a sandwich, you became his uncle. Alf wrapped up the second half of his sub and zipped up his coat. "I'd like to help you," he said, "but the thing is, I'm not exactly hiring."

"But I only—"

"Hey, do I look like Unemployment Canada? Quit being such a fuckin' whiner, okay?"

He stepped out to the cold of Eleventh just as Bill finished Kamil's sandwich. Unwrapping the remainder of his own sub while he walked, Alf felt the cold wind tickle his nostrils. He pitched forward and sneezed four times.

*   *   *

The King Eddie was a typical strip joint with loud music and watery draught beer. Alf waited for his eyes to adjust to the dim interior, then pulled out some sunglasses.

A DJ's voice boomed through a loudspeaker, "All right,

kiddies, all the way from Moscow, Russia, let's give it up for Katya!"

A tawny, anorexic woman draped in a flag of the Soviet Union pattered onto the stage. She started a slow grind to the tune of Elton John's "Nikita". Damn broad was Hispanic. Alf imagined her real name to be Juanita or Conchita. The men near the stage responded to her gyrations with lacklustre applause and the odd smoker's hack.

The Cowboys weren't hard to recognize, all gussied up in loud blazers and expensive cowboy boots. There were four of them at a corner booth. Two of them had acne, bad, just small-town kids playing bigshot with all their pro-hockey moola. Alf sat down at the booth next to them and tried to listen in.

But Elton John killed their voices. A waitress approached him and asked if he wanted a beer. She stared at his fingernail-free hand.

"I don't drink," Alf said. "Gimmie a Coke. Light."

"Why the sunglasses?"

"Is there a bylaw against them?"

She said excuse her for living and clipped away. He strained to eavesdrop again. "Nikita" ended, and the players' talk drifted over. One of them addressed a second one as "Halkidis," said something about Halkidis getting shafted by the motherlovin' ref. But then the Beatles started in on "Back in the USSR."

Alf gave up and waited for his Coke. He adjusted his sunglasses and washed down a vitamin B pill with some Coke. One day his body would be optimal. No steroids, no protein drinks, both of which he'd tried and discarded after getting out of Bowden. They screwed your innards, even shrunk your dick. And all you really needed anyway was a lean, hardy body.

A ready body.

From the corner of his eyes, he saw the player named Halkidis cross the floor to the men's room. Halkidis looked like a boxer: flat nose, leathery skin around the eyes, mangled ears. Maybe he was the team's enforcer. Halkidis ignored Katya as he passed the stage. Alf waited a few seconds, gulped half of his Coke, then headed to the washroom himself.

He found Halkidis at the urinal. The hockey player was still looking down at himself when Alf let him have it, a stiff belt to the back of the head, bouncing the forehead off a wall tile. The player went down and Alf pounced, pinning him to the floor with a knee to the small of the back. He pushed the hockey player's face hard against the cold tiles. The man would not see Alf's face.

The mouth gurgled like a fish being squeezed.

"I'm looking for McAvoy," Alf said.

Nothing. Alf pulled the Browning and dug it into his neck. "I'll pull the trigger." He knew he could do no such thing. "Tell me where his house is. It's some cabin out on the prairie, isn't it?"

"Carseland weir," Halkidis said. "Only house west of the power station. What do you want with—"

"I'm gonna get off you now, okay? Slowly. But I want you to keep your eyes on those floor tiles. You move your head, I'll shoot you."

He stood up and dusted himself off. The player stared obediently at the floor. Alf was halfway to the door when common sense struck. The player would call the cops, and the cops would rush out to McAvoy's place.

Fuckin' retard.

Again, he'd acted before thinking, just like at the writer's place. The counsellors back at Bowden, one of them had said rash actions were often the deeds of demoralized people. Demoralized by failure, or by society's expectations, or by the fact that your old man had beat the hell out of you from the time you could crawl—which was the case with Alf. Demoralized by a fear of taking the time to consider truly painful things. Maybe the counsellors had been right, but at a point like this—a guy on the ground, breathing fast, his hands flat to the floor near his head—theories weren't worth a dime. De-moral suggested im-moral, and when decisions had to be made, life wasn't a question of good versus bad; it was a question of good versus survival.

Alf couldn't see the player's face, but he knew he was terrified. He didn't want to shoot him, but then he didn't want to shoot McAvoy either. He wanted to be in a quiet room somewhere counting the dough from his dildo scam. The heating ducts hummed overhead while he sought options on how to get out of this. After a while, Halkidis slowly turned his head for a peek at his assailant.

By that time, Alf had finally made up his mind on what to do.

Thirteen

A croupier at the Horseshoe remembered Randolph Skalky. Skalky had played a few hands of blackjack, lost maybe a hundred, and left unhappy. Executive Manager Marshall Toby was courteous, but said he had no knowledge of the man. Detective Eddie Woo left the casino hoping forensics would earn its high budget and toss him a lead he could sink his teeth into.

He was at the crime lab, hearing that the dent/hole in Behn McAvoy's Cherokee had been caused by a semi-jacketed projectile, 9 mm, when a tech working another case told him to pick up on line seven. He took the nearest phone.

"Wong, Christmas comes early this year." Cullen.

"How so?" Woo said.

"I've got your perp, and I've got your motive. I've got the whole case tied up with a neat little bow."

Fourteen

Behn lost track of time before he made it to the Western Holiday. Locking the door and drawing the curtains closed, he checked out his prison. The wallpaper was dingy beige. The crooked painting over the bed showed a wrangler lassoing a steer; another one over the TV showed a rustic barn and burnt-brown field beyond a barbed wire fence. The laminated card on the TV promised satellite television, including the Playboy Channel.

An unmarked Crown Victoria pulled into the parking lot. One of the cops inside stayed put while a second one, a constable Clyde Lents, knocked on the door and assured Behn the room would be watched around the clock.

When Lents was gone, Behn dialled Jimmy Teal's number, listened to the answering machine kick in and hung up. Then he took a long shower and tried to get some sleep. A nagging idea slid through the crevices of his thoughts as he lay between the sheets. Jimmy Teal's wisdom, Jimmy's nagging petition: maybe call it a day, retire at the end of the year. All things considered, the career had been hard won. Lately, it had become a case of the head saying go and the legs saying no. There had been arthroscopic surgery on both knees. There had been hip surgery and a thrice-separated left shoulder and a broken knee cap and roughly forty stitches at various points between chin and crown. The daily in-season grind of keeping the lungs as strong as bellows and the thighs free of lactic acid, the playing through injuries, the off-season regimen of cycling and weight-lifting and hill-running—there had been times when Behn could skate well but could hardly walk out of the rink afterwards. There had been other times when rookies half his age made him feel ancient thanks to their knowledge of nutrition and fitness and their well-heeled personal trainers and their obvious care for their bodies far beyond their concern for the welfare of the team. Thirty-five years old was different from twenty years old. Thirty-five wasn't even thirty. And it wasn't as if money was a problem...

His mind wandered further afield. What was the point in seeking out Jack Brigham? If Normand was pals with Brigham, then Brigham might know something about Skalky? Slender prospect. Even if Normand knew Skalky, how would any of this explain Skalky getting paid to kill Behn? Who was it that was to pay him?

Behn's mind took a dozen dead-end turns before settling on Alicia Fournier—not on anything she'd said or done, but on her alone. Something about her stayed with him. The way she held herself. The nanosecond of doubt that cropped up whenever her mask slipped. Her appearance in his mind helped to relax him. He drifted into a sleep unweighted by the day's events. It was a deep sleep, narcotically numb, but a sleep that took something new and pleasant away. He was left with nothing but darkness while time marched on.

*　*　*

The sun spilled through the curtains. Someone was knocking on the door. Behn roused himself to focus on an unknown and unknowable room. Just like the drinking days, waking up in a strange bed and piecing together the events that led you here. A second series of raps brought things into focus: Skalky, the gunshot at Jimmy's place. Real incidents, not hazy episodes in a half-awake dream. He pulled on his jeans, went to the door and asked who it was.

"Detective Woo. You sleeping, Behn?"

The clock said nine o'clock. He hadn't slept this late in years. He opened the door. Woo shook his hand and asked him if he was awake enough for some big news.

"Big meaning good?"

Woo was carrying a notebook. "You sleep well?"

"Sleep isn't the problem. It's the daytime hours I'm worried about."

Woo closed the door. "Two things. First, Archie Halkidis has been shot."

The shock of the statement took away any reply. The cop added that it had happened last night at the King Edward Bar. Halkidis had been out for a drink with Steve Lewington, Patrick Bouchard and Gerry Pelt. The bullet had missed an artery by millimetres. He was now on a respirator at the Mountainview.

"Archie?" Behn stammered. "What the hell's going on?"

"Whoever shot him laid a good one on him first. Clubbed him in the back of the head."

"Mugging?"

"His wallet was in his pocket, almost three hundred dollars."

"So some psycho with a gun is working his way through the Renfrew Cowboys?"

Woo paused over the suggestion. "Are you good friends with him?"

"Will he be okay?"

"They say maybe. You know if he's ever taken any trips to Boston?"

"Where you heading with *that* question?"

"Depends on your answer," Woo said.

Behn rubbed eyes that burned from stress and too much sleep. He said he didn't know Archie's travel habits.

Woo dropped it and moved on to news item number two. "Boston police have arrested Maria."

"Who?"

"Don't tell me you don't remember. You remembered her yesterday."

God. Of course he remembered. He sat down on the bed and buried his head in his hands. The feeling behind his eyes was one of a hangover.

"Correct me if I'm wrong," Woo said. "You ran around drinking and gambling. Atlantic City. You annulled the marriage the same day you told the Bruins you quit hockey."

"It was a mistake," Behn said. "I sobered up, we agreed it was my fault. She was just a kid. She was more my chauffeur than my wife. Why would *she* hire Skalky?"

"She didn't hire him, she married him."

Hangover, hell. "You weren't kidding about 'big.'"

"Five years ago, just before he got sent up for aggravated assault. She waited for him every time he was inside."

If it was five years ago, she was still a kid at the time. "How could a girl like her marry a guy like that?"

"No offence, Behn, but how could she marry you? And anyway, she isn't as sweet and innocent as you remember. Skalky came after you because of your will."

Now the cop wasn't making sense. "I didn't have a will. Not when I was with Maria."

Woo looked embarrassed for him. "When did you write one up?"

"In ninety-eight, when the Stormriders were still in Medicine Hat." Most of the estate was to go to a series of alcohol rehab clinics in the States. Nobody but his lawyer knew of the document.

"Well." Woo pulled a fax from the notebook. "This look familiar?"

The message was neatly typed:

LAST WILL AND TESTAMENT
OF
BEHN THOMAS MCAVOY

I, Behn Thomas McAvoy, a citizen of Koochiching County, Minnesota, being of sound and disposing memory, do hereby make, publish and declare this instrument as my Last Will and Testament, hereby revoking any and all Wills, Codicils and letters of testamentary import I formerly may have made.

Articles I and II dealt with administration of the estate. Article III, Disposition of Property, was worth reading twice:

I devise and bequeath all of my property of whatsoever kind or character and wheresoever situate, whether presently owned or hereafter acquired by me, to Maria Angela Blackwell.

Behn skipped ahead to the signature at the bottom of page two. His. There were also two signatures of witnesses: a Franklin Bradbury and a Nathan Milton. The executor was one Mervin Lane. The date, March 15, 2004, was impossible. The whole damn will was impossible.

"Let me guess," Woo said, "you're stumped."

"To understate it."

"An autograph," the cop said.

"A what?"

"You signed an autograph for Blackwell to give to her brother. She kept it. Then she saw a sample will on the Internet. You can guess the rest."

"She admitted to forging this thing?"

"Yes and no. The two witnesses, they're ex-con buddies of Skalky. She says she thought they'd never have the guts to work the scam. She admits telling Skalky about the idea, but she didn't think he and his buddies would try to kill you." Woo snapped the clipboard shut. "She swears they did all this without her knowledge."

"And this Mervin Lane?"

"Doesn't know him. She says."

Lane, too, denied complicity. He was a lowlife lawyer, a specialist in personal injury who'd had legal troubles of his own. Woo's educated guess was that Lane had signed on for a cut just like the two witnesses had.

"I guess I don't need to tell you, each of them stood to make almost a half million U.S. if you stopped breathing. Maria admitted knowing that your closest living relative is an uncle in North Dakota. That's motive. It shows that she—they—knew no one would contest the will."

Behn blinked, tried to bring some focus. "The shrinks back in rehab were right. Addiction hits you in unexpected ways."

Woo adjusted the Playboy card on the TV. "Boston police have the two witnesses. They admit they signed, but they're saying they didn't want anyone hurt, say they thought the thing was a big joke they'd shared over beers one night. They'll break down sooner or later, when they realize that their word as ex-cons isn't worth doggie do in court. Lane, he'll probably hold out longer." Now Woo straightened the portrait behind the Playboy card. "Nice room."

You were supposed to remember the past. That's how you

would stay off the bottle. Remember the bad times to give the good times more meaning. When the past came back at you, you were supposed to be ready for it. Theoretically.

"This feels like the Twilight Zone."

"Ooh, I like that."

"If it explains Skalky, then why was someone taking a shot at me outside Jimmy's place? And why's Archie lying in the hospital right now?"

"That's a big one for me, too," Woo said. "Why send two men? Whoever took that shot at your Jeep, it's as if he's unrelated."

Behn pulled on his shirt and buttoned it up. Marshall Toby—Jesus. "I dropped by the Horseshoe yesterday."

He told Woo about the visit and about Jack Brigham and about the photos of Normand Fournier in Boston. Woo wrote it all down.

"Playing flatfoot like that," Woo said, "is foolish. It can be counterproductive."

"You'd do the same if it were you. Now how about making some sense of all this—and soon."

"Hey," Woo said, "remember what I told you back at the station yesterday."

Behn thought back. "'Don't lie to me, or I'll put you in a deep, dark place for a long, long time?'"

"I said that?"

"You implied it."

"I told you we always get our man."

"Yeah, but no offence, detective, your man is the one who's doing the getting."

Fifteen

Larry Coyne reached Behn McAvoy's house at ten in the morning. It was colder today, minus fifteen, so he wore a down-filled jacket. The area was deserted and the door locked. He pulled a log from the woodpile and decided to go in through the frosted window next to it.

His last and only visit out here had been during his first week as a Renfrew Cowboy. Behn had invited him and his other linemate, Normand Fournier, over to do some fishing —Mr. Congeniality trying to start a fraternity. Like brotherly love would make it easier to play the neutral-zone trap. Behn and Normand caught trout, Coyne caught nothing. Not that it mattered. For entertainment value, fishing was up there with clipping the toenails. After the day on the river, Normand had discovered that Behn kept no booze in the cabin, in fact didn't drink at all, what with him being an ex-lush. He'd peeled off for the liquor store in High River and (Coyne found out later) ended up at a blackjack table down at the Horseshoe.

So after frying and eating the trout, Coyne and Behn had played some nickle-ante cards and smoked some cigars. Behn told him some war stories about the Bruins, about the tenacity of Terry O'Reilly and Stan Jonathan, about the legions of promising rookies, himself included, who came and went because they couldn't handle the pro game's demands. It was a myth that the NHL chewed players up. The players who didn't make it either couldn't adjust their heads or didn't have the talent. Behn told Coyne that no matter how many goals he'd scored in junior, no matter how many accolades he'd collected, he was a pro now. He had to earn his stripes all over again.

Whatever. Over a winning hand of Hearts, Coyne thought, you have your excuses, I'll have mine. He stayed until eight, when he'd won fifty bucks and had told the old warthog, in no uncertain terms, that he was full of it.

Which now was neither here nor there. Larry Coyne had thirteen hundred dollars worth of Brazilian cocaine in his pocket (better to overdo it than to go too light). He'd bought the stuff last night from three different dealers down in Queen Elizabeth Park, as no single one of them could scare up enough to please him. The cops, led to the cabin by a fisherman's—no, a hiker's—phoned-in report of someone breaking and entering, would see the B&E signs, enter the place, and find the merchandise.

Wells wouldn't approve of this, framing Mac, but the next time she read about her star forward in the papers, it would be about an ex-drunk who had graduated from booze to harder stuff. End of his love affair with Renfrew fans. The headlines would be delicious:

Cowboy Has Sweet Tooth for Nose Candy
Out with the Bottle, In with the Blow

Tabloids. He peeked into the window, took aim with the log, and punched out the glass. Climbing in, he saw that Mac kept a clean house. Bed made up, sink sparkling, big tape and CD collection in a nice shelf on the wall. He checked some of the titles. John Prine, Waylon Jennings, Jerry Jeff Walker. Dated, nasal crap, stuff the older guys listened to back in Piapot. Kris Kristofferson, Johnny Cash. McAvoy wasn't just old for hockey, he was old period. With a gloved hand, Coyne swept glass shards from the window frame, climbed in and went to work.

The coke was in a cellophane bag. First he tossed it onto the kitchen table, then he propped it up against the bread box. Then the right idea came to mind. He crossed to the sink, pulled a napkin from the roll beside the stove, and found a pen on the magazine stand beside the sofa. On the napkin he wrote, in childish, hand-printed letters that would look like someone else's:

You need the stuff so bad, here it is.

Then a flourish:

Pay what you owe or it gets worse.

Put the cops on a false trail. He pulled a knife from a drawer beside the sink and drilled the message and the coke to the wall over the table.

When the cops swung by, there'd have to be a nice mess to get their attention. He overturned the sofa, smashed a wall photo of Behn grinning with Ray Bourque, danced on the collection of country music before tossing a few titles out of the broken window. Then, with the same log he'd used to break the window, he shattered the window in the bathroom and beat the hell out of the kitchen table. The door to the one bedroom was locked, so he left that room alone. When the rest of the place looked sufficiently devastated, he opened the fridge, was disappointed by the sparse contents, and closed it. Crossing to the front door, he thought, Wells better make good on this. I'm not spending my whole career paying off a walk-in cooler.

The moment he pulled the door open, something leapt at him.

A beast. An immense, slobbering gargoyle of a thing.

The creature sent him onto his back and leapt onto his chest with sledgehammer paws. It snapped at his nose, nipped the skin between the nostrils. It took gurgling breaths, eyed him intensely. Its incisors, so close to Coyne's eyes, looked like slavering tusks.

The nose stung, would have been nice to rub, but Coyne didn't dare move. And didn't someone somewhere once say that you shouldn't lock eyes with a rabid dog? It seemed like sound advice.

"Nice puppy. Wanna Milkbone? Maybe a biscuit?" More snapping. "Walk? Wanna go for a car ride?"

The dog clicked its teeth. Awful breath. Coyne screwed his eyes shut.

And then the dog was off his chest, yelping.

Christ. Coyne opened his eyes. A man stood in the doorway, a man with blond-white hair and a swollen nose. He wore latex gloves and was holding a long handgun with a silencer.

It had taken twenty-four years of moderately hairy living before Larry Coyne truly understood fear. The dog howled and romped in circles. The man with the gun must have kicked it. The beast spied an opening and bolted from the cabin.

Coyne watched as the man gave him a confused, searching look. His eyes were bloodshot. His nose was spread halfway across his face in blue-green disassembly. Coyne gained his feet and raised his hands to show him there would be no resistance. The gun was impossible not to gape at. Guns were awful. Always had been. Farm kids out shooting gophers were sadists. Hunters were barbarians. Back in Piapot, Coyne had felt like a fag for thinking that way.

The stranger surveyed the cabin's destruction. He lingered over the trampled CDs and the cellophane bag knifed to the wall.

Then his eyes rested on the only other person present.

"This," he said, " is a damn weird sight."

Coyne nodded, eager to show that he agreed.

*   *   *

Alf Lundgren didn't know what to make of this. The guy standing before him wasn't McAvoy, and by the looks of the cabin, he was no friend of McAvoy's, either. Whatever he was, he couldn't pry his eyes from the gun. He kept crinkling his nose but wouldn't dare lower a hand to rub it.

"Why'd you do all this?" Alf asked, sweeping the shattered scene with a hand.

The guy reached even higher for the sky and said Alf had the wrong idea. Alf raised an eyebrow and the guy revised his answer:

"It's...a long story."

"Toss your wallet over here," Alf said.

The man obeyed, and Alf checked the driver's license. "Lawrence Daniel Coyne. I thought you looked familiar. I saw you after the game last night. You play for the Cowboys."

Coyne nodded.

"Take a seat on that sofa."

Coyne back-pedalled to the overturned chesterfield. Alf sat on a kitchen chair beside the refrigerator. He felt better today. Shooting the hockey player last night had freed something within him. He could do the job on McAvoy. No waffling, no doubt. Shooting Halkidis had been a choice he'd made. It was really that simple—a choice. There'd been indecision, but in the end he'd acted. If he hadn't, he'd have forfeited his chance to help himself. Action spoke volumes, interpretation was for people who had leisure time. Be a goddamn poster boy for self-confidence.

"Why'd you mess up his house?"

"We w-want to make him leave town. Please, I got nothing against you—"

"We?" Alf said.

"Me and Pamela Wells."

"Who's that?"

The player spat out the story. Wells owned the team, wanted to trade McAvoy. He, Coyne, would make Mac amenable to leaving in return for a shot with the Canucks. Getting the ex-drunk arrested for coke, that seemed like a good plan. Press'd love it. That was the whole truth, the whole story.

It was so absurd that Alf Lundgren almost believed it. But the owner of an NHL franchise would have simpler and safer ways of ridding herself of a minor-league contract. She wouldn't have a dickhead minion make it look like irate coke dealers had swung by. That was just plain goofy.

"It would have worked," Coyne said. "It's perfect timing since Behn killed that guy and he's on the front pages."

Alf's heart skipped a beat. "Since he what?"

"You know, Randolph Skalky."

"No," Alf said, "I don't know."

Feeling something hollow, he ordered the player to fill him in. Coyne told him about Mac's fight for his life at the Carseland weir, about how he killed a man named Randolph Skalky in self-defence and how the TV news this morning said maybe someone had hired Skalky to kill him.

Alf couldn't believe it.

Ed Newby had hired a *second* guy? No, that wouldn't make sense. Someone else had it in for the hockey player? Maybe Skalky had been acting alone, settling some past score most coincidentally-like. Who the hell was Skalky?

This assignment was starting to look decidedly buggered up.

But choices. Wars couldn't be won unless someone lost. Alf opened the refrigerator and pulled out a carton of orange juice. He popped the lid and asked Coyne if he knew when his teammate would be home.

"I don't know." Avoiding eye contact.

"Stand up and open your coat."

Coyne turned military and Alf frisked him, then sat down again.

"What are you gonna do with me?"

"This Pamela Wells, she's so rich and mighty, it seems odd she'd have you setting up McAvoy like this."

"We had a deal."

"Maybe she's the one sicced this Skalky on Mac?"

"I wouldn't know about that," Coyne said.

"If I call her up and ask her, think she'll confirm this agreement you have with her?"

Fear poured into the hockey player's face. "Yeah, but... I mean, she doesn't know *exactly* what I'm doing."

"You've been truthful with me, Lawrence Coyne?"

Coyne shook his head like he'd been zapped by electricity. "I swear, I wouldn't lie. You're scaring the hell out of me. I *wouldn't* lie."

Babbling. Shivering and blinking, pouring out his words. He'd have to be Anthony fucking Hopkins to be fibbing. So what was the deal? Maybe this Wells was the one who had paid Ed to pay him, Alf, to whack McAvoy? If so, who was paying Skalky? And what do you do now? Tell Newby it's getting dangerous, even futile, cops are now shielding the target? How would that help you run your dildo scam? And look at what you've already done. Shot a Jeep. Shot a *man*. Back away empty-handed?

"Gimme your gloves," Alf said.

"What?"

"Toss 'em over." Coyne obeyed, and Alf walked to the door. "Now go get that knife and the blow." Confused but obedient, the player unstuck the knife from the wall and pulled off the cocaine and the note. "Now stick it back in, all together, just like it was. Then come close the door."

Coyne's expression streaked to fearful understanding, but he did as instructed.

"Now you're wanted," Alf said. "The cops'll find your prints. You ever been printed?"

Coyne looked miserable. "You do this, I'm finished."

"You don't say."

"I'm a hockey player."

"Not any more. Now you're my helper."

Coyne said, "Your what?"

"You're gonna help set up a meeting with Wells. We'll have a whaddayacallut, a soirée."

"A soirée."

"And if I'm happy about the way things go, maybe I'll let you come back here and wipe down your prints."

Coyne said, "But what if someone comes over in the meantime? What if—"

"The longer you stand here nitpicking, the later it'll be when you get back."

Coyne hesitated. "But what about you? Why are you here? What do you want from Behn?"

Alf held out his watch-holding wrist to underline his point about time. The hockey player muttered something then started toward the door. Alf followed him outside.

At the woodpile, Alf said, "We'll leave your car here. Gimme the keys."

Coyne did that, and Alf led him to the apple-green '68 Mustang that the player had parked among some trees off the path. Alf opened the driver side door, put the keys in the ignition, and closed the door again. He wouldn't get caught possessing these keys; and if they were left in the ignition, they were good incentive for Coyne to want to get back here.

"We'll use my car," he said unnecessarily.

Sixteen

Behn opened the door, and Constable Clyde Lents poked his nose in.

"Want a McMuffin? I'm heading across to the McDonald's."

A wintry wind poured in, fresh and alive, like the air on the prairie.

"You mind stopping at the Co-op?" Behn said.

"Nope. What can I get you?"

A quick list: rye bread, chicken or turkey cold cuts, the greenest green veggies there. Also toothpaste, toothbrush and, sorry, a pair of shorts so he could exercise.

"We'll swing by your cabin this afternoon," Lents said, "let you pack a suitcase."

Behn gave him a fifty.

"And I'll get you some cutlery from the hotel."

"Thanks," Behn said.

Directory Assistance provided the first P.I. firm listed in the Boston yellow pages—AAA Private Investigations. The man there said he would be happy to sift through country bars, two hundred dollars a day plus expenses.

"I'll have the photos e-mailed," Behn said, "and I'll wire some money. Can you give me daily updates?"

"Phone or e-mail?"

"I'll let you know."

He put a call through to coach Ken Duguay.

"It's me, Ken."

"Jesus, Behn, how you doing?"

"I haven't skated for two days. My quads are knotting up."

"I mean, how are you *doing?*"

"Confused going on befuddled," Behn said.

"Yeah, God, what did Archie ever do to anyone?"

"Will he be all right?"

"Too early to tell," Duguay said. "They have him on a respirator. I'm heading over to the Mountainview right now—if I can get past the reporters."

He said the press guys were sniffing his door like drooling coyotes.

"There might be some nut out there," Behn said. "Could be that someone's going after not just me or Archie, but Cowboys in general."

"This Detective Woo, he called me and brought up that very possibility. I'm calling a curfew after the game. No bars." There was a short pause. Ken Duguay shouted away from the receiver, "Back off, you bozos!" Then he lowered his voice. "This is quite the thing, Behn. Who's using my players for target practice?"

"I wish I knew." He remembered there'd been a game last night. "How'd we do against Tacoma?"

"Seven to one." No need to say for whom. "Maybe the road will do us some good. Get away from all this."

"I feel sick about being off the ice."

"Don't worry about that," Duguay said. "You just take care of yourself. Call me at the Boise Super 8 if there's any news."

"Boise Super 8."

"Oh, I almost forgot," Duguay said, "Pamela Wells is in town. She wants you to call her."

"Wells? Why?"

"She didn't say. She dropped into the dressing room after

the game last night. She's staying with her daughter." Duguay gave him the number. "Behn, Woo said no one can have the number to wherever you're staying, so I won't ask for it. But keep in touch, okay?"

Okay. Bye. The clock over the TV sounded like the *60 Minutes* intro; it made the room feel smaller. Behn had to call the hospital, get a report on Archie Halkidis. He had to call Jimmy, see if he'd rounded up Rico. And Frank Sparrow at Tornheim—sorry, but the next chapter would have to wait.

And then there was exercise. Jogging was out, as was the weight room at the Agrodome. Stationary stuff would have to do.

His coat was hanging on the door. He pulled out his address book and sat by the phone again. The phone. Great bridger of distances. Interrupter of valuable time. He hated his cell phone; no person should *always* be available. He leaned over and dialled Scotia Bank.

Mariola Lacroix told him that no one by the current or former name of Jack Brigham currently had a credit card in Canada. So Behn phoned Jay Ireland at the newspaper, and the sports reporter had similar non-news from his phone-company check.

"I thought maybe Brigham had changed his name," Ireland said, "and that of course got me asking myself why. So I checked our archives and found some backstories on him."

Behn stepped to the window and peeked out the curtains. "And?"

"And apparently he's on the lam."

"That I know."

"Nine years he was a partner at Pullman and Shantz. Crème de la prestigious. Embezzled two hundred grand over a six-month period. The other partners call him in one day to account for his accounts, and the next day he vanishes. Has no wife, so it's easy to pick up and move."

There was no movement on the street outside. No black Taurus cruising the neighbourhood. What kind of bad guy drove a Taurus, anyway?

Ireland said, "You got something to write on, Behn?"

"Yeah." Behn pulled a pen from his coat and dragged the phone chord back to the table.

"Okay, Brigham is staying at the Cornelius Hotel down in Queen Elizabeth Park. Real rat hole. Registered under the name Lyle Mulholland. Room 12."

Behn pulled the Gideon Bible from the drawer. He scribbled the info on the so-and-so-begat-so-and-so pages. "How on Earth did you find that out?"

"I'm a bright boy," Ireland said. "I called some of the other partners at the firm. One of them, guy named Price, says Brigham contacted him asking for dough. Said he needed it to pay a debt, otherwise he'd be done for."

"Price gave him the money?"

"The partners themselves ponied it up. The plan was to meet him discreetly, talk things through, help him. Pullman and Shantz didn't want him in any more newspapers. A firm like that, they make their rain based on reputation. If one of their own is stealing, clients fly south in a hurry. They wanted to smooth things out."

"But it didn't work."

"Uh-uh. Price goes to meet Brigham for lunch at the Danube. Reservation is for one Lyle Mulholland. Brigham's all dishevelled, hasn't been bathing. Price deduces he's been staying in dives, looking over his shoulder. Brigham thanks Price for his help, takes the money and bolts."

"So how'd you find him at the Cornelius?" Behn said.

"Simple phone calls. The Cornelius was the fourth place I called. He's still using the Mulholland name."

"You oughta be a P.I., Jay."

Ireland chortled. "And die of boredom? Following guys' wives around? Digging through trash cans for credit-card receipts? Besides, I have bigger plans."

"Oh?"

"I'm gonna write about Tony Tran, maybe do a book on him, depending on how this turns out. You gotta let me in on everything that happens, Behn. If Brigham's running from Tran, if Tran's trying to dust him—"

"Tony Tran wouldn't smile on an unauthorized biography."

"Hell, by the time I publish it, he'll be in Bowden anyway. I mean, hey, maybe Tran put Skalky onto you, did you ever figure that? You owe him any money?"

"No."

"I know, but I had to ask anyway. You gotta promise to give me whatever you dig up. We're now partners in this, Behn."

"Okay," Behn said, "anything I get is yours."

Behn cut the connection and found the Cornelius's number in the book. The guy answering put him through to room 12. A ragged voice came on.

"Yeah?"

"Lyle Mulholland?"

"Who's this?"

"Front desk. Were you planning on checking out today? The note in the registry is—"

The line went dead. Great. Behn peered out the window again. One constable was still in the cop car, Lents was still off buying workout shorts. Calling Brigham had been dumb. Now the guy was spooked. Behn pulled his coat on and opened the door. Then the phone rang. He eased the door shut.

"Who is this?" the voice demanded. Brigham.

"My name's Behn McAvoy." Silence. "I just wanted to talk to you. I've got—"

"You were on the front page this morning," Brigham said.

"Didn't read it." Fearing Brigham would hang up: "I don't care about your problems. Whatever you owe Tran or anyone else, that's for you to settle."

"You've been talking to Tony?"

"Not yet."

"Fuck you." Then he thought it over. "Jesus..."

"I only want to talk," Behn said.

"About what?"

"I'll tell you that when we meet," Behn said.

"My ass."

"I found you, Brigham. It wouldn't be any problem finding you again. That means it wouldn't be any problem for Tran to find you."

Brigham laughed a hollow, defeated laugh. "Jesus," he said again. Behn waited. "Tonight."

"Where?"

"Queen Elizabeth Park. There's a pay phone outside the 7-Eleven."

"I'm not—"

"Be there at seven, and wait for the phone to ring."

"You sound like TV," Behn said.

"It'll have to do. If you're not alone, we don't meet. Any of Tran's boys around, we don't meet."

"Can't do that," Behn said. "You're not the only one on the run. Someone followed me from the Horseshoe yesterday."

Brigham said, "Black Taurus, right?"

Now it was Behn's turn to lose his voice.

"The Taurus won't hurt you," Brigham said, "but if it's following you tonight, we don't meet. Seven sharp. Any company, it'd be risky."

"For you or for me?"

"You're the smart guy who found me. Figure it out."

Again the line went dead. Behn looked at the note he'd scribbled. Seven. Queen E. Park. He might be setting himself up for something.

Tell Woo? Brigham would bolt. Bring Woo in later.

But Alicia should know. Behn took a deep breath and took up the receiver again. The phone. Great bridger of distances...

*   *   *

Again Alicia had spent half the night staring at the ceiling. This time, however, a new and more primitive issue kept her eyes open: fear.

Fear in the form of a mysterious black Ford Taurus. It was a good bet the boys in the car were after Behn, not some irrelevant woman he'd carted around for an afternoon. But good bets were not always safe bets. Innocent people died in this world.

Alicia shuffled out to the living room and peeked through the blinds to the street outside. Then she clicked on the TV. The Behn McAvoy Saga was just starting in the form of the CRTV morning news. The cops had made arrests in Boston: two ex-cons, names that meant nothing to Alicia. Another Cowboy, Archie Halkidis, had been shot. McAvoy was under police protection at an undisclosed location.

The Cowboys were a bore on the ice, but off of it, they were the best jazz in town. Alicia clicked off the tube and journeyed to the kitchen.

Her mom was watching Oprah when she called.

"No, baby, I don't know anything about Normand going to Boston. What's this all about?"

"It's a long story," Alicia said.

"Want me to ask around? There's still plenty of his friends from midget and junior around. They'd probably know better than me if he went down there."

"Thanks, Mom."

The phone was hardly down before it rang. Something made her stare at it before picking up.

"It's me," Behn's voice said.

"How very pleasant to hear from you."

"I have some explaining to do."

"I called my mother," she said. "Not to worry, sir, mom's on the case, gonna nail her own dead son."

"How about some lunch today?" Behn said.

"Lunch?" She pulled the receiver away and stared as if Alexander Graham Bell, not Behn, were daft. "Are you for real?"

"That sounds like a no," Behn said. "There are some things I want to tell you."

"I thought the cops were hiding you. You want to go for lunch?"

"I'm at the Western Holiday on second and eleventh, room 124. There are cops outside watching the room."

He added that there was an Indian takeout place on 48th Street. He'd call ahead, make sure the order was ready when she arrived.

The guy was being sought by a killer.

"I know what you're thinking," he said. "It's a loopy proposition. If you'd rather do this over the phone—"

"Why wouldn't *you* rather do it that way?"

"After I make a few more calls and work out, it'll be me and this hotel room. I'll go crazy."

"So you need someone to keep you company?"

"I'd like to see you again."

She absently twisted the phone cord. Her mind flashed on Walter, lounging on a Cretan beach, telling every Greek who would listen that he was Steven goddamn King. She beheld the aimlessness of her life since *Squeaky Wheel* had started paying the bills. She hadn't been on anything approximating a date for a year. Which proved how infinitely screwed up she was. She considered this a date.

"Alicia?"

"Yes."

"Like I said, there are cops protecting me. But if you feel uneasy, that's okay."

She glanced around her spotless kitchen. Her only goal for the day was to last it out. "What about your mystery car? At least at home I've got locked doors and Smith & Wesson to keep me company."

"I found out that the Taurus isn't a problem. I think."

"Oh?"

"And the garlic chicken is amazing."

It did sound like a talk better held in person. "You drink wine with your meals?"

"Not for over a decade," he said.

"Oh, I forgot."

"Say one o'clock?" Behn said.

"One's fine."

"And Alicia?"

"Yeah?"

"Don't bother with the utensils. I have some on order."

Seventeen

A psycho, that's what he was. The puffy-nosed albino was a certifiable puddin' brain. Larry Coyne watched him from the corner of his eye as he drove the '72 Charger past twisted silver trees lining the street. The albino rubbed his nose and coughed. Then he rubbed his nose some more. He pulled out two pill bottles and popped some red and yellow capsules.

"What are those?" Coyne said.

"Vitamins. P and C."

"What for?"

"What kind of question is that?"

"Prescription?"

"What do you care?"

"Vitamin P," Coyne said, "is hard to process. You been taking it long?"

"Just keep driving."

The albino had him stop at a Radio Shack, where he stuck close to Coyne inside, gun in pocket, and bought a microcassette recorder. Back in the car, he said to find a phone.

Those eyes were so glassy. What did he want? He wanted Behn? To kill him? Fuck.

Coyne choked back the thought of the cops finding his Mustang at the cabin. Only hours ago, he'd been poised to jump to the NHL. Now he was one passerby's phone call away from having the thin-wicked flame of his career snuffed out. The price of greed. Dumb desire to expect to kill a debt in one fast shot.

But if he could get away, maybe he could beat him back to the cabin. Maybe things could be cleaned up. Right?

At the albino's insistence, Coyne stopped the car at an ice-frosted phone booth outside a Mohawk station. The car, it seemed logical to assume, was stolen.

"Come with me," the big man said, and he led Coyne by the wrist and into the booth. There he punched in a number and said, to whomever answered, "Is it fucking Pamela Wells who's paying for this job?" Whatever the person at the other end said in response, it wasn't kind. Almost chewing the receiver, the albino said, "It is too my business. Things are going south in a hurry. I take a step forward, I take unplanned risks, and then there's some awfully coincidental surprises knocking me back. Do you have any idea what's going on down here?"

He listened for a moment. "You being truthful?" he said. "Can I trust you to be straight with me?"

Now the guy at the other end said something that took a while. Finally some air went out of the albino. "Fine," he said, "you're right, a deal's a deal. I just don't like the stuff that's happening *around* the deal. And I hope to hell you're not holding something back on me."

He hung up emphatically, still holding Coyne's wrist. Then he said, "Call Wells. Tell her you have to see her."

Coyne said, "And if she doesn't want to meet me?"

"Be convincing."

Wells was going to love this guy. Coyne found in the phone book the number for Georgia Wells—her daughter there at the ex-mayor's house—and dialled. The albino leaned close to listen. A woman, who sounded young, answered.

"Hello?"

"Larry Coyne for Pamela Wells."

"Who's calling?"

"I just told you. Larry Coyne."

"You're one of them, aren't you? You're a Cowboy." Dripping acid.

"That's right," Coyne said, "not that it's any of your business. Will you just tell her that—"

The line went dead. The albino pulled his head back from the phone. "That was real smart. You have a way with women."

"I think it was her daughter. She's this notorious flake."

He dialled the number again, and when Georgia Wells answered, he spoke before she could. "Listen, I'm sorry I snapped at you, I don't know what came over me. I'd really like to talk to Miss Wells, okay?"

There was a pause. "You forgot something."

"I did?"

"Were you raised in a barn or something? You forgot to say please."

"Please," Coyne said.

"That's better." There was a click, then a long pause. Finally, another line started ringing.

The albino leaned in closer, put a hand on the phone, just over Coyne's own hand. Cold. Felt like a corpse.

Pamela Wells finally picked up. "Coyne?"

"Miss Wells, something terrible's happened. I gotta see you right away."

For the second time in her impressive life, Wells was surprised into muteness.

"Get cancer," she managed to say, "and don't you ever contact me again."

The line went dead, and Larry Coyne gently removed the albino's dead hand from his. "Don't worry," he said. "That's just the way she is."

"Meaning we can go see her?"

"Do we have a choice?"

"No."

Please, Miss Wells, realize how important this is by the time we get there.

They drove out of Forest Park. The houses became larger, more upper class, with multiple stories and spacious, well-groomed yards.

"Nice district," the albino said. "She must really be loaded."

"Her house in Vancouver makes this one look small. John Travolta and Brian Adams have houses on the same block."

"Was she born to the dough, or she make it herself?"

"Made some," Coyne said, "married some."

"Tell me about it."

"Why?" Coyne said.

"Yours is not to ask."

Gauging her. Sizing up Wells.

"A few years back, she—"

"Not the life story," the albino said, "just how she got the money."

"She married this old fart in B.C., Robert Daley. Ran this piddly brewery and was croaking from cancer. He kicked off, it was hers. She built it into a beast."

"Which brewery?" the albino said.

"Prairie Dog," Coyne said.

"Get out."

"Look, I don't know what you have in mind, but what if she has some security? She can probably push a button or pick up a phone, have some gorillas—"

"Let me worry about that," the albino said. "What about her daughter? Why's she such a slag?"

"How should I know?"

"You're the one who called her notorious."

A psycho, but a conscientious one. Didn't want to go in cold. Coyne explained that if you believed the newspapers, Georgia Wells was a spoiled brat and a pill. Never worked a day in her life. Flunked out of every expensive school mommy put her in.

"Hey," the albino said, "even the best of us have trouble in school."

It was all very public. It was like Georgia Wells had a thing for getting arrested, got turned on by it. One newspaper story in particular—apparently she stroked off one of her boy toys at a Stampeders football game, a hand job right there in the stands, no real attempt to hide it. The nearby fans caught on, someone complained, some usher stepped in and tried to eject her from the stadium. She punched the usher in the schnoz, started a free-for-all, and wound up at a police station, where they found a half ounce of Afghani hashish in her purse. The affair had got her onto the front page of the *Sun*. It was only one of many such incidents in her rocky little life.

Coyne and Alf reached the house and stared at it like pre-teen boys who'd procured their first dirty magazine: a sprawling place with a glass poolhouse to the side and a stable off to the back—a stable and horses this close to downtown. A tall gate kept them off the property. Coyne rolled down his window, pressed the intercom button and said his name for the guy at the other end. The gates creaked open, and he drove up to the door and stopped the car.

The albino stuffed his microcassette recorder into his jacket's inner pocket. But first he pushed the "record" button and blew some test static into the mike. What was that supposed to achieve? Must have seen it on TV.

The albino said, "Okay, you're gonna tell her what happened out at the cabin, only instead of me walking in on you, there was McAvoy's neighbour. He came over to feed the dog and caught you busting up the place. You tried to smooth things out, but he ran off, probably to the cops. You wanted to report this to her."

"Why?"

"I'll take it from there."

"And who are you?"

"I'm your lawyer."

"My lawyer. No reason she wouldn't swallow that."

Maybe this shitforbrains had come from the nut house in Ponoka or Red Deer. Wherever it was that society had kept him, he likely wasn't allowed the normal privileges of citizenship.

The mansion's two front doors yawned open, and a manservant with a black suit and crew cut lumbered out. The guy wasn't armed, unless there was something under the coat. Larry Coyne didn't bother waiting for the albino's instructions. Before Puddin'brain even undid his seat belt, Coyne opened the car door and marched toward the house.

*   *   *

Alicia Fournier pulled into the Western Holiday parking lot and stopped next to the unmarked cop car outside room 124. She tapped on Constable Clyde Lents's window and held up a steaming bag of Raja's Indian food.

Lents was brusque. If it were up to him, neither she nor anyone else would be popping by for din din. That was crazy, McAvoy handing out his whereabouts. Defeated the purpose of watching him.

Brief tirade finished, Lents stepped out and carried the food to room 124 for her. A heavy silence followed his knock on the door, so he opened it himself.

Behind the closed bathroom door, the shower was running.

"You in there, Behn?"

The water stopped. "As opposed to where?"

"Miss Fournier is here."

"Tell her I'll be a minute."

Alicia handed Lents a beef masala and a chicken vindaloo. That made him happy. When he was gone, she sat on the bed. Maybe Behn had meant for her to wait outside, with the cops. Maybe he had no clothes in there with him, would prance out naked, singing "O Solo Mio" to his soap on a rope.

Or maybe she should stop fretting like a teenager.

A sweat-soaked pair of shorts hung on the chair next to the dresser. The dresser held a phone book open to Raja's. Alicia picked up the phone and dialled Information.

The computer gave her a choice of services and asked, "Which city, please?"

"New York," she guessed.

"Which office or residence please?"

"Gemological Institute of America."

She sat on the edge of the bed while the call went through. Finally, an elderly man with a French accent answered. She introduced herself, told him she'd found a diamond ring and wanted to track down its owner. Did the institute keep customers' names on file? Maybe she could find the owner through the jewellery store that registered the ring. She had the GIA number.

The Frenchman said to hold on while he checked the Institute's information policy. During the pause, the washroom door opened and Behn McAvoy, wearing the same jeans and T-shirt as yesterday, followed out a thin current of steam. His wet hair was combed straight back. His watchful expression said he'd overheard her request.

The Frenchman came back on. "Can you give me the registration number?" She did. "I must call you back," he said. "Twenty minutes or so, Miss Fournier."

He gave the surname its proper French flourish. She told him her number and set down the receiver.

Behn was now sniffing some curry. "What did they say?"

"They'll call back."

The bed would serve as the table. He pushed a plate across to her, popped some plastic lids and dug in.

"Something I don't understand," she said over a samosa. "TV news said they've arrested Randolph Skalky's accomplices in Boston. What did Archie Halkidis have to do with him or them or anyone?"

"Cops don't know yet," Behn said.

"What did *you* have to do with these people? Whoever's gunning for you, you *have* to know the guy. Or at least knew him back when you were in the States."

Behn tore some meat from a drumstick.

"What were you doing there, anyway? I mean, apart from playing hockey?"

"Boozing my way out of the NHL."

"You made enemies while doing that?"

"Seems to be the question, doesn't it? I was too busy to make enemies."

"What do you mean?"

He shrugged. "Just the way it seems in retrospect. I was a drunk, but a good-time drunk. I don't think I had time to make enemies."

117

"You don't think? You sound like it's someone else we're talking about."

Behn said that wasn't far off the mark. He'd been having blackouts, tending to check out fairly early into his benders. Which was how that will business with the ex-wife came about. Most people got drunk when they drank; he entered another dimension.

"Then why'd you drink for so long?" Alicia said. "You had to know it was hurting you." Again he shrugged. She leaned forward. "Teenager? Big contract? Too much too soon?"

"More or less," Behn said. "Actually, more. You want some of this rice?"

She shook her head. "Wanna change the topic?"

"Nah. Take Normand out from under the microscope, slide me in. I'm fine with it."

She pulled two Diet Cokes from the bag and handed him one.

"Okay, you said you wanted to talk, so talk."

He ran through his visit to the Horseshoe and the litany of phone calls. Normand had been gambling with a guy named Brigham. Brigham was on the run from both the cops and gambling debts. Brigham promised the black Taurus wasn't a problem. Brigham was a puzzle.

"I'm going to meet him tonight," Behn said.

"How will you do that if the cops are watching you?"

"I'll manage."

"Do any of you hockey players lack confidence?"

The phone rang.

"We have consulted our files," said the stately Frenchman from New York. "I think you are very lucky."

"How's that?" Alicia said.

"The person who brought us the ring was a private

owner, not a jeweller. This is very unusual. I'd say ninety-eight percent of our customers are jewellers."

"Who was the owner?" Alicia said.

"A woman named Pamela Wells, from Renfrew, Alberta. Is that the city from which you are calling? Judging from the phone number on my display—"

"Did I hear you right?" Alicia said slowly. "Pamela Wells?"

"You know this person?" the Frenchman said.

She found a pen and felt Behn's eyes shooting questions at her. "Do you have the date she came in?"

"March twenty-nine, 2004. I suspect she will be pleased to hear from you, no? The specifications say it is a very fine diamond. Indeed, one wonders how one might be so careless as to lose such a diamond."

"One does," Alicia said. "Thank you so much, Mr..."

"Leroy." More bang-up French pronunciation.

"I appreciate your help, Mr. Leroy."

The phone wasn't down before Behn asked, "Did I hear you right? The ring belongs to Wells?"

At first, she didn't answer. Too many questions darting around. Then, "He said she paid for the certificate herself. March twenty-ninth. That's three days before Normand died."

"What would Normand be doing with Wells' jewellery?"

Alicia drummed her fork on her plate. "Surreal."

"Someone's idea of a joke."

"Some joke," Alicia said. "I've never met Wells, but I do remember what Normand said about her."

"Which was?"

"All she needs to complete the outfit is a broomstick and a pointy hat."

They both took a moment to think things through.

"So what now?" Behn said.

"Isn't it obvious? Talk to Wells. She'll clear this up."

In terms of ideas, he seemed to have heard better. He snapped up the last samosa and gave himself over to some unshared thought.

"She will, won't she? She'll clear this up?"

He finished swallowing. "That," he said, "would be too easy."

Eighteen

When that imbecile Coyne had called, she was in the office
that she kept next to Georgia's twelve-seat home cinema. She'd
been going over Prairie Dog's October sales, but the tremor in
Coyne's usually cocky voice staggered her. Guilt flooded in, as
if the "terrible thing" he mentioned was her terrible thing.

But what *had* she done? She'd listened to him rant, that's
what. Hopefully the crazy bastard wouldn't come over now
—though she knew he would. He was a mistake from the
word go, the kind of mistake you invariably end up
regretting. Get rid of him ASAP.

She studied a just-faxed copy of the latest Prairie Dog ad.
The ad was to go in six newspapers, two sports magazines
and *Alberta Report*. It depicted a colony of gophers basking
in the summer heat, bellies to a sun surrounded by clouds of
frosty Prairie Dog Ale. A bubble over the cute little critters'
heads read, "It's a Dog's Life."

Minus fifteen outside, and they wanted to sell a summer
thirst quencher. She tore up the fax and called her head of
marketing with an order to fire the ad agency. Then,
standing at the window and watching a light snow start to
whiten the riding grounds, she pondered calling again and
firing the head of marketing.

Then someone knocked at the door.

"Come in."

It was Coyne, and he was with the blond man with the
swollen nose, the same one she'd seen loitering around the
Agrodome after the last Cowboys game.

"My God..."

"This is my lawyer," Coyne said, sounding embarrassed.

The blond man looked surprised that *he* recognized *her*. He stepped forward to shake her hand, but coughed instead and had to withdraw his nail-less paw to cover his mouth.

Lawyer? What was this, a prank? She backed away, but the blond man thrust out his chewy hand again and advanced.

"Don't touch me," she said.

"My client, Mr. Coyne, is in trouble," the blond man said. "You're in trouble, too. He's got something he wants to tell you."

Coyne stared at the carpet. "I went out to Mac's house this morning and—"

"No," Wells said.

"What?"

"Get out of my office. Now."

The blond man said, "Your deal with my client went wrong."

"What deal? We had no deal."

She turned and headed for her desk. When she sat down in the swivel chair, the big man was there again, breathing down on her. He had a hand in his coat pocket, appeared to be holding something.

With that same unnatural quality, he said, "As he agreed with you, Mr. Coyne went over to Mr. McAvoy's house this morning. He put some cocaine in the kitchen. He planned for the police to find it, make trouble for the man. Just like you planned."

Coyne's non-response confirmed the statement.

"You idiot!" Wells said to Coyne.

"Just like you planned."

"Stop saying that. I planned nothing. Coyne—"

"Just like we planned," Coyne said almost inaudibly.

"For God's sake, I thought you'd go tell some reporter a lie or two, make some bad publicity for him. I sanctioned nothing. I certainly had no idea you'd do *that*."

The blond man nosed forward. "Be that as it may, in a sense you did plan to hurt McAvoy. You planned to run him out of town."

"You stay away from me." She pushed off the desk and swivelled away. Predictably, he followed. She looked past him to her employee. "Do you really expect me to believe that this man is your lawyer?"

The blond man yanked out a hanky and blew his foghorn nose. "Okay, so I'm not a lawyer. Who I am ain't important. But if you're so surprised by this cocaine story—which did happen, by the way—then what were you doing leaving the rink with this guy last night? You always give your players lifts home after games? Give 'em a little something else on the side while you're at it?"

The ringing of the phone broke the strain. It was still on the first chime when the blond man snatched up the receiver and slammed it down. His eyes rolled in their sockets ever so slightly. Wells felt the same chill she'd felt upon seeing him at the Agrodome.

"Listen, if Larry made you think I planned...whatever he did, he misled you. All I'm guilty of is listening to his stupidity. I should not have spoken with him. Whatever he did, if he did it, he did it on his own. Is that clear enough for you?"

The phone rang again. This time the blond man waited two rings before picking up and slapping down. He turned to Coyne, who wilted.

"You lied to me."

The hand inside his pocket moved. A click and a high squeal preceded a muffled message.

"All I'm guilty of is listening to his stupidity..."

The blond man fumbled with the contraption and found

the "off" button.

It took Wells a moment to put things together. "Am I being blackmailed here? Was this whole thing designed to get me to admit to something I didn't do?"

When the phone rang for a third time, everyone just ignored it.

Maybe stand up, Wells thought, cool, walk to the door. Something told her that Coyne's friend would not allow her to do that.

The answering machine clacked on: "Miss Wells, this is Behn McAvoy. Ken said you're in town, and you want to speak with me. There's also something..."

The blond man's eyes were ablaze now. "Pick it up."

"What?"

His hand snaked into a pocket and jerked out a gun.

"Answer it. You want to meet him tomorrow, two o'clock, Regent Hotel lobby."

"But he's—"

"Pick up the phone!"

She did, telling herself that this wasn't happening, that there was no gun in his hand, that everything would be all right. That was the only way to keep herself together.

"Behn?" she said into the receiver.

"Miss Wells, you're there?"

"Can you meet me tomorrow?" Her tongue felt like concrete. "Two o'clock. Regent Hotel lobby."

The gunman hit the speakerphone button.

"I'm supposed to stay where I am," the hockey player's distorted voice said. "I'm sure you're aware what happened yesterday."

"Yes."

"So we'll have to do this over the phone."

Again the speakerphone button. Alf said, "Find out where he is. You'll go to him." And the blond man switched the intercom back on.

"I'll come to you," Wells recited. There was more pressure behind the gun, jittery pressure, like the blond man himself was nervous. Or maybe sick.

"Miss Wells, I've already invited one person over here. If I bring any more over, the police will—"

"Listen, Behn, I have to come to you, okay?"

"They won't allow it. And anyway, I don't think—"

"Take my word for it, the phone is not appropriate. We have to meet."

No reply.

"Behn?"

"What's the matter, Miss Wells?"

"I need you to say yes right now. It's that important to me."

Another loud pause. "The Western Holiday on Eleventh Southeast, room 124."

"Thank you."

"I have a friend who wants to meet you."

"I don't have time," Wells said.

"You'll want to make time for her. She has quite a story for you."

The blond man was motioning for her to get rid of him. "Tomorrow," Wells said.

"Morning?"

"Morning's fine. Nine o'clock."

"Don't you even want to know who it is?"

The blond man pulled the receiver from her hand and plucked the jack from the wall. Then he started to pace. Coyne watched without stirring. Wells opted to follow his example.

The pacing wound down at the window. The blond man watched the snow streak down in a hard slant. "Tell you what, I came here to...hey, that doesn't matter any more."

Wells picked at a loose thread in her sweater.

"Don't bother showing up at his hotel tomorrow."

"Okay," she said.

"And don't call the cops about this, or I'll know. Because I know certain cops at certain copshops. They'll find out about it and tell me."

"Okay."

"And I'll have to come back to visit you."

"I believe you," she said.

"Good." He showed some gapped, browning teeth to go with the chalky skin and mangled fingers. "I appreciate the cooperation."

He stepped forward and actually shook her hand. What a specimen. Coyne needed no instructions; he rose from his chair and followed his captor out. Even in a bind, even facing danger, Coyne was a poster boy for arrogance.

She watched the door for seconds that could have been minutes. Her breathing slowed to normal, but not without conscious effort. The blond man—this guy was in with Randolph Skalky, the man who'd taken that shot at Behn? What was wrong with him? Who on earth would waltz into the office of Pamela Wells and try to blackmail her like that?

And why cart Coyne around?

No, listening to Coyne after the hockey game had not been a brilliant idea. Wells wished she could take the decision back. But she couldn't take it back. Things happened to you, and you had to deal with them. You couldn't just bow to fear. You had to be active—"proactive," as they liked to say these days. Because if you weren't, it meant you were the opposite; it meant you were impotent.

Pamela Wells would not let anyone make her impotent.

Nineteen

Behn sat on the bed and replayed Wells' words in his mind. Wells jittery. Wells sounding distracted—or more like consumed—by something. Something was wrong.

He plucked up the phone and called Jimmy Teal's office at the university. There was no answer, so he dialled Jimmy's home number. The writer answered with a simple, "That you, Behn?"

"Yes."

"Where are you? I thought you were going to be staying with me."

"That was the plan," Behn said. "Things changed. I'm at the Western Holiday down on—"

"I know where it is. What are you doing there?"

"We'll go over everything when you get here. I'm in Room 124, unless you have an appointment you can't get out of."

Jimmy didn't. "Meet you in the bar?" he said hopefully.

"Nice thing to ask an alcoholic. Besides, they want me to stay in the room."

"They?"

"The police. They've got a car out front to keep me safe."

"From what? Skalky's dead."

"Just come over, okay?"

After hanging up, Behn laid back on the bed and felt unconscionably full of Indian food. He'd spent only one morning away from the rink, and already he was taking Jimmy's advice and getting fat. Surely the carelessness of retirement—the slothful disconnectedness with things that mattered—was soon to follow.

Someone knocked on the door only ten minutes later. Behn opened it and saw Jimmy standing there looking haggard, bleary-eyed, like he'd been hitting the dope hard this morning.

"The cop out front is fucking Jurassic," Jimmy said, pushing his way into the room. "He told me you weren't even here."

"I'm not supposed to have visitors," Behn said. "They don't want anyone to know I'm here."

"Why not? What's going on?" But before Behn could answer, Jimmy's indignation multiplied. "I'll bet he comes from a long line of cops. Daddy beat up the cons at Kingston, Grandpa ordered the beating of Negroes down in Memphis. Tell me, is there anything worse in this world— anything less intelligent and more sadistic—than a so-called peace officer? I think they have to be clinically brain dead to be accepted into the academy."

Behn filled him in on the morning's events: another assailant had tried to shoot him; Randolph Skalky had been married to Maria; the pair had hatched an amateurish will scam, which explained why Skalky had come to Renfrew, but didn't explain the second attempt on Behn's life. Someone had potshotted his Jeep this morning. And then there was an odd connection between Normand Fournier and Pamela Wells, which might or might not mean anything. Wells had paid for a wedding ring for Normand. Why? And who was Normand going to marry, anyway? He'd kept the planned nuptials secret. And how did they get the caramel inside the chocolate of the Caramilk bar?

Jimmy sat at the hotel dresser and absorbed the strangeness one curveball at a time. Then he dug a joint out of his pocket and lit it.

"Put it out," Behn said.

"Why?"

"Because first off, show some respect for a recovering addict—for once. And second, you look like you've smoked a dozen already today. Third, I can't stand the smell."

Jimmy took a deep hit, then gently snuffed the cherry on the bottom of an upside-down glass on the dresser. "None of this scans," he said. "Think hard. You have to remember at least *someone* in Boston who had it in for you."

Behn lay atop the bed again and draped a forearm over his eyes. "I have been thinking about it. That's all I've been doing. And the more I think, the less I can remember. All that drinking, all that confusion compressed into such a short period of time. It's like I had a death wish. It's almost like I..."

"Almost like what?" Jimmy said.

"It's almost as if I'm the one who sent those killers after me."

"That makes no sense."

"All those blackouts, who knows *what* I did when I was on those benders? The way I was, I could have done just about anything."

"Sure," Jimmy said, "so you must have paid two different men to patiently bide their time for a full decade, then journey up to Canada to kill you. Since you put it that way, it *does* make sense."

"Nobody likes a smartass," Behn said.

"Wrong. Nobody likes a crybaby. I made thirty-two thousand dollars last year."

Behn removed his arm from his eyes. Jimmy looked angry. "What's that mean?"

"It means get over it. You kicked the bottle, you made a pile of money, you persevered. You're in better shape than most people. If you want to cry about it, you won't get sympathy here. You sound like a bad Victorian novel. Rich man's anguish."

Behn sat up, rubbed his eyes and stretched. "Moment of doubt, that's all. Pardon."

"You're forgiven."

"Rico's still at the cabin. Can you go take care of him?"

"Mmm-hmm." Jimmy picked up the remote and started channel-surfing.

"I talked to Frank Sparrow this morning. He's expecting more chapters. We'll have to tell him—"

"Consider it done," Jimmy said, landing on an in-progress tennis match. "Is it true what they say? Saturday afternoon bowling gets higher TV ratings in the States than NHL hockey does?"

"I think I'm developing claustrophobia," Behn said. "I don't know how long I'll be able to stay in this room."

"Then don't stay here. Buy a plane ticket. Go lie on a beach. Spend some of that M-O-N-E-Y."

"You talk a lot about money," Behn said.

"And you don't because you've always had it. For you, it's never been an issue. Plus, I'm older than you. My earning years are numbered." More to himself, he added, "My years period, I guess."

Behn stepped to the window and peeked outside. "Will you do me a favour?"

"Sure," Jimmy said, surfing again and landing on the Oprah Winfrey show. "Ha, the dumbing down of society—as we speak. I do so loathe a good daytime television icon."

"Do a Google search for me," Behn said. "Run the names Pamela Wells and Jack Brigham together, see if they bring anything up."

"Why would they?" Jimmy said.

"Wells paid for Normand's jewellery, Brigham took Normand gambling. Maybe Wells knows Brigham. What it all could mean is anyone's guess."

Jimmy sighed. *The Way of the World.*

"Huh?"

"It's the title of an old William Congreve play, the most convoluted plot ever put on paper. That's what your current problems remind me of." Now Jimmy landed on CNN, where Larry King was kissing the feet of an octogenarian actress. Finally he punched the "off" button on the remote.

"Sure," he said, "I'll do what I can."

"Thanks," Behn said—and sought a delicate way of telling his friend to leave.

*   *   *

A few minutes later, Jimmy Teal drove home to water his bonsai trees, then pulled on a heavy coat, loped out to his car, and drove out into the blinding greyness of the winter prairie. He hated the drive to Behn's place. He hated nature. The eco-system was a dreadful thing. Creatures were out there eating other creatures, and everything was at the mercy of the weather. He hoped he wouldn't have to scour half of Alberta looking for Rico, who liked to wander the fields when he wasn't sleeping. There could be coyotes out there. Or bears.

While he drove, his mind wandered. He thought about Behn and about how fast time was passing. He thought about the Caymans. Lord how he craved to be on his little island, to be losing himself in his THC fog and to be forgetting about all of the things he no longer had the patience for.

Things like the kid from British Lit 225, who had lodged a complaint against what he, professor James Teal, considered to be an avuncular bit of advice: "Give up on literature, kid; take up bricklaying instead. Do something with your hands, because your head won't get you anywhere."

The kid, a C minus student, had stormed out of the room, found the dean, and demanded a transfer to another course. Where was the freedom to be honest any more? Everything these days was either an affront or a potential affront. It was a character weakness, a verbal assassination, to speak your mind.

And meanwhile, Oprah Winfrey was a font of wisdom. This, too, didn't scan.

The student could rot, for all Jimmy cared. He pushed the car down the highway and comforted himself with a daydream: a hammock; a brown-skinned girl who wore sandals rather than shoes; the death of the revolution; a mellowing; a dissipating. Let the rest of 'em go on fighting and straining and striving. Let Behn, if he's crazy enough to. Be through with them. Be through with them all.

Nearing the cabin, he caught a flash of green between the patch of elm trees.

He stopped on the gravel road between the cabin and the highway, backed up, then stopped again. A car, an apple-green Mustang, was parked in the woods.

The car looked familiar. He stepped out of his own car and approached the passenger-side window, the snow crunching underfoot. Rubbing frost from the window, he spotted keys dangling from the ignition. The charm on the key chain was shaped in a logo he knew very well. A red-and-white horse breathing fire through its nostrils.

The Renfrew Cowboys' horse.

Eddie Woo returned to the Horseshoe Casino and asked Marshall Toby to jiggle his memory.

"Yesterday Behn comes to see you an hour before I do, and the fact slips your mind?"

"An oversight," Toby said. "I was gonna tell you he came here."

"Well, then, let's try the interview one more time. This time, focus."

So Toby tipped himself over, but nothing juicy spilled out. He said he knew Behn, because he used to play the Horseshoe, and he said Behn had been asking about Skalky and Fournier, but he had left the joint unsatisfied.

"A lot of that going around," Woo said.

Back in his car, he drove through sparse traffic and a howling wind to the site of the gunshot at McAvoy's Cherokee. His cell phone rang.

"Woo here."

"Skalky came up on Air Canada," said Dante Spinetti, "day before yesterday. Boston-Toronto-Renfrew. The Sauer was stolen. Serial numbers matched up with an owner in Buffalo. Skalky had two thousand forty-nine dollars in his joint bank account with Blackwell. Blackwell was doing temp work as a receptionist."

"Thanks for nothing," Woo said.

"Not nothing. We also got a call from one Pamela Wells."

"Why's that name sound familiar?"

"She owns the Cowboys. She said Larry Coyne and—"

"Who's that?"

"One of Behn's teammates. Centreman, speedy little shit."

"I didn't know you liked hockey, Spinny."

"I do. I can't help it. Apparently Coyne and some blond man with a broken nose pulled a gun on Wells today."

"You're kidding."

"She said they're now heading out to McAvoy's hotel to blow his brains out."

"Jesus Christ, Spinny." Woo stared at the phone for a moment. "Everyone's involved in this thing except us."

"Yeah, that was my reaction."

The junior detective recounted the Wells call. Coyne and his buddy had blundered into her office, tried to blackmail her.

"Over what?"

"Something Coyne did to Behn."

"Something what?"

"She didn't make much sense. She said they didn't make it clear."

"Sell the film rights to David Lynch, Spinny. This logic is right up his alley."

"They demanded McAvoy's address. It looked like Blondie was leading, and Coyne was following. Blondie wanted Mac— at least, according to Wells. She's pretty confused."

"Gimme her address," Woo said, "I'll swing by her place."

"No can do. She's at a meeting downtown."

"Then have her picked up."

"Where? Her daughter doesn't know where the meeting is, and she's not answering her cell. Daughter expects her back late."

Great. And McAvoy—you go through the trouble of protecting a guy—hell, taxpayers' dollars hard at work—and the dummy invites half of Renfrew over to his hotel.

Woo said, "Move McAvoy and get some cars out there."

"I already made the calls."

"And tell him if he gives anyone else his address, we not only won't babysit him any more, we'll feed him to the damn grizzlies at the zoo."

"I expect Lents and Lemay have already made that point."

"Then make it again."

Woo stuffed his cell phone back into his pocket. Then it rang again. This time it was an enraged Lieutenant MacKenzie.

"Snarlin' Harlan called me."

"Great," Woo said.

"He said he keeps calling you, and you keep hanging up on him."

"He can call all he wants," Woo said, "but pretty soon one of us'll start to look silly."

"Why do you always have a burr up your ass?"

"I used to ask my wife the same thing."

"Hah."

"Harlan can go to hell, boss."

"I have a better idea," MacKenzie said. "How about you loosen up? Either that or start retraining in some other field."

"Retraining in some other..." *Chunk.* The boss resorting to lame threats. The boss was so very inferior.

*   *   *

The sky had darkened at four o'clock. A storm was barrelling down from the Yukon, the wind having spent the last hour whipping up excessive nerve. By the time Woo pulled his unmarked Caprice to the curb across from James Teal's building, the snow cut visibility to maybe thirty yards. Traffic lights were whited out. Cars crawled the six-lane street at maybe ten miles an hour. Woo zipped up his coat and stepped into the storm, leaving the car running. The few people on the street were bundled up, running errands over frozen sidewalks.

McAvoy's report stated that the Jeep had been parked on the north side of the street outside Ted's Deli, facing west. The bullet, according to the crime scene techs, had been fired from the north at a downward angle of about thirty degrees. Woo cupped his eyes against the snow and peered up the street. The shot could have come from one of two places: the roof of the six-story Hudson's Bay department store or the third or fourth floor of the adjoining carpark. Right, that's what the techs had surmised. The department store's roof would have been hard to access during store hours, probably locked off, but the carpark also seemed an unlikely place. What kind of fool would risk taking a shot at someone when vehicles were coming and going? That was a busy carpark.

And the bullet, likely a 9 mm—that meant a handgun. Who ever heard of an assassin using a handgun from a distance? Didn't he have a rifle? The guy was either very amateurish or very determined despite having poor tools.

Woo tore the keys out of the ignition and crossed the road to Teal's place. Stepping out of the elevator on the ninth floor, he wondered what the apartments in this building went for. The hallways were run down, needed paint here, light bulbs there. An English professor. Flashback to two years of history classes at the U of A before choosing the police academy: most academics couldn't care less about appearances.

Teal answered the door wearing white shorts and a silk shirt bedecked with mangos and bananas. He was not what Woo would call elderly, but he looked like an old fool, as though he'd been interrupted from dipping under the limbo bar, daiquiri in hand.

"I'm Detective Edward Woo, Buffalo District Station."

Teal offered his hand and said he'd heard his name on TV. Matter of fact, he was just about to put some clothes on and head down to the station to see him. He didn't look surprised by the visit.

The place was well-kept but had no warmth. No photographs or plants. No woman's touch. A dog, a German Shepherd, lay curled up on the sofa. The stereo sent out some odd sounds, a plink-plink twanging that felt familiar. Woo had heard his share of such music growing up. His grandparents played it incessantly, homesick for Tianjin, the port city they'd escaped during a famine in the 1920s. For as long as he could remember, he'd hated the stuff. Real music had a singer and at least one guitarist but preferably two, one of them bass. Real music was deep-driving. The blues. Stevie Ray or Jeff Healey. Real music wasn't some guy screeching like a cat and strumming a shoelace.

He said to the teacher, "You wanted to come down to the station?"

"I just got back from Behn's cabin. The place could qualify for disaster-relief funds."

So started a story about a visit to Behn this afternoon, a green Mustang, a trashed cabin and a dog with tender ribs. Teal also described cocaine tacked to the kitchen wall and droplets of blood on the floor by the door.

"Would you mind turning down that music?"

Teal used the remote.

"What time did you get out there?"

"About an hour ago. I just got back. I was going to eat something and head down to see you."

"Did you touch anything? Light switches? You clean anything?"

"No, I knew you guys would want to go over it."

The story had the same feel as the phone call from Samuel Cullen, the one in which the Boston cop had said he had solved the case. Too easy. David Lynch wouldn't buy these film rights after all.

It was almost odd how this fogy-hipster seemed to enjoy telling this chapter in his friend's tale of woe. He didn't raise questions and didn't make assumptions. He seemed a straightforward guy who was able to divorce his feelings from the case and to appreciate the peculiarities.

"You take down the license plate number?" Woo said.

Teal pulled a scrap of paper from his jeans and handed it over. Woo pulled out his cell phone and told Records and Information to run a check on the number. He already had an idea of who owned the Mustang.

But if the car did belong to Larry Coyne or his blond-haired friend, that uncanned some new worms. What was this cocaine business? Another curve ball. It wasn't a clue, it was an anti-clue.

Teal scratched the dog's belly. "I gotta put Rico in a kennel. The super gave me hell for dog hair in the elevator."

"I better go see the cabin."

"The roads are terrible," Teal said.

"I want you to come with us."

"Us?"

"Crime Scene Unit. Take me through what you saw out there."

"I don't like the idea of eating snowy fence post at sixty miles an hour."

"We'll take it slow," Woo said. A storm like this, it would bury footprints.

Teal hesitated, then switched off a kitchen light and went to the bedroom. When he returned moments later, he was wearing torn jeans and a brown sweatshirt. That was more like it. Now he was a fifty-year-old man who was losing some hair, seeing the remaining hair go grey and growing crevasses around his eyes. Gone was the old fool living out some Orientalized memory of Woodstock.

They were crossing the street to the car when Spinetti phoned again. Ken Duguay had called the Renfrew cops from Boise, Idaho. One of his wingers—one Larry Coyne—had missed the team flight.

Coyne couldn't be found, and the coach was worried.

*   *   *

At the albino's insistence, Larry Coyne pulled into the Wendy's drive-thru and bought some cheeseburgers and baked potatoes. After eating, he and the albino sat in the car for two buttocks-numbing hours, "waiting for a good, dark night," as the albino put it.

Coyne's legs felt like bent goal posts. Every now and then he flipped on the windshield wipers to clear the snow. Eventually, the albino told him to start driving, then told him to slow down, stick to the left where there's no ice, what the hell are you doing? The albino also kept playing with his gun, jiggling the trigger, coddling it.

The snow was awful. Coyne couldn't believe that (a) the albino wanted to head down to Mac's motel while cops were there, and that (b) he planned to kill him.

"I'm going to shoot him, and you're going to help me. If I have to, I'll shoot you, too."

Dumb but determined. He wasn't taking follow-ups.

He also didn't look too good. The glaze in his eyes had faded to a dull, unfocused look. His nose had deflated almost to normal size, but now was blooming from blue-red to lime green. Every now and then he reached up, gave it a short tweak, then scratched like a monkey.

"It's infected," Coyne said.

"What is?"

"Your nose. You need a doctor."

"If it was infected, it'd still be swollen."

"Okay," Coyne said, "it's not infected."

Maybe it'd go gangrenous. Whatever was making him sick, it wasn't your average Chinook-induced temperature swing. The cough was now deep and rasping, and the albino didn't bother covering it with his hand. Every now and then he spat some phlegm, right there on the Charger floor mat, and leaned forward to study it.

"Just what I need," he said, "a damn cold."

"It's worse than a cold," Coyne said.

"Just keep driving, Gretzky."

* * *

Behn rubbed the fog from his motel-room window and looked out at the gathering storm. The chalky ground and blowing snow gave the evening sky a dawn-like glow. Lents and Lemay were in their unmarked car. Behn checked his watch and asked himself if Jack Brigham would really show for the meeting. Then he stepped back to the phone for one last round of calls. The girl who answered his first call said Pamela Wells was unavailable—and would be all evening.

"You wanna leave a message or what?"

"Name's Behn McAvoy. I'll call again tomorrow."

When the line was free, he dialled Alicia's number. She was reading newspaper articles on the Internet. Did he know that Pamela Wells had never finished university? Dropped out in her second year, went to work at a Safeway in Edmonton. She was managing the place within two years.

"Did you know she got pregnant when she was nineteen? No husband, just wanted a kid."

"Alicia, I called her and—"

"What a woman. They say she married Robert Daley because—"

"Who?"

"He owned Prairie Dog. She married him after he'd had a quintuple bypass. The *Pacific Press* called her a 'Black Widow'."

"She'll see you tomorrow morning at nine," Behn said.

A beat. "You called her?"

"Yes, and she was...she sounded very odd." When there was no reply, Behn said they should go see her together.

"Wow, a man's presence. How chivalrous."

"Shining armour."

"Protecting the fair young maiden."

"She's expecting both of us," he lied.

"Did you mention the ring?"

"I assumed you wanted to do that yourself."

She thanked him for that.

"I'll call you after I meet Brigham," he said.

"And when's that going to happen?"

"Seven thirty, eight."

"I don't know about this."

"I'll call you," he repeated. "I have to go now."

After hanging up and looking out at the cop car out front again, he stepped into the bathroom and slid through the window to the alley. Slinking out onto Twelfth Avenue, he raised his collar to the wind and hailed a cab.

The taxi took him past warehouses and an old stockyard on the eastern fringe of downtown. Cars were parked up on sidewalks. The drive to Queen Elizabeth Park and Jack Brigham's 7-Eleven took twenty drawn-out minutes.

The convenience store sat across from a twenty-four-hour cold-beer vendor and the Cedric Hotel. While the rest of Renfrew closed its shutters to the storm, the bums and street toughs around the Cedric stuck to their rhythms, passing around wine, blocking doorways, trickling into the Salvation Army shelter. Behn stood by the phone. Seven o'clock came and went, and he stayed where he was, stamping his feet to stay warm. When the phone finally rang, he snapped it up and turned his back to the snow.

"I'm in the Cedric," Brigham said, "corner table." *Click.*

Behn looked left and right for traffic and crossed the street. At the Cedric's doorway, two bums blocked his entrance. They wore tattered coats, had snarled beards and bad breath. One of them had a fairly new scar on his cheek.

"Where you going, sweetheart?"

Behn squeezed between them and entered the smoky darkness. A grubby guy on the stage pawed a guitar and scratched out a Neil Young oldie. The clientele had money for beer and cigarettes, but clearly not for much else. The four pool tables were occupied, and the place smelled faintly of urine. Two of the four corners had tables, neither of them occupied. Behn chose one, sat down and ordered a coffee. The waitress who'd taken his order stared disapprovingly at him before retreating to the bar.

Then the two bums from the doorway entered. They surveyed the bar until they spotted him, then they walked over. They sat down across from him.

"I'm waiting for someone," Behn said.

The bum without the scar said, "Nice of you to come alone."

Jack Brigham, partner at Pullman and Shantz.

Brigham pulled out a pack of DuMaurier's. Jittery fingers suggested either withdrawal or fear, possibly both. The eyes were milky but alert. He pulled a cell phone from his pocket and pushed a couple of buttons, maybe checking something, maybe turning it off, maybe just keeping those shaky hands busy.

"Tell you what," he said, "you're not what I expected either."

Behn studied Scarface. The guy was advertising scabby knuckles atop the table. The gap-toothed smile was meant to frighten.

Behn said to Brigham, "Your friend can give us some privacy."

"Can," Brigham agreed. "Entirely within the realm of possibility."

The big guy didn't move. Behn addressed him: "You sit two tables down, you can still see if I pull anything on your friend here."

Brigham nodded, and the big guy got up and changed tables. The waitress came with Behn's coffee. She gave a doubly acidic scowl when Brigham, too, ordered coffee.

"So you're not working for Tony Tran," Brigham said.

"No."

"And you're not a cop, you're a hockey player."

"That's right."

"What do you want from me?"

"You and Normand Fournier used to gamble together."

"Yeah."

"I want to know what the name Randolph Skalky means to you."

"Skalky." Brigham's expression didn't change. "Who would that be?"

"The man who tried to kill me yesterday."

Still on his first cigarette, Brigham pulled out a second. "So the upshot would be, Normand and me, we were pals with Skalky?"

"Is it true you staked Normand at the Horseshoe?"

"Sometimes. Nothing big. Normand dug his own holes."

As did you.

Brigham lit the second smoke before stubbing out the first. "Fifty bucks," he said.

"What?"

"Price if we're gonna talk. I used to charge three hundred an hour."

Once upon a time. You couldn't fall much farther than Jack Brigham had fallen. Behn fished the money out of his wallet and slid it across the table. Brigham pocketed it without eyeing it. Chump change.

"Unfortunately," he said, "I wouldn't know Skalky from Celine Dion." Behn sought signals of deception. Brigham caught him doing it. "Look, do I look like I care about anything other than myself? Normand's dead, so I can't protect him by lying to you. And this Skalky is Chinese to me. You don't want to take my word for it, you're wasting energy that you should be spending elsewhere."

Behn sipped his coffee. Bitter. "These poker games, anyone from Boston ever sit in on them?"

"What do you think we did, exchange life stories? We played cards. High stakes. Up a grand, down ten."

"Did Normand ever mention taking a trip to Boston?"

Brigham shook his head. He looked ready to leave, like staying in one place for too long wouldn't be wise. "Buddy, I asked you down here for a couple of reasons."

"And what are those?" Behn said.

"Number one, to find out how you found me. So I won't get found again. Number two, to see if you're interested in siccing Tony on me."

"I already told you, I don't care about you and Tony."

"Good," Brigham said.

"But you're making it hard for me to care whether you get found or not. Who belongs to the Taurus?"

Brigham laughed through yellow teeth. "Tony's boys. You either learn to spot them, or you end up in the trunk."

"Why would Tony's boys follow me?"

"Well, let me guess. You go down to the Horseshoe, right? You ask the questions you're asking me, about Normand and this Skalky fellow?"

Law-firm equity partner. Brigham was no fool.

"And you come on strong, and they give you my name and say I was Normand's buddy?"

"How'd you know that?"

"If they were trailing you, it was either to see if you'd take their game to the cops, or, more likely, to use you to get to me. Tony would do anything to get to me."

"How much do you owe him?"

Brigham shook his head. "Luck," he said, "bad luck, that's all. A bluff when I should've folded. A bet too big, a bet too hopeful. Nothing too complex about it. When my luck turns, I pay Tony and square things with Pullman and Shantz. If you see Tony, tell him that. I've got a few things on the go."

Gambling, said the counsellors back in rehab, was not unlike drinking. You had to hit rock bottom before you could right the ship. For some people, rock bottom was many leagues down.

"You ever meet a woman named Pamela Wells?" Behn said.

"Who's that?"

"Never heard the name?"

"I've heard 'Pamela' and I've heard 'Wells,' but never the two of them in the same breath."

"Okay. I won't be passing any messages to Tony, because frankly I have no desire to meet the man. Take care of yourself, Brigham."

Leaving, he remembered Alicia Fournier's diamond ring. He asked back to Brigham, "You know if Normand had a girlfriend?"

Brigham actually spent a moment on this one. "He brought this redhead along a few times."

"Redhead?"

"She played the VLT's while we hit the back room. But it's not like we talked about love lives."

So there was a woman after all. Behn said, "You remember her name?"

Brigham's cracked lips dipped. "A million years ago. Everything's so long ago now."

"Age, figure, anything?"

"Young. She called him Normie. When I say young, I mean young."

So why hadn't Normie mentioned her? Locker-room boasts brought the Cowboys' women into lurid detail—it was part of being one of the guys. Normand had never been too shy to tell tall and vulgar tales about the model Randi.

Behn tossed a ten onto the table and headed for the door. Brigham offered no good-bye. He had his fifty. It'd be gone in an hour, just the latest small payment on the trip toward Rockbottom.

The storm was worse now, hard to see across the street. Behn trudged to the corner of the Cedric and held a hand up to keep the snow from his eyes. A cab would be a miracle. Better to find a pay phone and—

A white light went off in Behn's head. His brain stopped sending messages to his legs. Falling forward into the snow, he blinked his eyes to the suddenly blurry world around him. The last thing he saw before blacking out were the lights of the Cedric's neon sign, fading and receding.

Twenty

Larry Coyne saw the cop cars a mile away, even in this darkness, even in this blizzard. Two across the street at the McDonalds, one parked on each side of the street itself, another one farther down on the left side. He hoped the albino wouldn't notice them.

But the albino said, "Turn here, don't go near those cops." He ordered the hockey player down a side street, then said hang a left, get back to Eleventh, park thirty maybe forty yards from the cops, close enough to see but not be seen in all this snow. What are they fuckin' stupid, think they won't be recognized?

Parked, Coyne said, "What now?"

"We watch."

"Watch what? The guy's being protected. One car, ten cars, I don't see the difference. They'd catch you if you tried anything."

"No, they'd catch you," the albino said. "That's the point."

"What?" Coyne said.

"You'd create a diversion."

"A diversion."

"Smoke screen. And I'd go in through the back."

Coyne drummed the steering wheel. He had the defrost on low, hoping to aggravate the albino's illness. His abductor looked sweaty and pale—pale even for him.

"To hell with it. Head back the way we came."

Driving slowly, Coyne asked himself what was next. The albino fell into another coughing spasm, worse than before.

"How can a doctor not sound good to you right now?"

The albino doubled over, spat more phlegm onto the floor mat.

"Do you have to do that?"

Then he started to retch, clutching his stomach, making sickening throat noises. "Stop the car," he groaned.

Coyne stomped the brakes, and the car slid a good twenty yards, careening off a curb before stopping. The albino opened his door, leaned out, and sent a biliary stew of Wendy's cheeseburger and baked potato onto the snow.

Coyne turned away and felt nauseated himself, hearing the awful sounds. Then a reflexive bolt of adrenaline struck. It was a feeling like being fed a pass at the opponents' blue line with no defense men in sight. He shifted in his seat, braced his left foot against the door for leverage, and shoved the still-vomiting albino out of the car.

When he hit the gas, the door closed on its own. The Charger's tires whistled atop the ice, taking forever to scrape up some speed. Coyne hunched low to the dashboard, fearing that bullets would soon start flying.

But there would be no shooting. The albino was still barking onto the road, and there was a corner to turn only a few yards ahead.

My God, that was easy!

He had to laugh. He welcomed a delirious jolt of joy, the likes of which he knew the average person felt only once or twice in a lifetime. So free. So lucky to be alive and breathing the air here on planet Earth. No troubles, nothing out there to put a wrench in your enjoyment of the rest of your now-to-be-very-appreciated life.

And yet there was his car out at Mac's place.

Shit.

He punched the defrost on high and pointed the car

toward Highway 22x. He tuned the stereo to AM 109, caught the voice of Harvey Bailor, the Renfrew Cowboy's play-by-play man. Bailor said there were six minutes left in the third, and the Boise Blues had left their get-up-and-go at home tonight. The Cowboys were leading four to one.

The team didn't even miss him. Duguay, that old hardass, was probably glad his centreman had missed the trip. Probably hoped he'd caught Ebola or fallen down a well or something.

Well, if the albino opted to make that phone call to the cops, and if the cops headed out to the cabin to investigate a break-in, falling down a well would look good.

Coyne stomped the gas, despite the slickness of the road. He prayed, audibly, asked a God in which he didn't believe to keep the cops and that albino fuck and everyone else from heading out to Mac's place. The storm was a good sign; it would keep most folks inside tonight. But he knew—and he didn't know why he knew this, but the knowledge was crystalline and brutal —that this long, dangerous drive was a wasted exercise.

*   *   *

After having the writer show him what he'd found and the order in which he'd found it, Eddie Woo had James Teal wait in the car. Then he consulted with the techs who examined the cabin. There were prints on the coke-holding knife, and there was confirmation that the coke was indeed coke, not something else. Research and Information said the Mustang belonged to Lawrence Coyne, who in the last few hours had been eminently unfindable.

The snow was letting up by the time Woo had seen enough of the place. He asked himself for theories. Okay, Coyne has a grudge against McAvoy, he comes out here, wrecks the place. But he leaves the coke on the wall for us to find? If so, why leave the car? Maybe he wanted to leave it. Maybe he wanted it known that he'd done this. Love to hear the motive that would explain *that*.

Driving back to town, Woo thanked Teal for coming out.

"A guy like you, how'd you get involved in writing a jock book? Isn't that more in the line of a sports reporter?"

"Everyone asks that."

"What do you tell them?"

"That academic writing doesn't do you any favours you can cash." They turned off the gravel road and onto the highway. Teal said, "You write a study of a literary genius, and they throw the thing back in your face."

"I'm surprised they'd even try to sell such books these days. How'd Behn dig you up?"

"Uh-uh," Teal said, "the book was my idea."

"Yeah?"

"I knew his story, Boston, drinking, rehab. I was younger, I had my own problems, did some abusing of my own. Fact is, I still…struggle with it."

"Birds of a feather?" Woo said.

"You could say that. And I knew people would go for a story about staying power and redemption. This is, after all, Canada."

Lights flashed up ahead. Woo eased the car to thirty and passed a snowplough. "What's that mean? You American?"

"I'm from Hamilton. I only mean that Canadians are a very tough audience."

"I still don't follow."

"Yeah. In the States, it's almost expected that the people of demonstrable brilliance, say a top athlete or a movie star, have a bit of a self-destructive streak. A booze problem? So what? Booze is almost quaint these days. Beats up photographers? Laugh about it on Leno and then forget it. Brilliant fuck-ups are a dime a dozen down there."

"We get all the American media up here," Woo said. "Hell, who watches the CBC any more? I don't see how we're all that different."

"We are different. You see it when you live abroad for a while and then come back. Canadians prefer to kick their heroes when they're down."

"That's pretty harsh."

"The only thing we hate more than a hero who doesn't fit our image of a hero is a hero who doesn't care that he doesn't fit it. Look at the way the Stormriders left town. Owner threatens to move them to Houston, the city turns out in droves to buy season tickets."

"Bought one myself," Woo said, "for the nephew."

"Owner keeps them here another year, the press and the public brand him a patriot and shower him with love. So when he moves a year later anyway—because he has to, because there's no way he can make the business work in this market at this time—he gets keelhauled. The greedy bastard had the audacity to want a return on his investment. He had the audacity to want to stay solvent."

"Interesting."

"There are courses at the university devoted to crying about it."

Woo said, "But what's it have to do with people buying Behn's book? I fail to see how another hockey player's memoirs are going to make you rich."

Teal rubbed his bleary eyes. "Behn's spent ten years in this country trying to keep his career above the waterline. He's persevered, but he hasn't made it back to the NHL. *That's* what the public likes about him. He's one of them. He's kept at it, but he's not quite good enough for the bigs. Heaven forbid that he actually make it all the way back. Heaven forbid a trade to the New York Rangers and a condo in Key West rather than a cabin out on the frozen prairie. He'd be just another selfish asshole who graduated to the United States. Like our erstwhile Stormriders."

"My guess," Woo said, "is that you don't own a Canadian flag."

He kept his eyes on the road. He wasn't sure he bought Teal's wisdom, but whatever the teacher said, the book did sound like a good one. Money, youth and pressure translated into wine, woman and song—the oldest brand of self-destruction out there. An attention-getter every time.

"How you holding up with all this?"

"With what?" Teal said.

"With what's happening to your friend. It's gotta be stressful."

Teal pulled out a tissue and blew his nose. "I just want to get back to work on the book. Sell the thing, pick up some royalties, get the hell out of Dodge. Does that make me a jerk?"

"It makes you honest. Can you drop by the office tomorrow morning?"

"Why?"

"So you can fill out a statement about your visit out here. Something for the files."

"Ah, cops and paperwork."

Woo dropped him off at his apartment and headed for the station. The snowploughs and salters had already been through the streets, leaving grey slush where ice had covered the asphalt. It was almost midnight when he lugged himself into the station. Most of the constables were out writing up storm-related fender benders. Spinetti was at his desk, size-elevens high on the desk and chin to his chest, nodding off.

Woo made noise unbuttoning his coat. Spinetti's eyes blinked open.

"Surveillance at the Western Holiday drew a big fat zero."

Woo poured a coffee. "Why don't you go home, Spinny. Get some sleep."

"Why don't you?"

"Me? It's a sad story."

"Yeah?"

"Afraid so. All I have at home is an empty fridge, an unmade bed and a broken stereo that won't play my *Muddy Waters Live in Chicago*."

"Right," Spinetti said, "sad."

"Very."

"All you need to complete the picture is a floppy-eared dog to keep the ex-wife's side of the bed warm."

"Who'd feed the thing?" Woo said. "I mean it, go home, get some sleep."

Spinetti shook his head. "The man we're supposed to be protecting has disappeared." Woo froze halfway into taking a seat. "Lents went to check on him and found the bathroom window open. Opened from the inside."

"He upped and left?"

"Looks that way."

"Any theories why?"

"You're the boss, you tell me." A yawn, Spinny making a production of it. "Also, Lieutenant MacKenzie was looking for you. Mad as a March hare."

"That mean crazy or pissed?"

"Crazy and pissed. I had to tell him to bug off. I was too busy getting the lowdown on Wells's albino."

Wells's albino? So that's why Spinny was still here. Just full of news tonight.

Spinetti said, "A rink rat down at the Agrodome said a pale blond man with a swollen nose was poking around after the Titans game looking for players. The rink rat steered him to the King Eddie. So Blondie goes there, a waitress remembers serving him, he didn't hang around long. When they found Halkidis in the can, Blondie had vanished without finishing his drink."

Spinetti finally pulled his feet down from the desk. Standing up took a theatrically embellished effort.

"Spinny, I want you to dig into some phone records tomorrow. See if anyone's been calling Boston from the Agrodome."

"When do we drop by Wells's place?"

"I'll take care of that. You stay here and do your usual stellar job."

"Taking statements and checking phone records? Gee, I can smell the promotions already."

Woo untied his tie. It felt like days since he'd slept. "If it's a promotion you want, there's always something else you can do."

"What's that?"

"Put that sterling wit under wraps and go find McAvoy."

*   *   *

Behn felt something tugging at him. He forced his eyes open, but the brain was still shorting out. Everything numb, nothing communicating. A prickle on the crown was the only sensation.

Voices drifted in. Cars passed by in the distance. The prickle bloomed into a piercing ache. Concussion. Fourth of the career, only this wasn't the career; this was a back alley during a winter storm. Finally, the eyes inched open. He was face down on snow-covered concrete, his head inches from a dumpster. The hazy voices in his head blended into a single female accent.

"Can you hear me? Try to say something."

He felt himself being rolled onto his back. He blinked up at Alicia, the outline of her sable hair turned yellow by the alleyway light.

He raised his head and looked down at himself. No coat. It was a safe bet there was also no wallet.

"Can you stand?"

"Can't sheel my handzh," Behn said.

She moved behind him, grasped him under his armpits, and sat him up. "Your're half-frozen." He saw her car down the alley. The engine was running.

"Might want to cancel your credit cards," she said. "It was a big guy who followed you out of the bar."

"What he hit me with?"

"His fist."

"You're kidding." Another bolt of pain tore through his temple.

"Think you can walk now?" She helped him to the car.

Inside, the heater hurt his hands and feet. Good sign. Pain meant the flesh was still alive.

Alicia drove carefully. "The storm started," she said, "and I figured you could use a ride."

"I'm glad you did."

"I also figured something might happen, and there I would be, cozy on my sofa while you're out there stirring up trouble."

"Sure," Behn said, "reverse chivalry."

"Your knight in shining armour."

She flipped on the signal light for a turn.

"No hospital," Behn said.

"Why not?"

"I've self-diagnosed. Soft bed and silence, that's what I need."

"The Western Holiday it is."

"How about your place?" he said.

She gave him a double glance. "Is this your usual way of getting girls to take you home? What about the cops?"

"I'll call them from your place."

He hunched forward and rubbed his feet with his burning hands. He felt better, almost clear-headed, by the time she reached her house, led him inside and showed him his bedroom. She pointed out some men's clothes in the closet and disappeared into her own room to change. He pulled on a flannel shirt, woollen socks and a surprisingly well-fitting pair of Wranglers. After leaving the room, he examined the locks on the doors and found the phone in the kitchen. He called Jimmy Teal's place.

"Hi, I'm either asleep or ignoring you. Either way, I'll get back to you."

A beep. "Jimmy, if you're there, pick up..."

Nothing. After hanging up, Behn stepped into the living room and studied the fireplace. Charred lace sat among ash and blackened wood. He opened the flue, started a fire and waited for Alicia. When she did appear, she looked good, wearing frayed jeans and a much-too-large-for-her T-shirt advertising JayBob's Grill.

"What were you burning earlier?" Behn said.

"Nothing."

"It looked like a dress."

"Like I said."

"A wedding dress."

"Make sure what's left of it burns, okay? I'm going to fix

myself a drink. I know you'd probably like a milk or a cream soda, but I'm going for the scotch." She stepped to the counter that separated the living room from the kitchen. The Dewars was just under the counter. "Actually, scotch-es. I could use them in the plural."

Behn tugged at his shirt. "It's just my size."

"Glad it's good for something. How's your head?"

"Better."

"Call the cops, dummy."

"Brigham was a dead end," he said.

"I know."

"You do?"

Drink poured, she took a long, steadying sip. "My mother phoned me just before I went out to your 7-Eleven. That country bar in the photos wasn't in Boston, it was in Rhode Island. Normand went there for a wedding last spring."

Rhode Island. Of course. Providence had a Bruins team of its own, Boston's farm club in the AHL.

"The groom played junior hockey with Normand." She took to the recliner sideways, legs dangling. "Retired last April to open a sporting goods store back home. His mom still sees my mom from time to time."

"I'm glad," Behn said.

"You're a good liar. Something's still bothering you."

"Getting shot at still bothers me."

"You don't know where this leaves you."

Behn thought about it. "It leaves me with Wells paying for his jewellery."

And with the young girl mentioned by Jack Brigham. He started to tell Alicia about the visit with Brigham, but didn't get far. He was distracted by her untouched-up looks, by the way the firelight played on her face. He changed the subject.

"Why'd you divorce the guy?"

"Walter? How do you know it wasn't the other way around?"

"Educated guess."

She took another too-long sip. "Because I came home with Cornish game hens, and he had two hookers in our bed."

That'd do it.

"I guess he was selfish trash right from the start," she said, "but I was too blindly devoted to notice, too hopeful for that book he kept working on."

Hard to see her as a prototypical "wifey". Hard to see her as under the thumb of a confirmed cretin. But it wasn't hard to see what the cretin had seen in her.

"At least he finished the book," she said philosophically. "At least it worked out for him. He's making an obscene amount of money."

"Which doesn't hurt you, either."

"Yes, his alimony really does make my world go round, doesn't it?"

Behn looked around at her Walmartesque living room. "You do appear to have let it go to your head."

She tossed back the rest of her drink and crossed to the counter for a refill. Then she changed her mind, slid into the kitchen, and brought the cordless phone back to him.

"The cops, Behn. I feel like I'm aiding and abetting."

He called the police station while she poured a fresh drink. The conversation with Detective Woo took a convoluted half hour. The upshot: his cabin had been trashed, apparently by Larry Coyne, who had not only stuck a bag of cocaine in his kitchen, but had also made a bizarre visit to Pamela Wells along with a blond man with a broken nose and a gun. They had been seeking Behn's whereabouts—and probably not to wish him well during these most trying of times.

Alicia was on her third drink by the time Behn recradled the phone. He told her no cop car would be swinging by to make sure they slept safe and sound. Woo was not enamoured with Behn's movements today. She swirled her drink, then planted it on the carpet. Then she stepped over to him and lifted the glass of orange juice from his chest. She bent down and straddled him.

"They say you live like a recluse, Behn McAvoy. By definition, a recluse stays...apart, right?"

"Apart?"

"Alone. Lonely. Lonesome. You have many girlfriends?"

"You have many boyfriends?" Behn said.

She thought about it. "Right, dumb question."

"Real dumb."

She climbed off and went to switch off the hallway light. Now there was just the glow of the fire. Rather than move off to the bedroom, in the next instant she was atop him again. She crossed her arms and pulled JayBob's Grill over her head. After tossing the shirt behind her, she reached back and undid her bra, leaving it dangling over her breasts.

"I'm glad Normand wasn't playpals with Skalky," she said. "It simplifies things."

She lowered her head to his, and he felt a restorative warmth behind her mouth. When she pulled back, he looked up at her.

"Here's a question I learned in rehab. Will you tell yourself later that the booze had you doing this?"

She tugged his shirt, freed it from his jeans. "Dumb question," she said.

He agreed. "Real dumb."

Twenty-One

Nighttime wheat fields and frosted hay bales flashed by. Larry Coyne slowed the car as he neared the turnoff to the cabin. At the turnoff itself, tire tracks cut through the fresh snow. Not just one set of tracks, a multitude. He cut the headlights and let the car roll toward the outcropping of trees where he'd parked his car. Lights broke the darkness ahead. An idle cop car was shining its high-beams on the bushes where the Mustang abutted a snowdrift.

Great. What would they give you for wrecking a guy's house and tacking thirteen hundred bucks worth of coke to his wall? Would that get you prison time? Regardless, it wouldn't do your status as a Renfrew Cowboy any good. In fact, it would pretty well noose your freaking neck, career-wise.

The more you want it, Larry Coyne told himself, *the easier it can fall apart.*

*   *   *

Alf Lundgren sat in an all-night laundromat on Charolais Trail, a few blocks from the Western Holiday. He felt miserable. His health hadn't improved much in an hour of cradling his head in his hands, and hitting the icy road face-first hadn't done much for his mood either. He had a goose egg over his left eye and a pounding headache to go with the churning stomach. Only two people came in to do their laundry—a young brunette, looked dirt poor, and a mangy Indian who Alf figured washed his clothes annually. Everyone else was hunkered down in their nice warm homes, looking at TV, sleeping away the winter chills. The Great White North. Bullshit.

A doctor. Coyne had been right. Alf couldn't go on like this, coughing up solids, feeling nauseous, digging away at that prickly nose. A doctor would have a pill or a shot or something.

But Coyne would have gone to the cops by now, told them that he, Alf, was sick. Emergency-ward cops would be on the lookout, so hospitals were out. That left an all-night clinic somewhere, an out-of-the-way place.

There was a phone and phone book on the wall by the Indian's washing machines. The book listed a clinic in Medina, way out in northwest Renfrew, which was just fine. The farther the better. Around here, the cops would be swarming.

The brunette had two loads on dry and was reading a romance novel. The Indian was at the change machine, jostling it, asking it through clenched teeth to turn his fiver into loonies. Alf Lundgren sauntered over to the coat rack and made like he was reading a poster advertising a lost border collie. Slipping a hand into the Indian's coat pocket, he found a set of car keys. When he headed outside, the Indian was kicking the machine and calling it a cocksucking motherfucker. The phrase struck Alf as contradictory.

It was warming up fast, minus five or so, felt like another Chinook rolling in. The keys were for a Ford, and there was only one Ford out there, a rusting yellow F-150 half ton, late seventies model. It was parked in front of the Chinese restaurant next to the laundromat, and it started just fine. Alf backed it onto the street, hoping the Indian hadn't heard the engine.

On the road, he kept an eye out for cops. Goddamn Ed Newby. Handing out jobs like this. Wells and Duguay, they'd be relaxing in a copshop right now, sipping hot chocolate with marshmallows, yapping about him, Alf, giving the cops a fine description. Every cop in town would now be looking for him.

And McAvoy? He could be in Tuktoyaktuk for all Alf knew. How could you finish the job now? Maybe you couldn't finish it. Maybe dildo entrepreneurship was dead in the water. Maybe that beautiful, liberating idea of just making choices and sticking to them was something that appealed only to desperate bozos.

Goddamn Ed Newby.

The Medina Medical Centre was empty when he got there, just a receptionist behind a counter. She was a tiny thing, couldn't have been five feet tall. A little pathetic, actually. Alf smiled at her and felt sorry for her. She looked afraid he might take a notion to violate her.

"I need to see someone," Alf said. "I have a phlegmy cough and nausea. Been throwing up." He added that he thought his nose was infected.

She gave him a sideways look and had him fill out a card that asked about allergies, medication he might be taking, prior surgery, special medical conditions. He signed his name Jerry Butler and listed the form of payment as cash. Then he sat down and picked up a Renfrew *Times-Dispatch* while she took the card into the room where the doctor apparently saw patients.

The front page was about a storm that was expected to hit. Well, it had hit. Another story was about a firefighters' charity ball. The photo showed three firemen posing with some poor crippled little bastard, grinning those dead-eyed grins that cops and firefighters all seemed to roll out for the cameras. Such nice boys. So involved in the community. The story didn't mention that the clean-cut heroes liked to sneak hookers into the fire hall during the night shift. One of the guards at Bowden, an ex-fireman, had told Alf as much.

The receptionist returned through the same door.

"Doctor Walton will see you now."

"Thank you," Alf said. "Nights don't get too busy in here, do they?"

"Not tonight. Everyone stayed inside, rode out the storm."

"Then you have yourself a nice quiet evening, okay?" Poor little midget.

Doctor Walton was black, like an African, with these big round glasses. He looked amiable and had an easy-going smile. He asked Alf to sit down and tell him what was troubling him. Alf retold what he'd told the midget about his stomach and his cough. The doctor thwacked on rubber gloves and put a finger to his nose. Then he pointed a little light down Alf's throat and into his ears.

"How long have you had the cough?"

"Couple days," Alf said.

"The nose is infected, true. It didn't get that way by itself, though. Someone give you a bop?"

Alf thought back to his pistol-whipping of his own schnoz. If felt like a long time ago. "That's right. Same with the lump on the forehead. Guy came at me in a bar."

The doctor stared.

"What do I got, doc?"

"Take off your shirt."

That done, the doctor put a stethoscope to the chest and the back and had Alf take deep breaths.

"You have a nasty flu."

"But my nose—"

"Yes. There's influenza, but something's kept your nose from recovering from its trauma. On your card, you didn't indicate an immunological history."

"A what?"

"And you're currently taking no medication."

"None. Don't need it. Just vitamins."

"Vitamins?" Walton said.

"Yeah. C and A. Also E and D. And P."

"Why were you prescribed vitamin P?"

"Also B6 and B12," Alf said. "I wasn't. I just…got them."

Stole them, actually, from a clinic much like this one, in Brandon, Manitoba. Hid in the crapper till everyone went home, kicked out the glass door to get out and tossed back a kaleidoscopic blend of pills to celebrate.

"Way I read it in this magazine, P makes your cells resistant. And you have *lots* of cells in your body, right? So the stuff toughens you up."

"That's what you think?"

"Well, it's a good vitamin, isn't it?"

"No, not necessarily." The doctor now sounded angry, like he was accusing him of something. Alf gave him an innocent look.

"It's not like it's a drug or anything. It's not like it's hard-core medicine."

"Oh, but it is medicine," Walton said. "That's precisely what vitamin supplements are. How long have you been taking them?"

"A few months," Alf said conservatively.

"At what dosages?"

Alf went to his coat, pulled out five small bottles and handed them over. "Three or four a day, maybe five, depending."

"Depending on what?"

Alf shrugged.

The doctor looked twice at the bottles. "These megadoses. These are prescribed to fight specific illnesses. Where'd you get them?"

"Never mind."

The doctor dropped a beat. "Do you know why your nose trauma won't heal?"

"If I knew that, would I be here?"

"There's a chance it's because you're taking megadoses of Vitamin C."

"Yeah, right."

"These aren't Flintstones Vitamins, Mr. Butler. These doses, if you're body doesn't need them, they interfere with the white blood cells' ability to kill bacteria. That makes infections hard to fight. That's why your nose hasn't recovered. It's why your flu will get worse before it gets better. Now what I suggest is a urine test and a—"

"I don't have time for all that."

The doctor sat back and smiled—like those firefighters in the newspaper. Phony. "I suggest you find the time."

"I'm on my way out of town. I can't hang around for test results. How much do I owe you?"

"I don't think you understand."

"Listen, you don't want my money, fine. I know the problem, I'll stop the damn pills. Now get outta my way."

"Fifty-three dollars," the doctor said. "Plus GST. You can pay Lisa."

Alf hustled his shirt and coat back on and stalked out to the reception area to pay the midget. Then he got out of there. He drove the Ford down to the Greyhound station and parked it between two trucks that looked like they hadn't been driven lately. The vitamins went into a trash can outside the station's big sliding doors. So much for the optimal body. He bought a ticket to Edmonton, the bus leaving in three hours, then checked Ed Newby's address, which he had on a slip of paper in his wallet. Things had to be set straight.

It was high time to find out who was paying to have McAvoy killed.

Twenty-Two

Behn couldn't sleep. The night was dark but alive with the sounds of the apartment: the wall clock, a rattling heating duct, a dripping faucet. Alicia stirred and draped an arm over his chest. He glanced at the clock radio—still only eleven o'clock—eased Alicia's arm off, and slipped out to the kitchen, where he found the phone and dialled Jimmy Teal's number.

"Hello?" Jimmy said at the other end.

"Hey, it's me."

"Where are you? I've been calling the hotel."

"I'm staying with Normand's sister."

"Well. And how did *that* come to pass?"

"I saw Brigham tonight," Behn said. "He's got nothing to do with Normand."

"I wouldn't be so sure," Jimmy said.

"Oh?"

"Remember that Internet search you asked me to do?"

Behn had opened the fridge to peek inside. Now he closed it. "Yeah?"

"It seems Brigham's law firm works for Wells. They represented Prairie Dog in court last year. Unfair competition case. Prairie Dog was squeezing independent brewers out of the Red Deer market, signing non-competition ad deals with local magazines and liquor stores, also offering stores cut-rate prices on beer purchases. The local breweries couldn't buy any shelf space, so they went to the provincial anti-monopoly office. Prairie Dog lost the case."

Behn said, "How'd you find this out?"

"Online newspapers. It was in all the business sections. Mr. Brigham himself led the defence until he left the firm."

Behn opened the fridge again. "He told me he'd never heard of Pamela Wells."

"And that's not all I have," Jimmy said. "You sitting down?"

"Should I be?"

"Larry Coyne went out to your cabin today. He—"

"I know," Behn said, pulling out some apple juice. "He trashed the place. Woo told me he took you out there."

"And your detective appears to be positively flummoxed."

"He and others." Behn found a glass and poured himself some juice. "The more that happens today, the less I understand."

"Maybe the good Mr. Woo will put it all on a big whiteboard flowchart for you."

"I'll call you tomorrow," Behn said, "after we meet Wells."

"We?" Jimmy said.

"She's Normand's sister. She has a stake in this."

With Jimmy off the line, Behn chugged his juice, crossed to the living room, gathered up his clothes and got dressed. Alicia's car keys sat atop a stand beside the door. He scooped them up, eased the door open and left the house without waking her.

Driving toward Queen Elizabeth Park, he asked himself if Woo could indeed "flowchart" today's new information into coherent meaning. *Can he tell me why Wells was buying Normand's jewellery? Or why Brigham gambled with him? Or why all of them—Wells, Brigham and Normand—kept their relationships with one another secret?*

He parked in front of the Cornelius Hotel, stepped inside and asked the desk clerk if Lyle Mulholland was still staying here.

The clerk nodded.

"Which room?" Behn said.

The clerk gave him a long once-over. "Hey, you're Behn McAvoy."

"Yes."

"I thought you guys were on the road tonight. Boise."

"I'm injured," Behn said, thankful that the clerk wasn't a fan of the evening news. "Concussion." The lobby smelled like old cabbage. The counter was scuffed and pocked with cigarette burns.

"Would you mind?" The clerk pushed across the counter an upside-down registration form and a pen.

Behn signed it and slid it back. "Lyle Mulholland?"

"Yeah." Now the clerk's expression streaked to confusion. *What would Behn McAvoy want with a creature like Mulholland?* "Room 12," he said uncertainly.

"Thanks."

The elevator was out of order, so Behn climbed the stairs to the fourth floor, stepping over sticky patches and crumpled newspapers. Jack Brigham's room was on the third floor, toilet at the end of the hall. Behn cupped his ear to the door and listened for the sounds of conversation. Nothing. He knocked, then waited, then knocked again. He turned to leave, and finally the door clicked open.

Brigham's goon from back at the bar—the one with the forehead-to-chin scar—looked out at Behn and promptly began to close the door. Behn launched himself forward and knocked Scarface backward onto the bed, where he landed next to a recumbent, underweared Jack Brigham, cigarette at his lips and eyes wide in amazement.

"Easy," Behn said as Scarface scurried to his feet. "Don't do anything stupid, okay?"

Scarface steadied himself and glanced nervously past Behn. Behn followed the gaze and saw that they had been watching TV with the volume turned down—looked like reality TV, a bikini-clad contestant manufacturing tears for the supposedly nonexistent camera.

He also saw a wallet—his own wallet—sitting atop the dresser, open. He glanced back at Scarface's clenched fists. One of those fists had just clubbed him unconscious outside the Cedric.

"There was a hundred, a hundred twenty in the wallet," Behn said. "Give me a few minutes with Jack here, and we'll call it even."

"Stay here," Brigham said, sitting up on the bed.

"Wait outside the door," Behn said to Scarface. "I don't leave the building unless you let me leave."

Brigham said, "What do you want?"

"I want to know why you lied to me."

"I didn't lie to you."

Now Scarface lunged. Behn bobbed to his left and the big man sailed past him and crashed into the mirror, spiderwebbing it. He spun around blindly and lashed out. Behn waited, then clipped him high on the forehead and followed up with another shot, aiming for the same spot. Scarface's legs buckled, but he stayed up. Behn took hold of his shirt collar and clouted him twice over the left eye. Then he pulled Scarface to his feet, dragged him to the door and tossed him into the hall.

When he finally turned around to look at Brigham again, he was surprised to see the lawyer chuckling.

"I forgot you were a professional barbarian," Brigham said.

Behn locked the door, knowing it wouldn't stop Scarface

from returning. Best thing would be to get straight to the point.

"You told me you don't know Pamela Wells."

"That I did," Brigham said. "I hope you're not forgetting my going rate for interviews."

"Didn't your friend share the contents of my wallet with you?"

Brigham shrugged. "It didn't last."

"Why did you lie to me about Wells?"

"Why are you so sure I did?"

"Your firm represented her. I'm also unclear—now that I think of it—on why you hung around with Normand. Hockey players and law-firm partners don't run in the same circles."

"In games of hazard," Brigham said, "everyone is equal. There's no social strata at a blackjack table. You plan to beat me up?"

"The way I'm thinking right now, I could go either way."

"We didn't use your credit cards, by the way."

Behn stepped to the dresser and snapped up his wallet. Everything except for the cash was still in place. A heavy shard of glass fell from the mirror, startling Behn as it slapped the wood. He saw that a splinter of glass had settled on a magazine—on a Renfrew Cowboys media guide.

He picked up the guide and saw that it was open to his profile. Adjacent to Behn McAvoy's career stats and scouting report, someone had scribbled in pencil: *Carseland weir. Cabin. No phone.*

How did the lawyer know he had no phone? Had he sent Skalky out there?

"Talk to me," Behn said, "or I'll drive you over to Tony Tran's house and dump you on his front lawn."

He tossed down the media guide, advanced on Brigham —and then found himself being hurled through space. Scarface had burst back through the door and heaved himself at Behn. He pinned Behn to the bed, Brigham vacating the space in time to avoid being plastered. The big man dug his fingers into Behn's neck, squeezed, shook Behn's head up and down. Behn pawed at his wrists, heard Brigham scream something in the background. He kicked his legs, tried to raise a knee, but was sandwiched flat. In his peripheral vision, he saw Brigham standing there holding a pistol, aiming it at him—at them. Behn punched at Scarface's ribs, but had no room to wind up. Such was the big man's hard-breathing fury that he slobbered through his clenched teeth, the saliva settling on Behn's fast-whitening cheek.

Then, as quickly as the assault had started, it ended. The big man climbed off, and Behn coughed and gasped and rolled onto the floor and rubbed at his burning neck. When he could finally breathe again, when he finally looked up, Brigham's protector was gone, ordered away by Brigham, and the lawyer was standing in the doorway, still levelling the gun.

"At first Normand and I sat at the same table without knowing each other. Then we hit it off, what can I say?"

Behn coughed and gasped.

"I needed money one night, he lent it to me. He needed it another, so I returned the favour. Then I started really lending him—until he started getting in too deep." Brigham chuckled sadly at the recollection. "I helped him until I saw how things were working out for him."

"Everyone," Behn croaked, still on one knee, "can identify the addict except for the addict himself."

"I had Lenny pick up the media guide after you called me this afternoon. I wanted to know who I'd be meeting with tonight, that's all. I don't know what else you're dying to read into my motives, but it's the truth."

"And Lenny knew where I lived?" Behn said. "He knew I have no phone line to my place?"

"No phone line? The Telus operator told me you're unlisted. If you didn't show up at the bar, I was going to call you. As for your address, I jotted that down from your bio in the media guide. Your PR team celebrates your distinctive rusticity. You mean to tell me you haven't read your own bio?"

Behn coughed again, the fire in his throat still burning.

"Near the end," Brigham said, "I wanted nothing to do with Normand. He was out of control. I don't know what you want from me, but it's making me nervous. I just want to be left alone. You can—"

"If Normand was out of control, who paid for his gambling near the end? Wells?"

"Why would you think that?"

"Because she paid for something else of his. Why did you lie about knowing her?"

"Reflex," Brigham said. "You don't talk about clients with outsiders. It's called confidentiality."

"Then how did Normand gamble? Ran up IOUs?"

"In part," Brigham said. "He was into Tony for a good amount. He also had another benefactor."

"Who?" Behn said.

Brigham lowered the gun and tucked it under his belt. "At the very end, the only person who could still tolerate his losing. His sister."

Behn stopped massaging his neck. "Who?"

"That's what he told me. I can't tell you if it's true or not." Now Brigham stepped forward and leaned in to study Behn's neck. "You wanna know something funny?"

Behn blinked.

"You've been coming on like gangbusters, but I still don't know what it is that you're after."

*   *   *

He drove back to Alicia's house, climbed into bed with her and pressed up against her back. She stirred and mumbled, "Where were you?"

After a while, he said, "Learning that Jack Brigham really does have nothing to do with anything." After another long pause: "Why did you give him gambling money?"

She moaned sleepily and lay silent. Finally she murmured, "I signed over Walter's alimony cheques."

"Why?"

"Spite, partly. I pictured Walter being satisfied that I myself was spending the money." He stroked her hair, and she breathed in and exhaled deeply—long but laboured—a failed seeking of release. "Also, Normand pleaded with me. I couldn't bear to see him that way—so desperate. That makes me an enabler, right?"

"It makes you human," Behn said.

"No. I enabled him all the way to the grave."

Behn watched her body rise and fall with the rhythm of her breathing.

"Funny thing is," she said, "until you woke me up, I was having the best sleep I've had since his funeral. Now there's no way in hell I'm going to fall back asleep."

*   *   *

The cops? Larry Coyne thought. Tell 'em the albino, for reasons known only to his own Lilliputian mind, had forced you to put that coke in Behn's cabin? Which in a sense was true?

Or come clean about the coke, hope they go easy?

Or how about this? Find a way to round up the albino, "bring him in" like Steve McQueen hauling in riffraff in *The Hunter.*

Right. If Mac were around, you could at least do some gut-spilling to *him.* Let him get steamed, call you Beaker if he likes. Warn him about the albino, tell him there's this crazed half-wit out there who wants to blast him, and that you did everything in your power to stop him.

Would he go easy if you did that? Would he help when it came time to clear the coke up with the cops? The cops weren't something that could be ignored for long.

Coyne drove aimlessly, endlessly, and willed himself to stop thinking so much. He fed the car more gas and turned the radio on. He worked the stations to find something loud and mind-numbing. Heavy metal, the music of choice while working the weights. Attitude music. Screw-you tunes. Back in Piapot, you were considered either full of long-haired attitude or deeply disturbed if you didn't live and breathe country and western. So be it. Larry Coyne clubbed the steering wheel in rhythm to the brilliantly anaesthetizing noise.

Back in town, he stopped at the first phone booth outside the first roadside strip mall. The book listed a J. Teal at 906, 1313 5th Avenue Southeast. He tore out the page, pocketed it, and dialled 911.

"Emergency services."

Now motor-mouth it: "An hour ago there was this big blond guy with a busted nose at the Western Holiday down on Eleventh. He wanted to shoot Behn McAvoy. Probably still wants to. He's real sick, has this infection, some kind of flu, got him barfing. He's also on foot, unless he stole a car. Actually, I bet he stole a car. He has a gun."

"Sir, please slow down and—"

Click.

The cops would bequeath no medals for judgment for having made this call, and certainly not for what was coming now, but maybe they could be massaged after the fact. Hell, he could tell them he was in shock, that's why he didn't go straight to the station after dumping the albino. There'd been lamer excuses.

The car's clock read one a.m. The Renfrew roads were cleared and salted, but the sidewalks looked to Coyne like Ken Danby doing Norman Rockwell. Teal's building was across from the Bay and a multi-story carpark, two bucks for half an hour, nine bucks for the day. He parked on Level One, crossed the street, and waited for someone to pass through the glass-door entrance.

A long-haired biker type with a Kim Mitchell patch on his jean jacket barrelled out of the building. Coyne caught the glass door before it closed, took the elevator up to the ninth floor, and rang Teal's doorbell.

When Mac's writing buddy opened up, he was drowsy, sagging in the shoulders, wearing this goofy kimono that made him look silly. Pathetic, really.

The teacher stood there in a fog. "Yeah?"

"I have to talk to you."

"You!" Now he was wide awake.

"You know, don't you?" Coyne pushed open the door.

"I know what?"

"That the cops are after me. You're wearing it like a sign. But you're not gonna call them, okay?"

"The cops?"

176

"All I want is a minute of your time, hear me out. Then maybe you can do me a favour."

The teacher stepped back and rubbed his eyes. He didn't look afraid, just really, really surprised. He wrapped the kimono tighter around himself. What a goofy-looking bastard.

He finally said, "What kind of favour?"

And he bought it, every word—or seemed to, anyway. Sitting in his living room sofa, that awful kimono resting on a skinny lap with bony, protruding knees, a trusty glass of rye and seven in his right hand, Mac's writing buddy believed that he, Larry Coyne, was mortally sorry about all of this and wanted only to help his besieged teammate.

Coyne kept the story simple, winnowed it of its central truths: He'd gone out to the cabin to warn Behn about this wild-eyed albino who'd been asking after him down at the Agrodome. But the albino had trailed him all the way out there, pulled this gun that had a big silencer, scared the ever-lovin' crap out of him. He'd given him this coke to stick to the wall. Absolutely, indescribably daft. Who knew what was going on in his amoebic, flu-ridden mind?

"A double whammy," Coyne said. "Near as I can figure, the idea was to frame me for the coke and the cabin so he'd have some leverage on me—I'd have to help him find Mac. And I guess I was a hostage for if the cops got too close."

He sipped the Wiser's that Teal had poured for him. The story sounded so good that maybe Coyne could use it with Mac and the cops. If the albino got away, or if luck struck and the cops killed him dog-dead, he could probably make up all sorts of nonsense. If not, if the albino got himself caught, the truth would have to come out. And in that case, best that it be directed to Behn first—because Behn was the one who decided if B-and-E charges would be pressed.

But would it work? Would Behn be moved by phonied-up contrition? Coyne thought that unlikely, but saw no alternatives. Play it by ear, choose the right option when the time comes. But first win over this gawking bozo in the silly chink get-up.

He looked Teal in the eyes. "You see, I spent the whole day trying to stall the albino guy, to keep him off Behn's trail. He had me take him to Pamela Wells' place, figured she knew where he was."

"Why's he after him?" Teal asked.

"Wouldn't say."

The writer's hair—that which remained—was sleep-mussed. He got up and turned the stereo on to a low volume. A whiny oriental plinking came on.

"It helps me think, music. Relaxes me."

Yes, like fingernails on a chalkboard.

The writer sat down again and closed his eyes. He looked like maybe he would start meditating. Finally he asked, "How did you get away from…the albino?"

This time the truth: "I booted him out of the car."

"What?"

"We were stopped at a curb so he could yark up his dinner. I kicked him out the door while he was heaving."

"You gotta be kidding." The writer put his head in his hands. Odd that the only true part of the story was the hardest part to believe. "What do you want from me, Coyne?"

"Two favours, actually. Number one, don't call the cops. I've already called 911 and described the guy, so they know who to look for. But if he gets away, none of what I've said here gets substantiated—and I go straight up the creek. It's no secret that Behn and I have had our differences. Right now it looks like I *wanted* to make that mess out at his place."

"Evading the police isn't smart," the teacher said. "Withholding information on crimes is illegal."

"I'll take my chances with that. Besides, I called 911." A pause to study the teacher, then time for the second request: "You gotta tell me where Mac is. If I can just talk to him, I can explain my side of things. If we go to the cops together —me and Mac—things won't be so bad for me."

"Well, it doesn't look like they'll be good no matter how you cut it."

"Hey, don't I know it," Coyne said.

Teal nodded—maybe the music helped him to think after all. Well, if it calmed him, it calmed him. To each his own.

Finally, the teacher said, "I don't know."

"You gotta believe me."

"I don't know where Behn is. That's what I meant."

"Then who does?"

"Only the cops."

"You're sure about that?"

"Do I look unsure?" The teacher now acting insulted. "But if I did know where he was, I wouldn't tell you. Consider yourself lucky that *I'm* not calling the cops."

Coyne watched the teacher shuffle toward his bedroom.

"Where you staying tonight?" Teal said.

"I hadn't thought about it."

"I want you gone by the time I wake up tomorrow. Otherwise, I *will* call the cops."

He slammed the bedroom door behind him and Coyne sat still until the light under the door went out.

Coyne found the living room light switch, flipped it off, and sat down in the darkness, half a drink in his lap. The room swam in blackness around him. Eyes closed, he remembered a morsel of home-spun wisdom that his dad had liked to recite. "Well, son, you been busy as a one-legged man in an ass-kickin' contest, but the only chances you got left are slim and none."

Naïve bastard. Why'd he have to listen to his fucked-in-the-head kid about those gas-station renovations? Why couldn't he have made his own damn decisions?

Coyne set the drink on the table. Yawning, he leaned onto his side and rubbed eyes that were red-hot and itchy. You don't, he figured, resist drowsiness at the end of the worst day of your life. He willed himself to drift off, his coat still on, his head resting on a sofa cushion. His feet were still on the floor.

*　　*　　*

He awakened before seven, a slice of daylight between the curtains and the wall. He opened his wallet and checked his pant pockets. Seven dollars and forty-six cents. With Teal still in bed, he examined the coffee table and the stereo top. Then he went through the cabinet drawers. Maybe the teacher kept some emergency cash squirreled away.

He rummaged through CDs, lighter fluid and toothpicks. Batteries, a Rubik's Cube, a pile of old junk mail. The third drawer held a tablecloth that looked like a Christmas gift from Grandma. He reached underneath and felt cold steel. He knew the thing was a gun even before he pulled it out and held it to the light. It looked like a .22 or a 9 mm. He shoved the gun back before it burned his fingers. Guns were the bane of the devil (the devil himself being Charlton Heston and all of those inbred, perpetually riled up *Deliverance*-type dudes that were forever whining about the gun registry and Kyoto and the Wheat Board and anything at all that impinged on their moronic notions of "freedom"). He tiptoed into the kitchen and opened some cupboards.

It took little thought to settle on Beefaroni. After opening the can and finding a spoon, Coyne slopped the gluey contents down his gullet while leaving the apartment. He finished most of the can before the elevator let him out on the ground floor. For the last bits, outside the building, he tossed the spoon away and swabbed the can's inner wall with a finger, careful not to cut himself on the rim.

Much of last night's snow had melted. New Chinook. It'd wreak havoc with the albino's flu, and bravo to that. He slopped through the slush on the street and considered leaving the Charger where it was. No doubt it was hot anyway, stolen by Pukey the Wonder Albino for use in the Behn hunt. What was there to do now? Any miraculous new options since yesterday? The constructive choices had expired, and all that was left now was decency.

Go to the cops. Wells had probably called them. She had no doubt—

Pamela Wells. Yes. How had you missed that?

Wells had to have noticed that he'd been the albino's hostage. Wells was a witness who could help him, tell the cops the albino was setting the agenda. So drop in on her, set that point in stone, *then* call the cops.

He found the car's registration in the glove compartment Michael Magruder, local resident. Well, Mikey, today's your lucky day, you get your car back—after I'm done with it. He started the engine and headed toward Chartrain Drive. The morning rush hour had yet to start. He rolled down his window and breathed the air with relish. He even stuck his head out the window as he drove, catching the day full on and asking the world to give him more of the same.

Then he opted to cool it. Chinook or no Chinook, this was winter. The only good thing about winter was hockey.

At Wells' place, the poolhouse glass was painted white eight or nine feet up so passersby couldn't peek in. Above that, it was fogged up. Coyne stared at it from the driver's seat. Must be odd to have a pool. Must be odd to worry about things like chlorine content and water filters. Money did weird things to your perspective. You didn't even have to have it to let it twist you. You just had to exist within its world. Meaning you had to exist.

Twice he stepped out of the car and locked it, and twice he climbed back in. Butterflies batted his ribcage. Wells was no fool. Was she really going to be in a mood to grant him favours?

A black Jetta stopped at the gate outside the mansion. The car idled for a moment before the driver killed the engine and opened the door. A woman stepped out and moved around to the front of the car. She looked familiar, but Coyne couldn't quite place her.

Then the passenger door opened, and a man stepped out. Coyne's heart thumped in his chest. He leaned over the steering wheel and squinted.

What was he doing here?

Behn McAvoy was following the woman through the mansion's big gates. They reached the door of the house before Larry Coyne recovered from his shock and splashed out of his own car. By the time he found the presence of mind to call out, Mac and the strange woman were inside the house.

Twenty-Three

Breakfast had included boiled eggs, toast, orange juice and coffee. Peering down at her barely-touched whole wheat, she didn't look hungry. She handed Behn the key to the Jetta and told him that he'd be driving. She was strangely distant, maybe going over last night.

"Don't worry about me," Behn said. "I don't need us to book a church."

"It's not that," she said. "My head's pounding. I haven't tied one on like that for years." She flashed a smile saturated by hangover pain. "I don't regret it, by the way."

"A ringing endorsement."

Driving to the Wells mansion, neither of them gave the parked Charger a second glance. They parked outside the gated, serpentine driveway and got out and pushed the intercom button. The gate buzzed, and they walked in and followed the path to the mansion. A man in a dark blue suit opened one of the adjoining front doors and told them Pamela Wells was in her office down the hall to the right.

"I'll need some ID," he said. Behn showed him his driver's license, and the man said he had to frisk him.

"Frisk me?"

"Frisk you. New policy."

He was thorough around the back and the legs. Satisfied with Behn, he scrutinized Alicia's ID and patted her down, too. Finally, Behn and Alicia started down the sterile hallway, no art or plants, only a cool, brown carpet and neutral ashen walls with a high ceiling. They stopped at a just-open door to what looked like an office. Voices carried through the crack.

"Don't be cheap," said a young woman. "Your cars cost a lot more than this one."

"But you already have a car, two of them." The second voice belonged to Wells. "You spend money like it's printed just for you. Instead of buying everything in sight, why don't you get a job? Or go to school? Find something, anything. Sink your teeth into something."

"And you'd know about sinking your teeth in, wouldn't you? Ever since Robert died—"

"Don't use Robert like that. To make points."

"Why not, you used him? Could hardly wait till they packed the topsoil over him before you went off and bought hockey teams and built your own little Camelot out on the coast."

Behn felt Alicia's elbow in his ribs. "Sweet family," she said.

Now Wells. "— don't have to take this. I don't have to sit here and—"

"Mother, unless you cut me off, there's not a damn thing you can do about the car. Don't let emotion cloud your judgment. Robert would frown on it."

There was a long pause filled by a theatrical exhalation. Wells' daughter, Georgia, must have been smoking. She sounded like a smoker. She sounded like an enjoyer of long, cool drags and sweltering facial expressions.

"I'm going for a swim," Georgia said. "If you don't like the Mercedes, tough. Eight more weeks, I don't have to live under your roof. And you won't have to act so damn maternal."

There was a pause before Wells said, "It's not an act, it's never been an act." Honest-sounding words, words of surprising pain, coming from Wells.

The door swung open. Behn stepped back to avoid being steamrolled by Georgia Wells. She was wearing a turquoise, one-piece bathing suit and a white bathing cap. One hand held a towel and the other wielded a cigarette. She pulled the door open wide to give her mother a view of the eavesdroppers.

"Well, aren't *you* nasty little spies." Puffing the cigarette, she brushed past them and headed for the poolhouse.

They stepped into the office. Wells watched and blinked. "Behn."

"Miss Wells."

She swivelled in her chair. "You enjoy listening in?"

"Not really."

"You have children?"

"No."

"Then I bet you enjoyed it."

Alicia stepped forward. "Miss Wells, I—"

"How is it that you can make company presidents squirm, bend CEOs to your will, but when it comes to your own daughter—" her hand swatted air "— no, I don't think you'd understand."

Behn waited. He knew that she knew why he was here.

She said, "The cops tell you your teammate dropped by yesterday?"

"They said he tried to blackmail you," Behn said. "With some tall blond man who threatened you with a gun."

She nodded.

"Over something Coyne did at my house."

"Cocaine," Wells said.

"But why? Why would he want the cops to think I'm a dope fiend? I can't figure that—"

"He's *your* teammate. How should I know?"

"Then why would he come to you?" Behn said. "It's like you knew he was doing what he did."

Behn felt Alicia staring at him.

"They taped the conversation," Wells said. "They tried to trick me into saying something that could…well, that could suggest that I asked Coyne to frame you. It was all very amateur."

"Yet they also wanted to know where I was."

"Yes."

"Why?"

"That's for the police to answer," Wells said. "I don't know, but I don't think they wanted to extend best wishes."

Behn gave her a few seconds. "Miss Wells, there's something missing here."

She laughed. "There's a *lot* missing. You ever have a gun pointed at you, Behn?"

"Yesterday."

"It felt a lot worse than you thought it would feel, didn't it? A lot more frightening?"

"Yes."

"Things happen so fast. Sometimes you're in your pattern, living your life here on planet Earth, and then someone has to throw their agenda on your lap. And then you barge in here like Joe Friday asking all sorts of—"

"Ken told me two days ago you wanted to see me," Behn said. "He told me to call you ASAP. What was so urgent before all this happened?"

This time the response stalled in her throat. "I…wanted to know you were all right. After Randolph Skalky."

The den mother. To her, hockey players were one step removed from Cro Magnon man—and degrees less loveable. Behn turned to Alicia, who pulled out the ring.

"You recognize this?" Alicia said.

"Should I?" Wells said.

"Since it's yours, yes."

She gave the ring a good look. "Why don't you two slow down. This is all moving too fast for me."

"The Gemological Institute keeps good records," Alicia said. "You brought them this ring on March 29 last year. They gave it a grading report, and you paid with your Visa card."

She showed Wells the GIA serial number. Wells paused, looked like she was thinking hard.

"My Visa card," she finally said, "was stolen."

"Oh?"

"I don't remember it as being in March, but…yes, maybe it was. If I recall correctly, there were four or five purchases, maybe three thousand dollars all told. They were made before I knew the wallet was gone."

"You live in Vancouver," Behn said. "Somebody stole your card, went to New York to grade a ring, then brought the ring back to Renfrew?"

Wells turned to stone.

"I found it in one of Normand's coats," Alicia said.

"Who's that?"

"My brother."

Wells stared blankly, took some time connecting jewellery to dead hockey player. "I don't know what you're insinuating, but—"

"I'm insinuating that you're a liar," Alicia said. "I'm insinuating that you gave Normand this ring for some reason, but that you don't want to admit it."

Wells nodded, the gesture seeming to say, *You've got guts.* Then: "The fact is, I spent the last week of March in Vancouver. *That* can be confirmed. As can the fact the card was stolen. Now why don't you start being a little nicer to me? I'm getting tired of all this...moxie."

Alicia stepped forward. "When I find out what interest you had in Normand, believe me, I'm going to—"

"Never mind," Behn said.

"Never mind?" Alicia stuttered.

"You're right, Miss Wells. We're off track. Sorry to waste your time."

He tugged Alicia from the room. Wells looked confused but amused by the sudden pull-and-push exit.

In the hallway, Alicia swatted his hand away. "What the hell was that?"

"It's all right here," he said. "Young girl, likes to spend mother's money?"

"Georgia?"

"Georgia."

Alicia said, "Georgia clearly has money of her own. Why would she steal her mother's Visa card?"

Behn said that was a good question; the answer had to be just as good.

They found a door to the grounds out back. They walked the snow-cleared path to the poolhouse. The warm air inside the poolhouse left water streaks through the fogged glass walls. There was a jacuzzi at the far end of the pool, and in the pool itself, Georgia Wells swam freestyle laps, the cap snug to her head. Behn and Alicia stood at the edge of the pool, watched the water ripple over her. They waited for her to see them, which she did in mid-lap, stopping and dog-paddling for a moment. She didn't say anything, didn't looked surprised.

"Your mother's not happy with you," Behn said.

"What else is new?"

"She's upset about your little trip to New York last March."

Georgia absorbed the statement, kicked with her legs, and finished the lap, touching home at their feet. After pulling herself from the pool, she headed straight for a table that held a stack of towels, a pitcher of orange juice and a pack of Player's Lights. She shouldered a towel, lit a cigarette, and took a long, mellow drag.

"You must be persuasive," she said.

"How do you mean?"

"To get Mother to talk about that."

*   *   *

Alf Lundgren rang Ed Newby's doorbell and checked his watch. Nine thirty-five a.m. It was frosty up here in Edmonton, maybe minus twenty, no mountains to push toasty air down at you.

There'd been no sleep in the bus station or on the Greyhound, but Alf felt better now. The cough was still there, but the nausea had retreated. He liked Edmonton. The city was so grey, so…isolated, its own town. The closest big city was a thousand klicks away, and the folks here saw that it gave them some status. The sign on the road in from Renfrew proclaimed "City of Champions"—juvenile chest-thumping, maybe, a statement more about ancient sporting history than about present-day reality, but it was a nice middle finger to Renfrew nonetheless. It said, "We are thus and so, and we don't care what you jealous twits think about it." Edmonton seemed more like an American city than a Canadian one, an accident of geography.

Ed Newby's house was a three-room bungalow in a

middle-class neighbourhood. From the doorstep, it looked like the home of a teacher or a postman, not of a guy who said he sold coke for Peruvians. Alf checked the address again, wondered if he'd written it down wrong way back when he was a friend and an equal sharing a cell.

A blonde in a nightgown opened up. "Who are you?"

"I'm looking for Ed."

"He's sleepin'," she said. "A guy's gotta call before he comes over. A guy should show some common decency."

She had siliconey breasts and vacant eyes. Alf pushed the door open and let himself in. He had to straight-arm her into the hallway to do it. She protested by calling him an asshole and trying to claw his eyes out.

"Hey, stop that, girl."

Before closing the door, he made sure she was on the other side of it. She danced out in the cold, pounded the door, screeched at him to open up. He left her there and found Newby's bedroom, saw his old cellmate leaning up on his elbows in bed, trying to put things together. Newby was still too close to sleep to say anything lucid, so Alf told him to sit tight for a while. Then he snatched a long winter coat from the closet and raced back to the front door. The girl stopped pounding when she saw him through the slats of glass. He opened the door and tossed out the coat.

"Here's some dough. Go get a doughnut or something." He tossed out a twenty, regretted it wasn't a ten.

"Lemme in, asshole!" He found some women's boots and threw them out, too. Then he pushed the lock in and headed back to the bedroom.

Newby was now in jeans beside his bed, uncrumpling a T-shirt to pull over his head. He was a slim guy with a sunken chest and long, wiry hair. Looked harmless, even a little nerdy, but he was good with the mouth, and he knew how to handle himself despite his physical limitations. The Indians and the bikers and the Vietnamese at Bowden had given him space the moment the cops put him there for pimping in Renfrew. The way Alf saw it, Ed had this uncanny way of making himself look dangerous. Toughness through hard-to-define charisma.

Newby glared at him. "I told you never to come see me. Never means never. Wanna see a dictionary?"

He brushed past Alf on his way to the kitchen. Alf followed, watched him fit a filter into the coffee maker. Man, the guy kept a middle-class home. Inside, too, it looked like a mailman's place. The oven mitts over the stove even matched the dish towels. Alf took a seat across the counter in the dining room.

"You hear about this Randolph Skalky?"

Newby peered into the coffee maker. "It was on the tube. Is this why you're intruding on my privacy?"

"It's not normal," Alf said. "How come you send me after a guy who someone else is after?"

"How was I supposed to know this Skalky was out there?"

"You didn't?"

Newby sighed. "God, Alf, you always find these answers before the question's even asked. You gotta slow down and be logical. What happened to your face?"

"Nothing," Alf said. "I'm plenty logical. Don't tell me I'm not logical."

A chuckle—so damn superior. "You still working on your dildo scam?"

"What the hell's that got to do with anything?

"How exactly are you going to market those things, anyway?"

"Magazines ads and billboards," Alf said.

"Yeah?"

"Yeah."

"Alf, you ever see a forty-foot dildo? They have laws against that kind of advertising."

Alf sulked, wasn't going to say anything. Then: "They'd have sold like stink. But I guess I'll never know for sure. Because I'm through with this McAvoy business."

"Ah, come on, Alf."

"You want him dead, kill him yourself."

The statement triggered a coughing fit, the first in a while. Alf doubled over, really leaned into it.

The coffee machine spat out sounds of its own. Also a nice aroma.

"You got a contract, Alf. You have to fill that contract."

"Says you. And you're not getting your ten grand back either."

"Oh?"

"Not after you sent me out on this b.s. job. I wanted to do this quietly." Which was comical, now that he thought of it. "The cops are hiding the guy. I try to work around that, it almost gets me caught."

"Alf, you don't finish what you've been paid to do, there's gonna be trouble." Newby crossed to the fridge, pulled out a box of pizza and took one of the three leftover slices. He didn't offer the visitor any. "We've been paid up front for this. The job doesn't get done, someone's gonna be real mad."

Alf leaned over the counter. "Who? Who's gonna be mad?"

"Listen, I take on lots of risk in this job. It's the nature of it. Someone's gotta handle the money, deal with the parties, that's me. This party paying, they don't know my name. I'm careful about that. But you, you know me. I figure you're a friend, but that's still not any kind of guarantee, you know? And you know what would really be dangerous?"

Who was he, talking like this, the Almighty?

"If *you* knew *them,*" Newby said. "That would really cook us. I can just see what you'd go and do. A deal's a deal. Make good on the contract, and I'll send you another ten grand."

"I told you, the cops are watching him."

"Then lay low," Newby said. "Go somewhere nice for a few weeks. They won't watch him forever." Newby worked on the crust now, talking between chews. "I swear, sometimes I think maybe your head's full of cement. Slow your mind down. A guy like you, you shouldn't be thinking like this."

"Like what?"

"Thinking period. You're not a planner of things, Alf, you're a doer. I chose you for this because you're good at watching out for yourself, at following through on a straightforward job. Do that. See this as a straightforward job."

Alf said, "If I get caught, I tell them you sent me. That doesn't worry you?"

Newby shook his head. "Ratting me out? I haven't seen you since Bowden. You're just an ex-cellmate, got a hard-on to see me burn so you can save yourself."

"You better cool it, Ed."

"And if the cops did get me for this, well, you know I have more friends inside than you ever had."

Alf choked back a cough. "You're a real asshole, talking so big."

"Let's not call each other names."

"You weren't such a prick in Bowden. What happened to you?"

"Come on, Alf, what do you want me to say, sorry?"

No, sorry wouldn't cut it. Alf gained his feet and wiped his nose with his coat sleeve. "Screw it. As of now, I don't work for you no more."

"That'd be dumb."

"Stop telling me how dumb I am."

"Well, you're acting that way."

"I don't take talk like that from no one, Ed, not even you."

"Yet I'm your boss, whether you like it or not. So take it you will."

Boss. That did it. Things clarified once you stopped seeing the underlying facts the way he saw them. Alf yanked out his gun.

"Whoa, Alfred..."

Now there was a sense of calm, not even a sneeze itching at the back of his eyes. "Where you keep your money around here, Ed?"

Newby did a double take. "What?"

"Hotshot like you, you done any big dope deals lately, you're bound to have some dough kickin' around. I'm thinking... I've got this idea."

"Put that thing away."

"I'm thinking you're gonna pay me the rest of what I'm supposed to get for McAvoy. You're gonna do it because that's gonna make us square."

"Only way to be square," Newby said, "do the job and take payment later."

"Uh-uh, there's another way."

"What?"

"Tell me who's paying for this job."

"Why?"

"Because instead of messing with the hockey player, I'll go kill him."

Newby's eyes narrowed to slits. The idea held an insane

hint of logic: in a deal gone sour, get rid of the only party who can cause trouble.

And no, they wouldn't have to mess with McAvoy any more.

Alf crossed to the pizza box, snapped up a slice and stuffed half of it into his mouth. The nausea wasn't quite gone, but he had to eat something.

"I get a feeling these guys who paid us, they had something to do with Skalky going after McAvoy."

"And what if they did?" Newby said.

"Well, you can't do that to a guy, make it so dangerous for him to do his job. What kind of business is that? Now where do you keep your coin, Ed?"

"You're being emotional," Newby said. "Being emotional never helps."

"Fine, I'll just shoot you, then rummage around until I find it."

The coffee pot was now full. Newby kept whatever fear he felt well hidden. He poured himself a cup, then led his hired help back to the bedroom. In the walk-in closet, he elbowed aside hanging pants and shirts and blazers—hell, he dressed like a history professor—and pushed on the back wall where it met a side wall. The wall slid inward a few inches, pushing the other end outward. Newby bent down and reached for something in the darkness.

"Hold on," Alf said. "Stand over here, let me do that."

Alf reached in with his left hand and searched the darkness. His thumb caught a strap and pulled out a black CCM gym bag.

"Sit on your bed, Ed."

"That money's not mine."

"I know, it's mine."

Alf unzipped the bag and held it upside down over the bed. Three bags of white powder tumbled out, followed by five stacks of money in paper bands. Nice red fifty-dollar bills. Four stacks of them, plus a partial fifth. After computing the math at twenty grand plus the partial stack, maybe twenty-six or twenty-seven grand all told, he stuffed two stacks into his coat pockets and put the rest back in the bag with the coke.

"We're even," he said, and he tossed the lightened bag back to his boss, hitting him in the chest with it. "Now the other thing."

"I don't know the man's name," Newby said. "I dealt with him, it was through Saleem, guy who makes deliveries for me."

"How'd he link up with you?"

"How do you think?" Newby said. "Through a friend of a friend."

"What's his name?"

"I don't have a name."

"Ed, I know you. You'd have checked him out."

"You think he put an add in the *Sun*, Alf? You think that's how these things get done?"

Alf moved to Newby's side of the bed, put a hand on his shoulder, and generally did his best to look benign. Then he smashed the butt of his gun over his former boss's left ear.

Newby pawed once at his head, then became wobbly. Alf held him like that, sitting on the bed, the barrel to his left cheek.

"I want his name and address, Ed."

Newby didn't answer—or couldn't answer.

"If you didn't know him beforehand, you had this Saleem guy or whoever follow him. You cover all the angles."

Alf slapped his cheek and told Newby to snap out of it. Then he gave the cobwebs a moment to clear.

"Duh droa," Newby finally said.

"Huh?"

"Droa." The drug dealer motioned to the dresser. Alf

stepped over, opened the top drawer, and dug around inside. The address book was at the back, under a stack of woollen socks. He handed it to Newby and told him to flip and find. Fighting to control his hands, Newby picked out the page and turned the book around for him.

Alf couldn't believe what he saw.

"Archie Halkidis, Ed? I just *shot* Archie Halkidis." Newby licked a finger that he'd dabbed in the blood at his sideburn. Alf slapped the book away.

"If you're steering me wrong, you're gonna regret it."

Newby blinked past him.

"I mean it, Ed."

"'kay."

"And Ed—listen to me now—if you decide to send someone after me, it'll turn into me versus you, and neither of us wants that, right?"

Newby nodded, then slumped back onto the bed and closed his eyes.

"Sorry I had to hit you, but you were being an ass."

Alf pulled back the gun and moved to the door. Newby stayed where he was. His bimbo would be returning soon, probably spoiling for another eye-scratching episode, so Alf moved down the hall to use the back door. Once outside, he watched his breath rise before him as he walked. Crisp, excellent air, sharp and hot in the fur-covered lungs.

Shouldn't have whacked Newby like that, he wasn't thinking straight.

But Archie Halkidis? One of McAvoy's teammates?

If that was the case, then there really was justice in the universe. Karma. Everything you did meant something. Halkidis was either dead or getting dead, Alf was certain of that.

Which meant things were really starting to look up.

Twenty-Four

Behn watched Georgia Wells puff her cigarette and drip
water at poolside. Georgia would talk at her own speed—if
she talked at all. She was watching Behn and Alicia for signs
of impatience.

"So?" she finally said.

"Your mother—" Behn started, but the clack of the glass
door opening cut him off. Pamela Wells paced in, followed
by Detective Woo. The cop's gaze went straight to Behn.

"You get around, don't you?"

"We do what we must," Behn said.

Alicia was staring hard at Georgia. She showed her the
ring. "You gave this to Normand..."

"Well."

"Look at it," Alicia said.

"I've already seen it." Georgia stubbed out her cigarette
and unpeeled her swimming cap. Deep-red hair. She faced
her mother. "Well, Mother? Shall we?"

"Georgia..." Wells stumbled forward, seemed to lose her
balance and deflate all at once. To the cop: "Normand was a
gambler and a loser." To Alicia: "Sorry, but he was."

"But my loser," Georgia said with a sad laugh aimed at
Mother.

"No," Alicia said.

"We were going to get married, just before he—"

"That's crazy," Alicia said. "He'd have told me. He'd have
told *someone*."

Georgia's cigarette trembled between her fingers. "No, he

wouldn't have. No one was to find out, including—especially —Mother here."

"Georgia, I—"

"But you're such a bitch! You tried everything with him, didn't you? Even threatened to trade him, right? Are we being open about this? Are we telling about how you threatened to cut him, but he told you to stuff it? He'd have quit hockey if you'd driven him that far, because he wanted to be with me!"

Wells looked pained by her daughter's obtuseness. "He wanted to be with your money, Georgia. You still can't see that?" To Woo: "Robert left her a trust. She turns twenty-five, she receives a lot of money."

"How much is a lot?" Woo said.

"After tax, four million dollars."

The number soaked the air for a moment. Wells explained. The idea was for Georgia to finish school before collecting the trust, but the date was approaching irrespective—and Georgia was so damn irresponsible. She wasn't preparing for it. She was going to waste it on some broken-down hockey player with a gambling addiction.

Wells said, "When she took the ring to that gem institute, they were in New York. Sightseeing, going to plays. Guess who footed the bill? Guess who dumped whom at the Waldorf for a few days to go drinking with some friends up in Rhode Island?"

Alicia massaged her temples. "I think I'm going to be sick."

"Meddling witch," Georgia said to her mother. "The one thing I ever wanted in life, and you had to destroy it!"

Silence.

"It's not meddling when it's for your own good."

"My own good!" Georgia butted out her cigarette, went still for a long moment, then hurled herself at her mother, flailing with open hands.

Wells twisted sideways. Georgia lost her balance and fell hard to the ground. Woo stepped over and held her there, her squirming, fighting to bound back up and resume the attack.

Wells smoothed out her dress with her palms. "They planned to get married in Vegas. She had a drive-thru chapel picked out. Elvis was to be the pastor."

"Oh, gimme a break," Alicia said.

"You know why? So they could send me photos of it and drive me crazy. She admitted that. She wanted so badly to hurt me that she'd turn her own wedding into a joke to do it."

Georgia struggled against Woo. "You'll rot...in hell."

"She lifted my Visa card because hers was maxed out. The ring was to be from Normand to her. That's how badly he was playing her. He wouldn't even pay for a ring." She turned to Georgia. "You have your whole life in front of you, baby, and having the last name you have, you're susceptible to all sorts of confidence swindles."

"He loved me!" Georgia cried. "He wouldn't have killed himself if you hadn't made him feel like such a loser. He wouldn't have..." The words trailed off into a sobbing spell. Woo let go of her wrists, then tried to help her to her feet. She wriggled and swatted his hands away, content to lie curled up at pool-side.

Behn looked at Alicia for the first time in a long while. Her face was chalk-white. Her eyes lacked focus.

"Are you okay?"

"I need...some air." She lurched toward the door. The impulse was to follow her, but then Woo spoke: "Why would

Coyne and his friend be visiting you, Miss Wells? I don't understand that."

"Detective, let's all just...slow down. Let's gather ourselves, shall we? Continue this inside the house?"

"All right." Woo again offered a hand to Georgia, who was now deadly silent. At his touch, she coiled into a fetal position, tucked within a shell of back, shins and elbows.

Wells squatted down next to her. "Georgia, you'll catch a cold, lying here like this."

Muffled words: "You go to hell."

"You can't just stay here."

No answer. Wells pulled a towel from the table and draped it over her daughter. She said, "Don't stay out here too long. Please."

She turned away, toward the door, and at that moment Georgia vaulted to her feet and sprinted past her, her bare feet slapping the concrete. Leaving the poolhouse, she slammed the glass door behind her. The clatter echoed in the enclosed space.

For a moment no one spoke. Then Pamela Wells offered, "She'll be okay. She cracks up like this regularly."

The desperate humour was lost. Georgia was a battle she wouldn't win.

They walked to the door, nobody saying anything. It didn't occur to Behn that Alicia might no longer be there when they got outside.

Twenty-Five

Larry Coyne did not want to be grabbing anyone, certainly not kidnapping anyone, but Normand's wigged-out sister made the decision for him. Pouring herself out of the poolhouse like that, floundering down through the gate to the sidewalk where he sat in the car. At first, Alicia hadn't seen him. She'd stopped on the sidewalk, bending over, hands on her knees, catching her breath as if she'd done some punishing windsprints. He was slinking low in the driver seat, uncertain whether he wanted her to see him (would she recognize him?). Only minutes earlier, Larry Coyne had seen her and Behn—and then Wells and some cop—enter the poolhouse. Now, as she passed the car, she became not a question mark, but a...a what? What was she?

She was a last chance to get to Mac.

But when she spotted him—crouched low in his seat and eyeballing her—when he stepped out and told her who he was, she panicked. She started a mad dash up the snowy knoll to the poolhouse. He had to intercept her before she reached the door.

He smothered her mouth with a gloved hand. Her legs kicked. The hand slipped, and a muffled scream escaped before he bottled her up again. He had to drag her, kicking, wriggling, back down the slippery knoll between the fence and the street. She was easy to handle despite her struggling. Good thing. And good thing Wells' daughter hadn't come blasting out of the poolhouse ten seconds earlier (and what a sight *that* had been).

He stuffed her into the car through the driver-side door, shoved her over the console to the passenger seat, and kept a clump of hair in his right fist as a safety measure. With his left hand, he turned the ignition and began to steer. She wasn't struggling now, at least not with any strength, but he didn't trust that. He got the car moving quickly enough to keep her from jumping out.

Her fight soon fled altogether, air from a blown tire, but he kept his eyes on her anyway. He stayed at forty on the waxy road. Her right hand reached for the door, but it was a motion to steady herself, not to escape. She leaned forward and vomited.

"Jesus H.," Coyne said, "what are all you people eating!"

He hustled his window down, slapped off the heater, and turned away from her floor mat. She let heave a second time, and he dug a tissue from a pants pocket and slipped it into her left hand, which cradled her cheek. Her black hair had pitched forward over her pale forehead. She wiped her mouth with the tissue, sat up slowly and croaked out something barely audible.

"What?" he said.

"I said thank you."

Then she looked at him full on, with red, watery eyes. She seemed to sense his anxiety. He tried to look friendly, beseeching, anything but dangerous.

"You calm now?" he said. Her window was all fogged up. "I'm not going to hurt you. I didn't wanna grab you, but you went snaky like that, you left me no choice." He added, "I don't want the cops picking me up."

"I gathered that. Water..."

"We'll get you some."

"Where are you taking me?"

"I don't know yet."

"*Why* are you taking me?"

"Let's just drive around a bit. I need some time to think."

She gave him a long look. "They said you were after Behn..."

"They're confusing me with someone else."

"Sure, that's why you're kidnapping me."

"I'm not kidnapping you, I'm protecting myself."

"Hah."

"Strange as that sounds," he said, "it's the truth."

"Protecting yourself against what?"

Well, at least she wanted to hear it. If he told it smoothly enough, really piled on the sincerity, she'd forgive his little trespass here. Maybe even set up that meeting with Mac. There was some real work to do with her. She'd no doubt heard about what he'd done at the cabin. Surely there was no poster of Larry Coyne, centreman for the Renfrew Cowboys, pinned over her bed.

"It started the other night after the Titans game," he said. "There was this pale-looking guy down at the Agrodome. He was looking for Behn, so I..."

*　　*　　*

The bulletin went out—one Alicia Fournier was missing. After confirming her absence from the mansion property and calling it in, after reassembling both Wellses and Behn McAvoy in the office in the mansion, Eddie Woo listened to a story about a tape recorder, a gun and a blond man's desire to find Behn McAvoy.

"Stay available," he told both Wellses. "Please stay home." Then he led Behn out to his car and radioed for an unmarked car to watch the mansion.

The sun splashed a glare onto the soaked roads. Woo donned his sunglasses, Behn flipped down his visor.

"You sleeping with her, Behn?"

The hockey player said, "Does all that paperwork aggravate the piles?"

"I have to clear things up. Something's missing."

Behn didn't answer.

"Correct me if I'm wrong, but before all this started, you didn't know her—or knew her superficially—but then last night you're sleeping over at her place?"

"Maybe she ran off," Behn said. "She was shocked about Normand. She didn't know what she was doing."

Woo thought, *And she literally ran away from the property at the speed of light?* She wasn't going anywhere alone—at least not as quickly as she would have had to move in those few short moments before everyone else had followed her out of the poolhouse. Someone had driven her away from Wells' house. The jumble of footprints down to the road suggested a struggle on the way to the vehicle.

And McAvoy knew it, or would know it once his own shock wore off. His wrinkled brow, his emphatic concentration, his desire to make this incident into something it wasn't—he wasn't much good for anything at the moment.

A few minutes later, Woo pulled into the station parking lot and led Behn inside. He had him wait in Lieutenant Lloyd MacKenzie's office while he went to leave a message of his whereabouts on Dante Spinetti's desk. MacKenzie was out of the office, speaking at some powder-puff crime-detection conference down at the Four Seasons. As Wells was an interview subject today, they could use the office rather than a sterile interview room. The rich were to be afforded amenities.

At Spinetti's desk, Woo called the lab.

"Anything?"

The lab tech said, "The blood from the cabin floor matches Coyne's type."

"How'd you get Coyne's type?"

"Vancouver Canuck training-camp fitness tests."

"Nice. Wouldn't have thought of that."

So it was Coyne's blood. No surprise.

The tech said, "We also have a face for our Halkidis suspect. Jerry Ward—"

"Who?"

"Spinny's rink rat. He came in for a computer sketch."

"And?"

"Blond, pale, nose like a tractor-tire print. I'll fax a copy over. Suspect looks more like a sketch than a sketch does, if you get what I'm—"

"I get you," Woo said. He hung up and returned to the office. McAvoy was on his feet perusing wanted posters.

"Have a seat, Behn."

"Mind if I smoke?"

"You'd think a hockey player would be a militant non-smoker."

Behn said, "Guy Lafleur, Mike Bossy, Rocket Richard, all smokers."

"That's an excuse? Maybe if they didn't smoke, they'd have been better."

"Or maybe they'd have climbed walls. I started smoking in rehab. Booze or cigarettes. One a day. I need it."

Woo hesitated, then slid open a drawer and pulled out a pack of cigarettes. After lighting one for himself, he slid the pack over to Behn, who lit his own.

"What are you doing to find her?"

"Everything we can," Woo said. "Did she say anything to suggest someone might wish her harm?"

"I just met her two days ago. But no. She would have mentioned it."

"Did she have any visitors yesterday?"

"No."

"Any phone calls? Did she go meet anyone?"

"Not when she was with me," Behn said. "If you're asking if she's involved with whoever has it in for me, then the answer is no."

"Does she socialize with any of your teammates?"

"She hates hockey players."

"Present company excluded?"

"I'm growing on her," Behn said. "Where are you going with all this?"

Your guess is better than mine, thought Woo. He sighed and stubbed out his cigarette. He smoked only with interview subjects. Smoking created a bond that was sometimes useful.

"Your dog'll be at a kennel by now," he said. "Jimmy Teal said his building super wouldn't let him keep it."

McAvoy sucked greedily on his own death-dart.

"By the way, why didn't you tell me that Archie Halkidis threatened to kill you a couple days ago?"

"Archie's not involved in this."

"Look at it this way. We have you in here, we grill you about who might want to kill you, and you tell us you haven't the foggiest. And yet just one day before that, one of your teammates threatened to kill you? It's curious that such a thing could have slipped your mind."

"Archie doesn't want me dead," Behn said.

"I have it right here." Woo shuffled some papers on his desk and pulled out a witness statement. "According to one of the janitors at the Agrodome, Halkidis said, quote unquote, 'I am going to kill you.' This was stated in the concourse after practise. It was not said in jest."

"It was an idle threat."

"Oh?"

Behn sighed. "It's the way he talks. It's the way a lot of the guys talk. When you want to hurt someone, you don't say, 'I plan to hurt you,' just like when you get hurt you don't say 'ouch.' You scream or swear or look for something to hit."

Woo nodded. You didn't have to be an athlete to have that mentality. "So why would he want to hurt you?"

"He wouldn't. He just has a problem with me. I embarrassed him."

"Oh? How so?"

"He's been floating, hasn't been accountable. Last week I called him on it in the dressing room after practise."

"What do you mean you called him on it?"

"I told him the world didn't owe him a thing. I told him Vancouver demoted him for a reason—he wasn't fighting, wasn't protecting his teammates—and unless he was willing to accept that truth, he would be no good to himself or to the Renfrew Cowboys. I told him to grow up. And for what it's worth, lieutenant, he told me he was going to kill me after that practise too."

"That's it? Habitual hyperbole?"

"I got him right in the ego, that's all. He's twenty years old. He has a lot to learn."

Woo said, "Tough love in the Renfrew Cowboys' dressing room."

"If you want a murder suspect, you should hear how

coach Duguay threatens us."

"The thing is," Woo said, "Halkidis threatened you, and then he ended up getting shot by the man who's running around with Larry Coyne. It's a terribly coincidental coincidence."

"Then ask him about it as soon as he's awake," Behn said. "You'll know what I'm talking about. Rub him the wrong way, he'll threaten to kill *you*." Behn looked at the clock, then checked his watch as if any discrepancy between the two would be vital. "In the meantime, please find Alicia. And find Coyne and his friend."

"Do you think Larry Coyne is capable of wanting you dead?"

Behn thought about it for a minute.

"Larry Coyne," he said, "is capable of just about anything."

Twenty-Six

It was one thirty in the afternoon when the Greyhound pulled into the station. The sun was out, pricking Alf Lundgren's eyes and tacking wings onto his hacking, gasping coughs. The laundromat Indian's F-150 was still in the parking lot between the two other trucks. The mercury had shot up to twelve degrees because of that fucking Chinook, and now sweat streamed from every pore. Alf found a cab and had the driver take him down to 5th Avenue Southeast. He waited at a booth in Ted's Deli, across the street from Jimmy Teal's building.

Archie Halkidis was still alive. The radio had stated as much. He was likely going to pull through, which was terrible news. It meant he would have to be shot all over again. In fact, he had to be shot *in addition* to McAvoy. As long as McAvoy was around, he would want—look for, seek out—the identity of the hitman. And if McAvoy wasn't staying with his writer buddy right now, then there was a good bet that the writer knew where he was staying.

It was Wednesday, so maybe the teacher was at the university, schlubbing with the eggheads. Maybe wait till you see him coming or going, be sure he's there before you go flashing your face around that apartment building. The cops no doubt now had a description of him, Alf. Maybe they'd even run a sketch on TV.

But a half hour passed, and Teal didn't come or go, so to hell with patience. Alf gobbled down a Bavarian smoky and slurped an orange juice (*this* vitamin C wouldn't hurt,

210

would it?). Then he crossed the street and entered the
building alongside a lady struggling with three plastic Co-op
bags. He carried the bags for her and handed them back
when she got off on eight. She thanked him tentatively,
staring at his beat-up face. His nose itched.

He rang Teal's doorbell and sounds from within the
apartment said the teacher was home.

Alf readied himself. The door drew open slowly, and Alf
stepped up and kicked it hard, knocking the teacher back
into his living room. He raced into the place and slammed
the door. His next impulse was to grab the guy by the hair
and demand to know where his hockey-player buddy was.
But the guy didn't have any hair—or anyway, not much—
and there was something numbingly awful about this place.

There was this music in the air, this high-pitched ting-
tang clamour that burred into Alf's flu-ridden head like
termites.

He glared at Teal, really looked at the man for the first
time. White cotton pants with string for a belt. A T-shirt
reading "Chulalongkorn University, Bangkok". Alf showed
him the gun and said, "Make it quiet in here, or I'll shoot
your stereo."

Teal used the remote.

"Now sit down." Teal did that while Alf endured six
rapid-fire sneezes. The illness was starting to interfere with
things. "You have anything for a flu, James?"

Teal looked confused.

"For a flu. Starve a cold, feed a fever. You got anything?"

"In the washroom cabinet."

"Show me."

Alf followed him into the washroom and started some
water running. Two Coldrex's, one Contac and three

Panadol's for the aching joints. Alf slurped water from the tap to wash the mixture down. Then he marched Teal back to the living room sofa, levelled the gun at him again and watched him blink once. It was hard to tell what Teal was thinking.

"You know where McAvoy's staying?"

"No." The answer came too fast.

"You feel like going peckerwood up?"

The teacher locked his hands together and leaned forward, his elbows on his knees. He was so calm. He looked as if someone pulled a gun on him every day of his life.

"Behn's my friend," he said. "If I did know, I wouldn't tell you."

Alf toyed with the idea of blasting a toe off, then thought maybe a pistol whipping would do the trick. But it was tiresome, unoriginal, like any meathead off the street. He paused for a moment. *Something* had to be done.

Well, there was that music. Maybe strap some headphones to the teacher's melon, crank up the volume, and blow his eardrums to sawdust.

Alf stepped to the stereo and leaned over to read the CD in the tray. The writing was in some odd, loopy language, words jammed together without spaces.

"It's Thai," Jimmy Teal said.

"What is it, bells?"

"Xylophones."

"Xylophones?"

"Why do you—"

"Precious," Alf said, giving up the music-torture idea and moving back to the teacher. He sank into the soft leather across from him. "Do you remember when you were a little schoolboy, James? Back in Grade Five?"

A slow nod.

"Then you remember how you used to answer questions back then. You recall how you used to sit up so straight that even a fucking ant wouldn't be able to crawl between your back and the chair. The teacher'd ask a question, and you'd answer so clearly and not nod or mumble or do anything unclear or dishonest. Because you wanted the approval. Because your teacher would give you this big smile or a 'Thank you so much, James' and you'd feel so damn proud of yourself you could just burst."

He waited for Teal to respond. Another nod.

"Well, I'm your teacher today, James. Loud and clear now, okay? Answer my question, and I'll go home, and you can sit here and listen to all the cat-scratch xylophone nonsense you want."

The teacher said, "I'm not lying. I don't know where—"

"If you don't tell me the truth, I'm going to hurt you. Honest."

The doorbell warbled.

The fact of the sound hung heavy in the silence that followed it. Alf's breath quickened, but he didn't move. Neither did Teal. The teacher didn't even glance at the door. Frozen. Alf brought a finger to his lips and shushed any potential sounds. The bell rang again.

"Sit tight," Alf whispered.

A voice from the hallway said, "Open up, it's me! I heard you in there."

Larry Coyne's voice. What the hell…

Alf whispered, "James, what's *he* doing here?"

"He came by yesterday," Teal said, "after he threw you out of his car."

"I can hear you through the door," Coyne said. "Open up."

It couldn't be Coyne. Coyne should have been somewhere safe and warm, recovering from his escapades yesterday. Alf tiptoed to the door and motioned for the teacher to remain still. A squint through the peephole said yes, it was in fact Coyne. There was a woman with him, a good-looking thing, like this red-haired movie star whose name escaped Alf.

He drew open the door, staying behind it. When Coyne and the girl were well inside, he slammed it shut and slid the chain lock into place. The girl gave a start, but she looked more together than the player. The player looked like a bladder accident waiting to happen, the same way he'd looked out at McAvoy's house. Alf scratched his head with his gun.

"Good God," he said.

Coyne didn't say anything. Neither did the girl. They were waiting for directions, also asking themselves questions too quickly to find answers.

Well, you had to start somewhere. Alf sat down again. He fixed his eyes on Coyne and decided to start with an easy one. Putting a friendly tinge in his voice: "How's tricks, Lawrence? You throw anyone out of any cars lately?"

* * *

Alicia Fournier suspected that Larry Coyne was capable of worse than this half-assed kidnapping. Her hangover had died long before the hockey player suggested they swing by Jimmy Teal's place to leave a message for Behn—"just in case Mac calls," as he put it. The hockey player had spent the morning with her at an Alberta Tourism rest stop on Highway 2. The stop was closed for the winter and had picnic tables around back, away from the road. She had nowhere to run while he spat out a riddle: this albino guy had abducted him at the cabin and made him leave cocaine and fingerprints and his car there, then carried him around like insurance against cop attacks while he tried to blackmail Wells for cash and find Mac to kill and there was nothing that could be done to stop him and no way of alerting cops or overpowering him or doing anything at all that you would think you might do when something like that happens to you.

"What?" she said.

After he went through it a second time, all she said was, "I see." The man was clearly insane.

But this so-called albino did exist. He was now waving a gun at her. He was asking Coyne if he'd thrown anyone out of any cars lately. Teal, on the sofa, was obedience incarnate. When the albino stepped toward Coyne, the hockey player raised his arms and flinched. The albino reached past him and tugged at the door's chain lock, testing its strength.

"Just stay where you are," he said. "I'm having a talk with James here." He returned to the leather chair across from Behn's friend. "James, you owe me an answer."

"I don't have one," Teal said. "I don't know how many ways I can say it."

The albino eyed Teal's stereo. "Let's not have to fire up that Grundig, James."

"What do you mean?"

A sneeze erupted, followed by rasping coughs that sounded like a motorcycle being started. Alicia glanced at the chain lock, but her feet felt plastered to the carpet. Coyne was also catatonic. The albino recovered from his coughing spell.

"I'm waiting, James. He was in a hotel yesterday. He moved. Where to?"

Teal's eyes darted toward Coyne. The writer wordlessly

begged for help. Then he told the albino, "I can't tell you what I don't know."

Alicia turned to Coyne. The writer hadn't been giving the hockey player eye signals—it had been happening the other way around. Coyne's eyes were Morse-code ovals, understanding whatever it was that the writer had sought to convey.

The albino was wracked by a new seizure. On the third or fourth kick-start cough, he doubled over, releasing the gun onto his lap. There was a quick movement to Alicia's right. Coyne tugged a pistol from the drawer under the stereo, stepped forward and pointed it at the albino.

He held his arm plank-straight, shaking. The albino just kept coughing.

"Let that gun slide to the floor," Coyne said.

More coughing.

"I mean it, you...mutation."

Finally, the albino settled down and mopped his mouth with his left hand. Then he wiped the hand, front and back, on the chair. "Don't play with guns, Coyne. Some real bad stuff comes out the spittin' end."

His own gun stayed right where it was, on his lap, inches from his hand.

"You want me to count to three or something?" Coyne said. "Is that how you do it? Hands up!" Tight fear. The gun looked wrong in his hand.

"I was never going to hurt you, Larry."

"Larry? What happened to Helper? What happened to me being your toady? I oughta put one in your big greasy snapper right now."

"Larry, if I wanted to hurt you, I'd have done it by now. Right?"

"The voice of reason."

Teal gained his feet and stepped gingerly toward the bedroom.

"Where you going?" Alicia asked.

Behind the albino, Teal mouthed the word "po-lice" and disappeared into the room. When he returned seconds later, he drew a finger across his throat. What did that mean, dead phone line? She didn't dare to ask, not with the albino watching, not with Coyne looking so unsteady. Teal inched toward the hockey player, eyeballing the albino.

The albino grinned and brought up his non-gun hand to wipe his runny nose. Alicia expected a quick move for the lap-held gun, a hail of gunshots, one dead person, maybe two or three. She stepped aside, out of the line of fire.

Teal wrapped his right hand around Coyne's gun-holding hand. "It's okay, Larry. He so much as flinches, pull the trigger. Think of it as popping gophers out at the farm."

"We never had a farm. We had a gas station."

He unglued Coyne's fingers from the metal and replaced them with his own. By the time the transfer was complete, the albino's grin had fled. The big man eyed Teal cautiously, gauging the new gunholder's intentions. Teal stayed quiet, stepped closer to him. Finally, the albino shifted his left leg and let the gun fall to the floor. At last he raised his hands.

"Same goes for you, James," the albino said. "I could've shot you. Don't do anything dumb."

Then he started to cough again.

Teal picked up the gun and stuffed it under his belt. Alicia watched with mouth agape. Teal now looked so sure of himself, not at all squeamish about firearms.

"What's wrong with the phone?" she asked.

"Dead until three. Telus is switching exchanges."

There was a phone on the wall next to the kitchen. She

picked up the receiver and listened to a hollow echo. She punched in 911. Nothing.

"We have to frisk him," Teal said.

Alicia held up her hands. "I'm not going anywhere near him."

The albino gave her a you're-not-so-hot-either look.

"I'll do it," Coyne said. "On your feet, dickweed.'"

The albino spread his legs wide and clasped his hands around his head. He'd been through the routine before. Teal held the gun on him while Coyne ran his hands up and down the big man's legs.

The hit man said, "Don't touch my you-know-what. I mean it."

The hockey player gave the groin area a miss and patted the albino's back and sides. His hands stopped at a coat pocket. He pulled out a microcassette recorder and set it on the coffee table.

"You were going to tape him?" Coyne said.

"Uh-uh," the albino said. "That's left over from our talk with Wells. This was going to be question and answer, then straight home."

"And I wonder which penitentiary that might be."

The big man's wallet held ninety dollars but no ID. From coat pockets, Coyne pulled two stacks of money and dropped them next to the recorder. Big red fifty-dollar banknotes.

"My my, where'd all this come from?"

"A fellow in Edmonton," the albino said. "He's got a lot more than this. It's money you don't report missing. We can go visit him and get some more."

"Are you about done?" Alicia asked.

"Yeah, that does it." Coyne stepped back from the captive.

Alicia picked up the phone again, and again there was an

echo instead of a dial tone.

"Did you hear me?" the albino said. "A *lot* of money."

"Shut up."

"Let's tie him up," Teal said.

"What is this, calf-roping? I'll run downstairs and find someone with a cell phone."

"No," Teal said, "you'll help me tie. Just let me put him on the bed." He waved the pistol, pointing out the bedroom for the albino. "Slowly," he said. "You get in there, lie face down, hands out at your sides. No detours."

Teal stepped back, let the albino pass him, then followed him. Before he entered the bedroom, he turned to Alicia. "There should be some string in the kitchen."

"You want to tie him up with *string?*"

"It's pretty thick. The closet with the mop and the tools."

"This is crazy," she said.

"Just do it."

He sounded so determined. And better him in charge, him holding those guns. She started toward the kitchen and Coyne stayed in the living room. She spotted the closet.

A gunshot shattered the ether.

Her mind swam. She dashed back through the living room and into the bedroom. Muscling her way between Coyne and Teal, she smelled the sulphur. The albino lay face-down beside the bed, one hand twisted beneath him.

Teal was still aiming the pistol. "He jumped at me. He tried to...I had to..."

"You shot him in the back!" Coyne said.

"No, he spun around. He was grabbing for the gun. I think he's...God...dead."

Why hadn't holding the gun on him been enough? Alicia thought. Why wasn't keeping him in that chair, his hands on his head, enough? Jimmy Teal was not one hundred per cent there.

Alicia paced the carpet. What now? She dashed to the door, freed the lock and turned the knob.

"No," Teal said. The ice in the single syllable made her shiver. "Don't go out that door."

"I'll find a cell phone," she said. "We have to call the cops."

"Yeah," Coyne said. "What's the difference? Let's just call 'em."

A fugitive one minute, cop-happy the next. Alicia started out the door, then heard the brawny command again:

"Do not go out that door."

Now Teal was aiming the gun at her, the albino's gun, not his own pistol. The choice of guns seemed oddly significant.

"What's wrong with you?" Coyne said. "You blow a spring?"

Alicia closed the door. From this angle, she could see past the teacher and into the bedroom. The phone on the night table was off the hook. So that's why Teal had walked into the bedroom: to kill the phone line. The hollow feeling of being in danger returned. She watched, mouth agape, as the teacher reached into the bedroom and tugged out a heavy suitcase. He rubbed his nose with his gun-holding hand. "Move over there with her," he told Coyne.

"What the hell..."

He raised the gun. "Both of you, sit."

"What are you doing?"

"Just do it. I'm not feeling all that cosy with things."

They sat.

"We could have done this simply," Teal said, back-pedalling and recradling the phone, "but you had to keep at it, didn't you? You had to make it hard."

Alicia watched Teal. He was agitated, grasping for control after passing a boundary he regretted passing. She looked at Coyne. The hockey player appeared abject. Not abjectly afraid or angry or defeated, just abject. Maybe abjectly wretched.

"I can't believe this," Coyne said. "I can't believe my eyes."

"Believe them," Teal said. "Wrap your mind around it. It's what I'm trying to do."

Twenty-Seven

The door to Lloyd MacKenzie's office opened, and Detective Dante Spinetti stepped in like a king claiming a territory. He strode to the empty chair by the wall and sat down.

"Someone's been smoking," he said, sniffing the air.

"What is it, Spinny?"

"James Teal didn't come in to give his statement."

"Call him," Woo said. "Remind him."

"The phone rings busy." Now he addressed Behn. "When you started work on that book with him, when was that?"

Behn said, "Why?"

"Curiosity. I've been doing some routine checks. According to the phone company, James Teal made no long-distance calls from his home over the last three weeks, not a one. But from his office at the U, he made four calls: one to Thailand, to a buddy at a university there, and three to Boston."

"Who would you expect him to be calling?" Woo asked.

"Players," Behn said, "guys who were with the Bruins when I was there."

"The calls were to a pay phone in Chinatown," Spinetti said. "Do your old Bruin buddies take their calls at pay phones?"

Woo watched the hockey player's expression sag.

"And this particular phone is on Beach Street. Wanna guess where that is?"

"Spinny," Woo said, "just tell us what you found."

"It's a half block from Randolph Skalky's apartment, a few convenient steps."

Woo raised an eyebrow and leaned forward.

"And the Boston P.D., they're bringing the subject up with Maria Blackwell at this very moment. She gave up the will pretty easily, so I don't expect they'll have trouble getting her to give this up, too."

Finally, Woo thought, something makes sense.

Maybe Maria knew Teal. Or maybe it wasn't quite so A-to-B. Maybe Maria had come up with the will scheme, but Skalky had taken it over. Maybe Skalky had left her safely ignorant of the plan to kill McAvoy, planning to leave her out until she was needed to claim the money.

Woo leaned even closer to the hockey player. "When I met Teal, Behn, he seemed pretty eager to get out of town."

"He is eager," Behn said. "He's ready to build his own raft."

"He suggested all he needed was the money."

"Jimmy's got this notion the world owes him some comfort and quiet. This does not mean he was in on the will scheme."

"No," Spinetti said, "I didn't say it does—yet."

"How well do you really know him?" Woo said.

Behn sighed. "Well enough to know that this conversation misses the mark. Jimmy's many things, but he's not a killer. Talk to him. There's an explanation for those calls."

"Maybe," Woo said. "That's very possible."

Spinetti lowered his feet from the desk and faced Behn full on. "So you know him pretty well, huh? What do you know about his past?"

"His past?" Behn said. "You sound like a soap opera."

"Did you know, for instance, that he's been canned by three universities in the last nine years?"

"Yes, he's upfront about it."

"Did he tell you why he was fired?"

"Misconduct," Behn said. "Smoked pot with drama students. Flunked the dean's nephew. Raged against the establishment. He refused to toe lines. At Baylor, he took part in student protests to allow alcohol on campus."

"At Baylor," Spinetti said, "they fired him for stealing."

Behn opened his mouth but found no response.

"Stealing?" Woo said.

"Allegedly stealing. He worked with the drama department. The gate proceeds from a play went missing, and one of the stage hands said she saw Teal take it. He denied it, the campus cops found no corroborating evidence, it became a case of his word against hers. They couldn't charge him, but according to the dean of the apartment, his fellow profs made things so frosty for him that he quit and moved back to Canada."

Woo opened his pack of cigarettes but couldn't decide whether to take a second smoke.

"Go ahead," Spinetti said, "light one. You've already fouled my lungs anyway."

"You spoke to the dean himself?" Woo said.

"Yes."

"Then okay, get Teal in here, tell him all we want is his statement from yesterday."

"Like I said, his phone's busy."

"Then let's go for a drive." Woo roused himself from his seat and gave Behn his best Dutch-uncle glare. "Glue yourself to a bench out front until we get back."

"Where would I go?" Behn said.

"Judging from the last few days, anywhere but where I tell you to go."

He led Spinetti and Behn into the hall, and while Spinetti

peeled off to retrieve his own coat, he shepherded Behn to the Public Information and Complaints Desk near the entrance. He eased him onto the bench, a father making his boy sit still.

"You want coffee, there's a machine at the end of the counter. That one over there."

"Okay."

"Everything said in there stays between us."

"You're wasting your time," Behn said.

"Leave this bench, I'll have you marched into the courtyard and shot."

"You should be out looking for Alicia."

"Every cop in the city is doing that."

Spinetti bounded up behind Woo, one arm into a coat sleeve. "Let's go. Let's do some good."

"Do some good?" Woo said. "Did you get that from a movie?"

"*The Untouchables*," Spinetti replied. "It got the same reaction in the flick."

*　　*　　*

Behn picked up a newspaper from the bench and watched them leave. He gave them enough time to get unmistakeably gone, then stepped to the Complaints Desk and asked the constable where the nearest phone was.

He dialled Alicia's number knowing she wouldn't answer. Of course she wouldn't. Someone—Coyne? the mysterious blond man?—had snatched her. Still, he let the phone ring nine times, felt a little feeble for doing so. Then he hung up and asked himself what he could do to find her. She could be anywhere—and anywhere was not a promising place to start.

And Jimmy? *Jimmy?* In prepping for the book, who had Jimmy said he'd been calling in Boston? Harry Sinden, for one, but it was a safe bet that the Bruin's old GM didn't take calls at a booth. Also Mike O'Connell, Behn's roommate on the road in eighty-eight. And O'Connell ran the Bruins from the Fleet Center and lived in Jamaica Plain, far from Beach Street. Who else? Terry O'Reilly, Ray Bourque—big names to lend compelling quotes to the book. If there was a good excuse for those phone-booth calls, it wasn't springing to mind.

He dialled Jimmy's number, knowing he would get a busy signal, just as Spinetti had. But surprisingly the phone began to ring.

"Hello?" Jimmy said after the sixth ring.

"Hey, it's me."

"Behn! Were you trying to call earlier? Guess the line rang busy. I was busy. I know I told you to call, but I was all wrapped up in this—"

"Jimmy, why are you babbling?"

"What?" Jimmy said.

"You're all keyed up. What's wrong?"

At first, Jimmy couldn't answer, sounded like he was fighting to find words. Then: "I need to see you right now."

Something hollow settled in Behn's stomach. "Why?"

"Not here, no, I didn't mean here, no, not that." The line fell silent again.

"Jimmy, take it easy."

"We need somewhere private."

"Just say what's on your mind."

"The weir. Meet me at the weir."

"Jimmy, why can't you talk to me? You sound..." *You sound guilty.*

"I don't have time," the writer said. "Just believe me it's

urgent. Get out to the weir and don't tell anyone you're going. Certainly don't tell the cops."

"You're worried about the cops, Jimmy?" This was an entirely different person. All of Jimmy's usual window-dressing had been stripped away. "I'm not going to the weir. I'm not going anywhere."

"The weir's private. You'll go." Silence followed the imperative. Then Jimmy spoke freely, for the first time not fighting anything. "Go there alone," he said. "If I see any cops, the girl dies."

The line went dead.

Behn started away from the desk. The constable told him to wake up, don't pull the phone chord out of the wall.

The girl dies.

He fished thirty-five cents from his pants and dialled again. This time the answering machine clicked on. "*Hi, I'm either asleep or ignoring you...*" He waited out the message, then told the machine, "Jimmy, come on..."

No answer. *The girl dies.*

"Why, Jimmy? Why are you doing this?"

He heard a click while Jimmy picked up at the other end. "I'm giving you one hour to get there." *Click.*

Behn gritted his jaw. The constable was saying something else now, but the words didn't get through. Behn dropped the receiver and stepped outside to find a cab.

*   *   *

In the back seat, he calmed his breathing and told the driver Highway 22x to Carseland. The world started to flash by outside, a hazy and distant thing. Could you really misjudge a person so badly? When you were a pro athlete, you had to be careful in choosing your friends (the would-be sycophants and limelight seekers were crawling in through the windows). Maybe once you called a person a true friend, you slipped on a pair of blinders so that you could maintain that rare and precious commodity. Maybe cynicism was a healthy and necessary thing. At least cynics didn't turn trust into a weak spot.

So Jimmy and Randolph Skalky—partners in crime? The idea was hard to stomach. Money. Jimmy's voracious hunger for moving money. Was this whole thing explained by that?

The taxi turned onto Elkhead Drive and accelerated past the zoo, under the fangs of a plaster Albertosaurus Rex. The cabbie mumbled something into his radio.

Behn checked the ID card on the dashboard. "Mr. Milutinov?"

"Yeah?"

"I'll give you fifty dollars on top of the fare if you get me to the Carseland Weir in half an hour."

"What's the rush?"

"And another fifty if you wait for me where I tell you to wait until I'm finished my business out there."

The cabbie cast a doubtful glance over his shoulder. Behn reached into his pocket and remembered his wallet was now empty.

"I get a speeding ticket," the cabbie said, "you pay."

"Deal."

They turned onto Whitetail Trail and Milutinov's right foot became heavy. The taxi wove in and out of traffic, blasting past the other motorists. Behn sat back and pulled on his seat belt.

The least you can do, he told himself, is get there first.

Twenty-Eight

Alicia sat still, her hands on her lap, her mind flying reconnaissance over the current proceedings. Jimmy Teal leaned down to tie a boot lace while training the gun on his charges. He stumbled, rapping his head against the wall.

"We go outside together," he chattered. "You have a car, Coyne?"

The player pointed to the bedroom. "His car."

"Good, I know it's daylight out there, lots of people, but you're not going to try anything like running away or calling for help. You two are boyfriend and girlfriend. You, Coyne, you're going to hold her left hand with your right hand. And you're going to keep holding it until we reach the car. Then you're getting into the driver seat, and she's taking the passenger seat. I'll be behind you the whole way."

He was ready now, Kodiak boots under his light cotton pants, a heavy down-filled coat covering his upper body. Not much of an outdoorsman. He even pulled on a fat hat with a gaudy pompon that looked Sherpa-styled or hilltribe-ish. He opened the door to the hallway. Alicia gained her feet and held her hand out to the hockey player. Coyne took hold of it—too tightly.

"Stop squeezing, Coyne."

In the hallway, Teal skipped the simple mechanics of closing the door. He doubled back and pulled it shut. In the elevator, he was careful to stay behind them, his hands in his pockets, at least one of them clutching a gun.

"When we get outside, don't look back at me. Just keep

walking. And maybe think of this: right now I've got nothing to lose."

Coyne was still hand-crushing.

"Relax, Larry."

"Now everyone's calling me 'Larry'," he said.

The doors opened and they exited as planned, crossed the street, stopped at the car.

"Can I let go of her now?" Coyne asked. "The keys are in my left pocket."

"Fine."

The hockey player pulled out the keys and opened the driver-side door. A foul odour spilled out.

"Jesus," Teal said, jumping back, "what's that?"

"She puked. Everyone's puking around me these days." With the door still open, Coyne rolled down the window. He had disposed of the passenger-side floor mat back at the Alberta Tourism stop. He lowered himself to the driver's seat and pulled up the three other locks. Alicia took the passenger side, and Teal squirmed into the back seat and rolled down the windows.

"Where to?" Coyne asked. "You told Mac—"

"The weir. I believe you know how to get there."

The engine bellowed with each shifting of the gears. Teal had traded his gun for the albino's. The gun lay atop his lap like some strange tool that he didn't know how to use.

"He's not going to meet you out there," Alicia said.

"Why not?"

"You think he's crazy? Why would he?"

"I know him. He likes to carry loads."

"Loads? Meaning?"

Teal waved the gun at her. "Damsel in distress. He won't be able to leave you in my evil clutches."

Alicia's mind flashed on a statement from yesterday—an accusation she'd made about Behn being chivalrous. "That man back there—"

"The hit man," Teal said.

"You crossed him somehow."

Teal shook his head.

"Then why are you planning to shoot us?"

The car punched a curb. Coyne brought it back on line and watched her for an explanation.

"That's why he's using your albino's gun, Larry. He wants it to look like the albino killed us, then popped over to Teal's place to get *him*—but instead got himself gunned down. Self-defence. Teal here, he wasn't planning to kill Behn, at least not like this, not now, but he figured it a lucky strike when Behn called. He's going to kill all three of us, and it'll look like someone else did it. He chose the weir because it's secluded. No knocks on the door. And it's a head-scratcher. I mean, the cops'll ask themselves why on earth would James Teal drive two people all the way out to the weir just to kill them. It wouldn't compute."

Coyne blinked once to show he'd received the message; the words weren't information, they were a call to arms. They had to get that gun—those guns—away from Teal. Somehow.

"You have a good imagination," Teal said.

"I've been hanging out with writers."

"Just drive. No one's going to get hurt."

Alicia shifted in her seat. "That's pretty much the route you took with the albino, right? Got him to turn his back on you. You gonna have us do the same thing? Turn our backs just so you're able to do it?"

"You know what?" Teal said to the window. "You have a strange way of trying to help yourself."

Woo leaned against the wall next to Jimmy Teal's door while Dante Spinetti dialled the teacher's number on his cell phone.

"No one answering at his office either. Maybe he's on his way to school."

Woo sighed. "Forget it, phone him later, play it cool. Tell him all we want is his signed statement about what he found at the cabin."

Spinetti stepped back, his hands at his hips, then reached out and turned the doorknob. The metal tongue clicked and the door opened.

"You're out of line," Woo whispered, stepping between Spinetti and the door. "You're compromising the whole—"

"Mr. Teal?" Spinetti asked through the crack. He jostled the door open a few more inches. "Anyone home?" He rose onto his toes, peered inside over Woo's shoulder.

Again Woo spoke softly: "An invasive search without a—"

"Shhh," Spinetti said, finger to his lips.

Woo turned and looked into the room. Nothing curious in his line of vision. Spinetti opened the door wider, then the lead detective saw the feet in the bedroom doorway.

The two men drew their guns and entered with trained caution. The first thing Woo noticed, dead blond man aside, was the blinking red light on the telephone answering machine.

*   *   *

Behn had the cab-driver turn onto a gravel strip a mile away from the road to the weir. A few minutes later, the cabbie parked the car at an outcropping of trees a half mile from the house.

Behn stepped onto the snow. "This is where I want you to wait."

"How long?"

He pulled some Ray-Bans from his jean jacket. "About an hour."

He started across the field for the woodland surrounding the cabin. The Chinook gusts warmed his face. In the heat of the city, snow was melting. Out on the prairie, the fields were immaculate white. Behn high-stepped through the sticky drifts and bypassed two ice-covered alkali sloughs. Some of the sloughs in these parts ran six or seven feet deep, could be treacherous until late-December, when the ice solidified. The winter cover of snow and tumbleweeds made the water hard to distinguish from the fallow prairie. Careless passersby could find themselves deep in earthy muck before they realized what had happened.

Behn's exercise-starved body enjoyed the knees-high fullback romp through the snow. Nearing the woods, he slowed to a walk and glimpsed yellow police tape snaking through branches around Larry Coyne's Mustang. Closer to the house, he saw two strips of tape over the front door.

He snapped the tape off, pulled out his keys, and stepped inside.

The sofa was overturned and CDs and cassettes were scattered everywhere. Home sweet home. Someone had nailed a plank to the punched-out window, which explained the peculiar darkness. Behn pulled off his coat and went to the bedroom. Then he realized that the heat was off, so when he returned to the living room he tugged his coat back on. At his tackle box, he pulled out a combination knife-and-pliers set.

He glanced at his watch. Only thirty-five minutes had passed since his phone call to Jimmy. Outside, he retrieved his Stumpsplitter axe, brought it to the door, and leaned it under the light switch next to the door frame. Then he snapped up his binoculars from a nail beside the coats and walked back outside. After pulling the door closed behind him, he stepped around to the back of the house and cut into the trees. He started a measured jog to the weir, careful to keep his footprints far away from the path.

*   *   *

Alicia kept at Teal.

"How'd you work it with Skalky? How much money did you expect? What happened with Skalky, crossed signals? Said he wouldn't rub Behn out, so you hired this other guy? Then he changed his mind? You know that phony will won't hold up in court. The money's gone. If you're going to shoot us, why not say why?"

The only answer: "Who said I was going to shoot anyone?"

The teacher sat motionless and seemed interested only in keeping his charges tame. A marker with an arrow pointing right read, "Carseland Hydroelectric Complex." At the teacher's instruction, Coyne slowed the car and turned onto a snow-covered gravel road that showed no tracks from other vehicles. Alicia peered out ahead. The road dipped and rose over sloping mounds of frozen prairie. Coyne drove slowly, thirty miles an hour, postponing the inevitable. Every so often he looked furtively toward her, asking with the glance, Any ideas? Anything apart from the my-big-mouth-gets-Teal-mad-at-us approach?

When the weir came into view, Teal leaned forward between the bucket seats and told him to slow the car.

McAvoy wasn't around. And hadn't been. The snow along

the riverside path and the road itself was undisturbed.

"Stop here," Teal said. He peered through the windshield toward the prairie. "He's watching us."

"What?"

"Give me the keys, stay where you are."

Coyne handed over the keys. Teal donned sunglasses, stepped out of the Charger and climbed atop the hood.

Coyne whispered, "So Mac's got this book contract, huh? After the fruitcakes I've been hanging with, I should be the one writing it all down."

Teal hollered, "Your binoculars, Behn, they're sending off flashes!"

He waited a full minute for a response, then jumped down from the car, his boots crunching the snow.

He hesitated, then said back through the window, "Out of the car, one at a time."

Coyne climbed out first, and Alicia followed. Her hands flew to her eyes. The glare burned in from all angles. Blocking the sun with a hand did no good, and neither did squinting.

The eyes behind the teacher's sunglasses peered at a fixed spot on the snow. "Okay," Teal said, "get back in now."

As they followed the order, he climbed onto the hood again. His voice boomed out over the fields: "Behn, what happens to them is up to you!"

Alicia rolled down her window. A blue-jeaned form rose from behind a high drift maybe eighty yards out. McAvoy was alone, binoculars hanging from his neck. He was standing sideways, his head and torso visible over the drifts. His voice, when he spoke, was dimmed by the gusting Chinook.

"Why, Jimmy?"

"Let's talk," Teal shouted back.

"Leave them there, come over here, we'll talk."

Louder now: "They stay with me."

"Jimmy, the cops know you were phoning Skalky."

A pause to let it sink in. Teal scratched an armpit.

"It was an act, wasn't it?" Behn hollered. "The book, that beatnik routine, all the time we spent working. It was a way to put yourself beyond suspicion. Problem is, you can't... " The wind swallowed the rest.

"What?"

Behn made more of himself visible. "You can't get out of this, not any more. Let them go, Jimmy. It's over."

"We make a trade," Teal shouted.

"What?"

"I said we make a trade!"

The teacher hopped down off the hood and returned to his seat behind Coyne.

"Drive over there. I can't hear him."

"The snow's too deep. We'll get stuck."

"Then drive until we get stuck."

Coyne muttered something.

"What was that?" Teal said.

"I said you're fucking loco."

But the hockey player started the engine and turned the car toward the field. The path the vehicle cut was surprisingly smooth. Few bumps, no gopher holes. The tires clawed up enough traction in the fender-deep snow to propel them forward.

Alicia kept her eyes on Behn, waited for the inevitable loss of traction, tires scuffing packed snow. Suddenly Behn began running toward them, flapping his arms. He was shouting something.

"Jesus," Alicia said, "stop the car."

"What the hell..."

The shouts could now be heard over the chugging

engine. Behn was saying get out, get out of the car.

"Jesus Christ," Coyne said, "we're on a pond or something."

He slammed on the brakes, and the car slid to a standstill. Ice groaned all around them. Shivery whining grew to muffled snapping sounds. Alicia scrambled for the door lever, Teal already had his door open, was already either out of the car or well on the way to being out when she realized that something was very wrong and would never be right again.

The ground beneath them gave way.

The car plunged nose-first into the water. Jagged blocks of green ice spilled in through Alicia's window. The shock of the surge made the door lever impossible to grasp. She was vaguely conscious of someone crying out, of Coyne punching the gas and jamming the gearshift into reverse. The car shifted again, slamming her against the windshield and the dash. In seconds, most of the vehicle was submerged, the front end resting on the bottom, the tail end still perched against surface ice. Sunlight through the back window provided an eerie brilliance. Her hands mauled the door, her mouth sucked in a rush of glacial liquid.

Finally, she grasped that the door needn't be opened because the window already was open. But by that time, by the time she harnessed enough sense to pull herself through the window, someone pulled on her legs from the driver side, keeping her submerged.

Someone wouldn't let her reach the surface.

* * *

Ice cracked and moaned as Behn sprinted toward the half-immersed car. The tail lights flickered twice and died. Jimmy lay half on the snowy ice, half in the alkali water, holding tight to solid ground. He pulled himself up slowly without cracking the surrounding surface. Coyne and Alicia wouldn't last long. Even if they found an air pocket near the window, the shock would steal away their breath.

About thirty yards from the car, Behn slowed his run and chose his steps carefully. Teal tottered to his feet and staggered away from the hole, his clothes sodden and dripping. He also retched out liquid, one hand on a knee, the other still clutching the gun. Behn drew nearer, and the teacher raised the gun and fired it. He'd hardly aimed, hardly even glanced at the target, but the intention was clear enough. Behn started to back-pedal slowly.

Teal clutched his throat with his free hand and coughed out more water. He glanced back at the hole and at the Charger's protruding bumper. Then he studied Behn. Indecision played his eyes. He raised the gun and fired again, this time with marginally better aim. Then he let out one last cough, hesitated, and lit out over the ice, his boots spraying tufts of wet snow behind him.

Behn resumed his approach on the hole. He'd hoped the ice was thin enough to sink a man. He'd hoped he could lure Jimmy out here, not Jimmy and Beaker and Alicia and the whole car. Air bubbles were still popping the surface around the trunk. The slough water was a murky brown, impossible to see through. As he neared the car, the popping bubbles slowed to infrequent blips, then stopped altogether.

Then a head burst through the surface, the mouth pushing skyward, sucking air with hoarse urgency.

Coyne.

Behn crept to the edge of the ice and grabbed his wheezing teammate by the collar. Coyne was too heavy, stuck on something, bobbing downward each time Behn pulled up. He fought for breath while focusing his strength, pulling at something—Alicia—through the Charger's submerged driver-side window.

When the woman's lifeless body broke the surface, Behn traded his grip on Coyne for a grip on soggy Goretex enclosing a hundred and twenty pounds of dead weight.

He pulled the body out of the hole and dragged it ten or fifteen yards back. He laid her on her back, unzipped her jacket and tilted her head. His hands dug under her sweater, felt for the ribcage. She quivered and twisted onto her side. She gurgled some water.

Behn glanced back. Coyne had begun crawling toward them. Behn punched Alicia on the back and asked back to his teammate, "You all right?"

"That," Coyne croaked, "is the dumbest question I've ever heard."

"Take your coat and sweater off."

"What?"

"Trust me."

He guessed the temperature at eleven or twelve degrees, a lifesaving Chinook. He pulled his sweater over his head, leaving himself a white undershirt. Then he clapped Alicia's back again.

"Slow breaths," he said. "Don't rush it."

The breathing found a rhythm. He sat her up and pulled off her coat and sweater, replacing them with his fur-lined jean jacket. Tossing his sweater to Coyne: "Where's your blond-haired friend?"

Coyne rubbed his arms.

"We don't have much time, where is he?"

"The teacher, he sh-sh-shot him."

"Alicia?" Behn glanced toward the path along the river. "Can I leave you alone with him?"

"What's that mean?" Coyne said.

"Listen, Alicia, back at Wells' place, is Larry the one who grabbed you?"

She opened her mouth, but a watery cough delayed her statement. Finally, she managed two bumpy words: "Coyne's okay."

Behn stepped over to his teammate. "There's a taxi parked a mile away from here, that way."

"O-k-kay."

"The field slopes down a little. Can you get her there?"

"Yeah. God, I can hardly...get any breath." Coyne leaned forward and rubbed his hair with the lower end of Behn's sweater.

"Jimmy's heading for the cabin," Behn said. "He took the path along the river, so stay to the left of it. Stay in the sun."

Coyne continued to mop his hair. "Where you going?"

"Home."

Training discipline kicked in as he raced for the trees. He increased his speed gradually. Jimmy had a head start and had taken smoother terrain by choosing the path. But he would weaken in those sopping clothes. And a direct line across the slough and the fields would cut a quarter mile from the trip.

Jimmy must have put it together, panting and retching on the ice while Alicia and Coyne inhaled the deluge below. He must have realized that Beaker's wheels were now his only hope for escape.

Leaving the slough, Behn kept an eye out for ferret holes and gopher holes and for movement among the trees along the river. When he finally reached the woods at the east end of the property, he knew there would be no footprints to the cabin except for his own. He circled in from the back, the way he'd approached the place from the taxi, and bypassed the cabin and went straight to the Mustang. Jimmy would stumble through the trees any moment now, so Behn wasted no time in pulling his Leatherman from his pocket and slashing both driver-side tires. Then he fled into the house, snapped up the axe from inside the door, left the front door ajar and the light off, and entered his bedroom.

He pulled on a sweater, locked the bedroom door from the inside, crawled out the window, and headed back to the woods, taking another arc around the path. There was a nice spot behind a fat pine maybe twenty yards from Coyne's car. He pressed himself flat to the tree, guessed the angle at which Jimmy would appear down the path. When Jimmy did stagger into sight, huffing and looking back more than he looked forward, Behn adjusted his position for better cover behind the tree.

Jimmy ducked the police tape and tried the driver-side door. Locked.

He smashed out the window with the butt of the gun, reached in and flipped up the lock. He was in the driver's seat and reaching under the steering column when he noticed the imbalance. He sat upright, cocked his head and looked out over the hood. Then he climbed out and took in the sight of two flat tires.

No time to think things over. He tucked the gun under a soaked armpit and rubbed his freezing hands together. Then he peered down the path again. It took a good half-minute for the cabin to win his attention. He saw the broken police tape and moved to the open front door.

He walked guardedly, seeing the fresh footsteps in the snow. Behn knew he was going to fall for it. Cops and crime scene techs had swarmed the property, but that was yesterday.

The warm wind had robbed old footprints of detail and left today's prints clear. Jimmy would see the prints to and from the car, and to the cabin from the east, but not from the cabin. He would deduce that Behn was inside.

Reaching the cabin, the teacher stood to the side of the door frame and pushed open the door with the gun.

"Behn?"

He flicked on the light switch and stepped inside.

It wouldn't take long to conclude the place was empty. Behn dashed to the west side of the house, the side with no footprints to or from the door. Choking up on the axe, he peeked around the corner to the doorway. Jimmy would be pulling on dry clothes, and he wouldn't waste time. He'd head back to the path and make his way to the highway, his back to the property. A strong batter's stance, a timely wave of the axe, and he'd take a nice, blunt-end wallop. Go for the legs or the chest?

A blackbird cawed. The wind warbled through the pines. The next manmade sound was not of Jimmy leaving the cabin, but of a wall-rattling thump and a snapping of wood. The bedroom door. Behn's heart pounded. Inside the bedroom, Jimmy would peer out the open window, see the footprints to the woods and start to see that the cabin was a trap. If he opted to climb out the window and follow footprints, he'd see the prints from the woods to the house's west side. Either way—whether he left the house via window or door—he'd now be more alert.

The sun dotted the west side of the cabin. Behn stepped to the centre of the wall and loosened his choke on the axe, extra length to compensate for the greater space that now had to be covered. If Jimmy left through the door, it would feel more natural, swinging to the left, a switch-hitter batting from his preferred side. But the sound of feet crunching snow to his right told him the opposite. Teal had climbed through the window. And was now coming this way.

The footsteps were slow, cautious. They stopped just around the corner. Behn pictured Jimmy looking out at the tracks to the trees. He tightened his grip on the axe, knew his friend was squeezing his own weapon.

He waited out his own composure, then leapt to his right and swung.

He'd guessed right. Teal stepped fast around the corner and the axe-head crashed his chest, knocking the wind from his lungs and the gun from his hand.

He fell onto his back. Behn picked up the gun, aimed it into the woods, and pulled the trigger rapid-fire. Four bullets whistled from the silencer before the gun clicked empty. He dropped the thing to the ground, reached down to his wincing ghostwriter, and dragged him by the sweater around to the front of the house.

He propped him up against the woodpile and stood back from him while still gripping the axe. He gave Jimmy a few seconds to learn how to breathe again. The mouth clicked open and shut, a guppy gulping air.

Then Behn squatted down and jammed the Stumpsplitter under his chin, wedging his head against the protruding cuts of woods.

"So what was the trade you wanted to make? You give me Alicia and Coyne, I give you what?"

"You broke…a rib."

"I give you what?" Behn said.

Jimmy wrapped his hands around the axe handle, but had no strength. "Money. That money…you have in Bemidji."

The expected answer.

"Grand Cayman," Behn said. "I'd be sending it to your

account down there? What about Skalky? You were calling him at that pay phone on Beach Street."

"I can't breathe. You're blocking my—"

Behn pressed harder. The teacher's face twisted.

"No. It was the wife…I was calling her."

Behn eased off. "Her?"

"For the book, to interview her. She told me about the will."

"Yeah, just like that: 'Yes, Mr. Teal, I was his wife. By the way, how about if we kill him.'"

"It didn't happen like that," Jimmy said. "She thought you'd blown all your money. She was *admitting* she had the will. So I could write about it. I had to convince her to go along with…"

To go along with the hit.

"Looks like you did a good job," Behn said.

Cops in Boston wouldn't believe it if they were here right now. Hell, Behn wasn't sure *he* believed it.

"So you, Maria, Skalky, the two witnesses, that lawyer— that's a lot of people to split up one man's estate."

Jimmy dropped a hand from the axe. Moaning, he probed his sternum.

Behn said, "So who's this man you killed in your apartment today?"

Teal blinked. "How'd you know—"

"They didn't drown, Jimmy. They're on their way back to Renfrew." Behn leaned on the axe. "So who's this blond guy everyone's talking about?"

Jimmy gritted his teeth. "I flew to Boston to meet Maria. Skalky was in jail. Jesus, lay off, Behn."

"Fuck you, Jimmy."

"She was going to leave him. We were going to leave Skalky out of it."

"But he found out and wanted in."

"Yeah, after I met Mervin Lane."

"Lane?" Behn said.

"His lawyer."

"Ah," Behn said.

"He helped me find a guy, made some calls for me, hired…a man through this ex-con who lives in Edmonton."

"So why would Skalky come up here knowing that this other guy was after me? How many times were you hoping to kill me?"

Jimmy clenched his teeth and pawed at the axe. "I never told Skalky I'd hired a guy. I was trying to cut him out. He flew up here, he surprised everyone."

Which meant… "Skalky jumps me," Behn said, "and meanwhile you're warm and comfy back in my house, whipping up a nice breakfast for your good friend Behn."

"Behn, I never meant to—"

"Please don't finish that sentence. If you do, I swear to God, I'll do something awful."

Behn pushed harder on the handle, let his ghostwriter choke and slap at the tool, let him think this was going to be it. The cops or a backwoods execution? For a moment, Behn figured he could go either way on the question. Then he snapped the axe away and stood up.

"Was it money alone, Jimmy? Because if it was, I don't understand a thing about money." He peered down at the teacher. "Speak up."

Teal twined onto his side, still clutching his sternum. His other hand palmed the pillow of snow, a brace for an attempt to stand. But soon the hand drew away, behind his back. When it returned, it was clutching a pistol. Behn sprang back at the very moment a flaming heat stabbed his side.

Twenty-Nine

Smoke cut the high air. Jimmy's eyes, in a line behind the weapon, looked cold as steel. Behn reached down and fingered the hole in his abdomen. Something buzzed in his ears.

"Jimmy..."

He slumped to his knees. Teal clambered to his feet, still holding his chest together.

"You always had it all, Behn. Even when you were in Boston throwing it away, even then you had so much talent. You'd always end up on your feet. Some of us aren't like that."

Behn moved, but pain raked his body. "So what you're saying...you're saying it *was* only for the money. I'm disappointed."

Teal tucked the gun into his pants. He began to breathe more evenly. "I'm sorry, Behn, really. I do want that home in the Caymans. I *do* want to sit back and let the world go by. I'm so tired of the game." He stepped closer. "Believe me, if there were any other way..."

Now a laugh. Not a laugh with any joy, but a laugh all the same. It hurt.

"Glad you're amused, Behn."

"What you writer types would call irony. Finally get me shot, finally killed me, and what do you get? You get to be on the run. A province-full of cops gunning for you. But the money, that's what you don't get, none of it. So fuck you very much, you've screwed it up. I hope your prison stretch is *très* enjoyable."

Behn fingered the wound again. There wasn't much blood.

Teal tucked the gun into his jeans, which Behn now noticed were a full three inches too long for him—which made sense as they were fresh from Behn's bedroom. The writer stepped forward, raised a boot to Behn's chest, and pushed forward, sending him back against the woodpile. Behn tried again to stand, but pain again set him back. Jimmy watched with interest and took a while to decide that his friend would not be going anywhere. Then he turned and headed back into the cabin, leaving the door open.

Behn screwed his eyes shut and fought the fire in his side. Coyne and Alicia would be in the taxi now, halfway to Renfrew. The cabbie would be radioing cops and RCs, who would converge on the cabin from Renfrew, Carseland and Strathmore. Even if Jimmy gave them the slip, his photo would be flashed on every TV station province-wide before he reached a town that had an airport or a bus station. He was sunk. A man with his obvious smarts should have understood this.

Behn heard movement at the door. Eyes still screwed shut, he asked, "How much did the hit man cost, Jimmy? I hope I didn't come cheap."

A muffled reply came from inside the cabin—from deep inside. "What's that, Behn?"

Behn's eyes sprang open. The movement at the door, the creaking of a footstep—it hadn't been made by Jimmy. Larry Coyne stood inat the end of the porch, hunched over and panting.Coyne's hair was snarled and wet, and he was half-dead yet perfectly poised. His white-knuckled hands gripped a cut of knotted pine. His feet had to be blocks of ice, but he wore an expression that Behn never thought he'd see on the guy. Despite the breathlessness, despite the pain his half-frozen body must have been sensing, his face showed cool resolve. He was focused, unconcerned about himself. Larry Coyne, for God's sake. He wouldn't dislike clubbing Jimmy Teal, but he wouldn't drool over it either. He was going to do it in order to finish something.

Closer to the door now, but still inside the cabin, Teal said, "You say something, Behn?"

It took a moment to recall the question. "I asked what you paid the hit man."

"Why?" Teal said.

"Why not?"

"Thirty thousand," Teal said.

"You had that much?"

"At first, no." He was now just inside the doorway, his back to Coyne. One hand held a backpack—a small day pack that Behn used for fishing. The other rested on the inside doorknob.

"I used the advance money from *The Behn McAvoy Story*," Teal said. He laughed as if he could now enjoy a small —very small—victory. "Like you said, ironic. Get paid for the story before the ending's even written."

Jimmy stayed there, just inside the door. He seemed to be going over a mental checklist, seeing if he had all the clothes or whatever else it was he'd meant to pack. Maybe he planned to sleep out on the prairie, hunt whitetail deer for sustenance. Such a plan would be no less ineffective than any other. (Behn guessed that the cops and RCs would round him up in roughly five or six hours). Finally, he drew the bag over his shoulder and stepped through the doorway.

Coyne brought the cylindrical pine down onto his head with one steady swoop. The wood bounced right back up, but Jimmy didn't go down. He didn't look hurt or dazed, just contemplative, a little doubtful. Coyne swung the wood a second time and this time smashed the neck where it met the clavicle. The cracking sound was not unlike the sound of ice cracking back on the slough.

The teacher hit the snow, squeaked like a mouse and started a low, breathless moan.

"There's a gun under his belt," Behn said.

Coyne reached down and pulled out the pistol. For a long time he didn't say anything, just studied the gun. Then he did something that Behn found odd. He brought the gun to his lips, planted a smooch on the metal and tossed the thing into a snowdrift.

Jimmy's moans grew louder. Coyne looked out at the trees as if none of this had happened, as if he'd just awakened to a bright and clear morning.

"How's your side?"

"It hurts," Behn said.

"Do me a favour, okay?"

Behn waited.

"I messed up your home, trashorama. I'm guilty. I wanted to fuck you up big-time."

"Why?" Behn said.

Coyne doodled a semi-circle in the snow. "To run you out of town."

"Why?"

"For reasons that now seem...minor. But I'm hoping that when the cops get here, we can say the albino made me do it."

"The albino?"

"The guy your friend here hired—and then killed."

Coyne looked awful—bad-salad hair, ash-white face,

snot at his nostrils. Behn almost felt like laughing at the man who'd just saved his life. "No problem," he said, "I won't question whatever you tell the cops."

They both waited for the sounds of sirens. Too much talk would tarnish things. Coyne doodled some more, and Behn turned his thoughts toward surviving at least until help arrived. Then—for the sake of mental health—his mind switched to some less-solemn mechanics. Woo, when he got here, would look at the gunshot wound and say something akin to I-told-you-so; maybe next time you'll stay put. Spinetti —he would be ticked off at having missed all the fun.

Maybe they'd both be relieved that all this was over.

Thirty

The paramedics took Behn McAvoy to the General and James Teal to the Mountainview, to the same floor where Archie Halkidis lay breathing through a tube. Woo found the teacher's room, asked the doctor if the patient would be coherent, then started asking questions.

The only response: "I want a lawyer."

Woo drove back to the station. Dante Spinetti was going over Lawrence Coyne's statement about the events of the last three days.

"McAvoy's under the knife," Spinetti said.

"You believe Coyne? What did Alf Lundgren have to gain from framing him for that coke?"

"Space," Spinetti said. "Throw us on Coyne's trail."

"But how did he have the foresight to buy the coke before following him to the cabin?"

"Maybe they met in an Internet chat room."

"Good work, Detective."

"Well, how about he'd learned that Coyne hated McAvoy? I guess it wasn't a secret. He'd been watching Coyne?"

Woo didn't buy it. If Coyne hated Behn so much, why risk his life for him in taking down Teal? The chain of events was murky.

"Maybe this'll help," Spinetti said.

He passed over a note. "This was in Lundgren's pocket." *Ed N., 11425 116th St., Edmonton.*

"I ran a check," Spinetti said. "The resident of the address, one Edward Carlton Newby, was in Bowden in ninety-eight and ninety-nine, same time as Lundgren."

"Yeah?"

"Our good colleagues in Edmonton are plying him for info right now. They found Archie Halkidis's name in his address book—a name but no contact information."

"Meaning what?"

"The Edmonton Police Service got him to give a description of Halkidis: late forties, balding, Hawaiian shirt, even in winter."

"Teal," Woo said.

"Teal. Hired Newby to arrange the hit. Must have used Halkidis as an alias."

A constable popped his head in the doorway. "Eddie, pick up on two."

Woo sifted through desk papers to find the receiver. "Yeah?"

"Hello, Eddie, how you doing?"

"Sorry," Woo said, "you're breaking up."

"Eddie?"

"Static, can't hear you, you'll have to call back."

"Don't hang up on me, Eddie. I'll—"

Woo slapped down the receiver and looked at the phone's row of blinking lights. Another line began to blink. "Buy you lunch, Spinny?"

"Snarlin' Harlan?" Spinetti said.

"Snarlin' Harlan."

"What kind of lunch we talking about?"

"How 'bout some nice greasy ginger chicken?" He remembered the blinking light. Snarlin' Harlan would be so proud of the ethnic meal. "On second thought, maybe a steak and a beer."

*   *   *

Four hours before the Renfrew Cowboys' third game without Behn McAvoy, Pamela Wells had a message sent to the hockey player's hospital room.

If your doctor consents, meet me at my SkySuite at the Agrodome for today's game.

The doctor, a young surgeon named Laurie Benjamin, did not consent, at least not right away. The slug from James Teal's Colt Pocket .22 had punctured the oblique muscle, but had disturbed neither bone nor organ. Benjamin likened the wound to an appendectomy, where the main recovery issue would be scar-tissue formation. Only two days after the shooting and operation, she didn't want him walking around.

"How about crutches?" Behn asked, and they finally settled on a wheelchair. Andy Murray, the Cowboys' team doctor, had argued that Behn should be pushed to start rehab as soon as possible.

So Behn phoned Alicia Fournier and asked her if she'd like to go to a Cowboys' game.

She was at home reading the latest postcard from Walter, this one from Mallorca. Walter was making a swing through the Mediterranean, and each stop somehow managed to produce more vacationing Germans than the last one.

"A hockey game?" she asked. "Can't you think of anything more romantic?"

"Man of little imagination. See you at the players' entrance at seven thirty?"

She was there when the Yellow Cab dropped him off. She offered to wheel him into the dressing room to say boo to the players.

"Maybe later," he said. "This close to game time, it'd be a distraction."

The elevator hoisted them to the SkySuite Skywalk, a

concrete walkway leading to eleven apartments that overlooked an ice rink, a basketball court, or, depending on the schedule, a concert stage or motocross pit or rodeo ground. Six of the eleven suites on this side of the rink had been vacant since the Stormriders escaped to the riches of Houston. Wells had the best one, over centre ice, and she used it maybe six times a year.

A man dressed like a waiter answered the door and showed Behn and Alicia through the unlived-in living room to the SkySuite balcony. He brought them drinks: scotch and water for her, water for him, in Prairie Dog glasses. The host was still absent during the national anthem and when the teams lined up for the opening face-off.

"What now?" Alicia asked.

"The game."

"Oh, the game."

There was an early icing call against the Regina Tumbleweeds. The JumboTron flashed a green-and-red message: *Get Well Soon, Archie Halkidis!*

"Will he get well?" Alicia said.

"Depends on how you define the word. He probably won't play again, but he's awake and breathing on his own. I'm hoping that means yes."

Ken Duguay's shouts at his players carried from the bench all the way to the SkySuite. Each Cowboy penalty (there were four in the first period) elicited a new and ever-more-vulgar stream of epithets from the coach, which seemed to excite the docile crowd of 8,147 as much as anything that was happening on the ice. The period ended with the Tumbleweeds leading two to one.

And Wells still hadn't arrived.

The waiter stopped by.

"Another scotch," Alicia said.

Wells finally showed at 16:04 of the second period, with the game tied 3-3.

"I'll have a tea," she told her servant. She sat next to Behn and looked over his wheelchair. "How you feeling?"

"Fine. I'll be going home soon."

"And where's that, home? Your little cabin? You'll be able to take care of yourself out there?"

Alicia leaned over. "He'll be staying with me for a while." Which was news to Behn. "We'll have someone out there in the meantime, get it cleaned up for you."

"What's your policy on pets?" Behn said.

"Well," the boss cut in, "how are the boys doing tonight?"

While she checked the scoreboard, Alicia asked, "How's Georgia, Miss Wells?"

"On her third shrink since that...since your brother. Look, I didn't ask you here to relive old times."

"We didn't think so."

"I just got off the phone with my lawyer. I'm selling the Canucks."

The stadium erupted. The Cowboys on the ice converged on Larry Coyne for a goal celebration.

So she was selling. A year after the CBA that was supposed to save small-market teams, the dominos were still falling. Sooner or later Toronto would be the only Canadian town with a team. Behn could see it now. The Canucks in Portland, or maybe San Francisco, and the Renfrew Cowboys in—well, the Cowboys wouldn't move. The Central League was one of the two top minor leagues out there, a weak sister to the American League. There would be no reason to move to a less-competitive circuit.

"The organization goes on the block in March," Wells

said, "or later if the Canucks make the playoffs."

"And drive up the price," Behn said. "Why are you telling me this?"

"It was your coach's idea. You know the score, Behn. You know that whoever the buyers are, they'll be making changes. And you're no rookie any more. You have an inflated contract and an injury that will affect your play. And at your age, you're no NHL team's idea of a future prospect. Next year you'll feel the full weight of new ownership bearing down on you to move on."

"And?" Two days ago retirement had been an option. Today there was only the dry arena air and the echoes of skates slashing ice.

"Don's taken it upon himself to help you," Wells said. "He's talked to some people."

"About?"

"We can nullify your no-trade clause, help you find a home where you'll at least get a couple more years out of your career."

Alicia laughed. "The woman does have gall."

"I don't want to be traded, Pamela."

"Miss Wells."

"If I have to be in the minors, Pamela, I'll take Renfrew."

Wells sipped her tea. "Don's talked to Bobby Hartson."

"Who's that?" Alicia asked.

"GM," Behn said. "Amarillo Armadillos, Southern League."

"Hartson has an opening. Assistant coach, someone to work with the forwards and special teams. Ken says it's right up your alley."

Coaching. It didn't sound like a career change, it sounded like retirement.

"If I want to coach," Behn said, "I can always do it later.

I'm sorry, but I'd like you to honour my contract."

Wells snapped up her purse. "I thought you'd say that."

"You're leaving?"

"Let's not pretend we're socializing. You change your mind, take it up with Ken."

She strode past the Prairie Dog posters in the living room and left the SkySuite without closing the door. A moment of silence passed.

"Look on the bright side," Alicia said, "you get paid either way."

The Cowboys won the game six to three thanks to a powerplay anchored by its newest addition, Larry Coyne.

Afterwards, Alicia wheeled Behn down to the dressing room and waited outside while he went inside and exchanged backslaps and victory noise with his teammates, even with Coyne, who now looked like one of the guys instead of a lonesome hotshot. Off the ice for a week, but the feel of the dressing room never left you. The noise, the camaraderie, even the smell of the equipment strewn about the room. Behn knew he'd been right to turn Wells—Pamela, Pammy—down. He'd been wrong lately to be considering retirement. As long as he craved this scene, this was where he belonged. Recuperation from a gunshot wound seemed a long way off, a dismal, unsolicited delay from something vitally significant.

He rolled himself out of the dressing room feeling a little depressed.

Alicia stood at the door watching the last of the crowd mill toward the exits. She caught the look on his face and responded with a wide smile and exaggerated cheer.

"Buck up," she said. "If things don't work out, you can always write a book."

Steven Owad was born in Calgary, Canada, where he and his siblings played hockey. He studied journalism at Carleton University in Ottawa, later enrolling in the University of Calgary's English program, where he began writing poetry and short stories.

After graduating, he began travelling and teaching in Southeast Asia and in the newly democratic countries of Eastern Europe, eventually working as deputy managing editor of *The Warsaw Voice* weekly.

In the early 1990s, Steven began writing plays, which have been produced at small North American theatres. *Bodycheck* is his first novel.

He and his wife, Aleksandra, reside with their daughter Sara, in his native city.

You can visit his website at
www.stevenowad.com